ISLAND OF TIME

ISLAND OF TIME

Davis Bunn

SEVERN HOUSE

First world edition published in Great Britain and the USA in 2022
by Severn House, an imprint of Canongate Books Ltd,
14 High Street, Edinburgh EH1 1TE.

Trade paperback edition first published in Great Britain and the USA in 2022
by Severn House, an imprint of Canongate Books Ltd.

severnhouse.com

British Library Cataloguing-in-Publication Data
A CIP catalogue record for this title is available from the British Library.

ISBN-13: 978-1-4483-0844-6 (cased)
ISBN-13: 978-1-4483-0856-9 (trade paper)
ISBN-13: 978-1-4483-0855-2 (e-book)

All Severn House titles are printed on acid-free paper.

Typeset by Palimpsest Book Production Ltd.,
Falkirk, Stirlingshire, Scotland.
Printed and bound in Great Britain by
TJ Books, Padstow, Cornwall.

This book is dedicated to
David Lipman
Sharing the vision

ONE

J ackson Burnett was seated in the ready room, observing the watch officer field-strip a weapon that had never been fired. Jackson was supposed to be off duty, but Interpol's headquarters in Brussels had appointed him liaison on a possible police action. Dawn was less than two hours away, and the alert had never come. Jackson did not mind. He had arrived in Geneva twenty-two months earlier, after frontline action had reduced him to wanting nothing more than a few safe days. As if quiet hours might make a difference and heal the wounds nobody saw.

Interpol was the international agency tasked with policing magic and Talents, those gifted in the arcane arts. But Switzerland had outlawed all magic seven hundred years earlier. As a result, Interpol's presence in Geneva was limited to sixteen officers and four support staff. They occupied two floors in a nondescript building a block from Geneva's main train station. The ready room held a coffee maker, kitchenette, battered sofa set, three scarred tables, and the weapons safe.

Tonight's duty officer was Krys Duprey, a recent transfer from Brussels. Krys possessed a hard-edged beauty and a wealth of mystery. She was just thirty years old and had already been with Interpol for seven years. Normally, Interpol only accepted seasoned veterans who had served their home force with distinction. Jackson could not recall another agent who had shifted straight from training to a field position, even one in Geneva.

Krys used a soft cloth to rub off the excess gun oil and began reassembling the weapon. Her actions were swift, practiced, and utterly pointless. The Geneva office had not seen a major bust in five years.

Except for Jackson and Zoe Meyer, chief of the Geneva office, the local agents came in two flavors. Either they had failed at their duties or they had applications pending to be relocated. There was no overtime. The chance for advancement was nil. Zoe Meyer was retiring in eleven months. Everyone assumed Jackson was hanging around to be named the new chief. Meyer herself treated Jackson as an unofficial deputy. Jackson saw no need to correct them.

Jackson's Geneva assignment came in the wake of some very hard years. He had seen postings in several of the globe's most intensely contested regions. His file was two and a half inches thick, much of it blacked out. He had fought against some of this era's darkest Talents. He had survived cases in Singapore, Malta, Cairo, Lagos. Two years back, Jackson's wife had been felled by a sudden illness while he was off on assignment. By the time Jackson had been alerted, his wife was already gone. Afterwards, he had slunk into this backwater posting, wanting nothing more than to be forgotten.

Jackson watched as Krys set the weapon back in the gun rack and locked the door. Then she just stood there, staring at the painted steel surface, her features slack, her eyes blank. Krys Duprey possessed a rare blend of bloodlines. She had been born in Ethiopia to an Egyptian mother and a Canadian father. She was fluent in six languages. Krys was a poster child for the agency's global reach. Which only added to the mystery of how she had landed in Geneva. Serving the midnight watch in a nowhere office.

She said to no one in particular, 'I'm dying here.'

There was nothing Jackson could say to make things better, except, 'Go home.'

Krys blinked and focused. 'What about your raid?'

'It's an hour to dawn. The strike was timed for midnight. It's not happening.'

When he was alone, Jackson carried his coffee back into the central office. He didn't mind staying because he didn't have anywhere else to go. He rarely slept more than a few hours. Sitting here was better than in his cramped studio apartment, waiting for another empty sunrise.

He had scarcely settled behind his desk when his phone rang. The read-out said it was the chief, who had been called the previous day to Brussels. The wall clock read a quarter past five. When he hit the connection, Zoe Meyer demanded, 'Are you still in our offices?'

'Eight hours and counting.'

'Good. The Geneva police have been called out to a fire. They're classing it as suspicious and have asked for our input.'

Suspicious was Geneva cop-speak for possible magical ties. This meant the serious crimes squad would roll out. The serious crimes detectives included Jackson's principal ally on the local force. 'Why contact Brussels and not our office here?'

'Because the request came from the federal government in Bern.'

Zoe Meyer was former Swiss military intelligence, with a grand-mother's build and a cop's merciless gaze. 'HQ wants you to team up with a temporary staffer on this call.'

'Brussels is sending us another agent?'

Meyer answered carefully, 'Luca Tami is not an agent. He has been seconded to our Brussels office.'

'Where from?'

'I am not at liberty to say.'

Jackson pondered this. There was not nearly enough work for the current staff. To have Brussels formally ask the Geneva head of station to make room for an outsider made no sense. 'We don't have any cases that could possibly draw that sort of outside attention.'

A voice behind him said, 'You do now.'

Jackson sprang to his feet, overturning his chair. The Interpol offices were isolated from the outside world by bulletproof glass barriers and portals that were electronically sealed. 'How'd you get in here?'

The man was an inch or so taller than Jackson's six-three and had no eyes. The holes were crudely gouged and old enough for scar tissue to fill the space. He pointed behind him with the hand not holding his long white staff. 'I asked, it opened.'

Jackson heard his boss calling. He lifted the phone and said, 'Tami is already here.'

The call-out address was on Rue Gambord, a stubby lane rising from the lake's eastern rim. Jackson took the Mont Blanc Bridge and headed down the lakefront highway. For once he ignored the Alpine peaks glistening silver in the moonlight. Jackson drove and inspected the man seated beside him. At first glance, it appeared that Luca's pale hands were wrapped around a chest-high white stick. But passing streetlights flashed glimpses of half-seen carvings and a script Jackson could not read. When he stopped for a light, Jackson asked, 'That thing you're holding, is it a cane or a wand?'

He did not actually expect the man to answer. Luca had not spoken since they had left the station. But the head came around, and the sightless face met him straight on. 'Why must it be one or the other?'

Jackson remained as he was, confronting a blistering array of unasked questions. Talents did not ally themselves with Interpol. The seven global Institutes of Magic were determined to police their

own ranks. They considered Interpol a threat to their way of life.
Yet Jackson now shared his ride with a man sent from headquarters
who used a wand for a cane. And doing so in a country that had
outlawed all magic seven centuries ago.

Finally, the car behind him hit the horn. Jackson accelerated into
the night.

Rue Gambord climbed a steep rise off the highway hugging the
lake's southern rim. Although the city officially ended about four
miles back, Geneva's cops were responsible for patrolling all the
villages leading to the French border, which was twelve miles
further on.

The Rive Droite district was home to numerous corrupt diplomats
and rapacious financiers. Swiss gendarmes stood guard by a set of
tall open gates. Jackson showed his badge and was directed into a
graveled forecourt. At first glance, the house appeared to have been
built entirely of glass. From this perspective, Jackson could see no
visible support. The house lights glared overbright, illuminating
windows streaked by smoke.

As Jackson cut the motor and opened his door, Luca said, 'Wait.'

'What for?'

In reply, Luca rolled down his window and took a long, slow
breath.

Jackson felt his hackles rise once more. 'You can smell magic?'

Luca took another breath, then nodded slowly. 'I can and I do.'

'It's here?'

'Thick as sulfur. Tell me what you see.'

'The house—'

'Not the house. The surroundings. Do you see a sculpture?'

He did. 'An obelisk – looks like black granite. Maybe thirty feet
high. In a pool of water, surrounded by flowers, in the center of the
drive. Shaped like a giant black spear.'

Luca kneaded the handle of his cane. 'Is there anything strange
about the lake?'

'The lake . . .' Jackson swung in his seat. The city of Geneva
wrapped around the western tip of a lake seventy miles long, curved
like a crescent moon. On the lake's opposite side, the Alps rose in
shadowed majesty, silhouetted against a cloudless sky. As he
watched, an army of mist spread across the lake, like tongues of
silver beasts. He said, 'There's a fog coming in from the west.'

Luca replied, 'It is not fog.'

Jackson watched the mist-figures approach, swirling like slow-motion dancers over the lake's surface. 'What is going on?'

Luca reached into his pocket and drew out a phone. 'Go see to the police.'

'You're not coming in?'

'I can shield you better from here.' Luca coded in a number by touch. 'That is what partners do, yes? Watch each other's back.'

TWO

As Jackson walked up the graveled drive, mulling over Luca's words, a police officer stepped through the home's front door and called, 'Jackson! I hoped it would be you.'

Simeon Baehr was senior detective in the serious crimes division of the Geneva force. Jackson considered him both a friend and a very fine police officer. Simeon's English was perfect, except when they were together in public. Then he liked to play the Swiss clown. Whenever Jackson tried to respond in French, Simeon held his ears and groaned. Then he called Jackson the butcher.

Simeon clapped Jackson on the back. 'So good it is, dealing with, how you say it . . .'

'An officer of vastly superior intelligence,' Jackson said.

'No, no, what is the word I am seeking.'

'Someone to teach you manners.'

'A murderer,' Simeon said, then slapped his forehead. 'Wrong, wrong. Forgive me. An officer who *knows* murder.'

Jackson ignored the grins of the police within hearing range. 'You're treating this as a homicide?'

'Why don't you come inside and tell me.' As usual, Simeon was dressed in rumpled elegance, sports jacket and gabardines and loosened silk tie. He smirked at Jackson's outfit of jeans and polo shirt. 'That is, unless you are concerned about staining your extremely limited American wardrobe.'

Jackson saw no need to respond. He stepped aside as the two crime-scene investigators came padding out. Their paper booties and coveralls were stained black with ash.

Simeon asked, 'Anything?'

'Questions only,' the CSI replied. 'I have never seen a place so full of mysteries.'

'No prints?'

'Not only no prints,' the investigator replied. He brushed back his hair from a weary face, streaking his forehead with ash. 'No clothes. No toys in the children's rooms. No footprints other than our own. No personal items. No documents of any kind. We'll come back tomorrow and go over everything once more. But I am not optimistic.'

Simeon must have expected this, for he merely grunted and wished the CSI a good night. Now that they were alone, he dropped his jocular shuffle. He pointed to stacks of white disposable protective garments. 'We must suit up.'

Jackson donned the coverall, hairnet, gloves, and booties. He then followed Simeon inside. They stood in an open-plan middle floor that contained a kitchen, dining area, and a living room whose interior walls were charred and blackened. The floor was covered with a thin veil of ash that lumped and clung to his feet and legs. Simeon watched him bend over to touch the ash, which felt treacly and gooey. Jackson asked, 'Fire retardant?'

'The house has a sprinkler system, but it was not activated.'

'You mean, they had turned it off?'

'I mean, Jackson, the alarm did not sound. Their system is linked to a professional security agency. They were not contacted. We only know of the incident because neighbors on all sides reported a bomb going off. A silent one. Two passing motorists called in the same report.'

Jackson checked the nearest window. There was no sign of cracking. Even bulletproof glass would have been punctured by such compression. 'A quiet bomb that doesn't blow out the walls?'

In reply, Simeon gestured towards the home's interior. 'Tell me what you think.'

Jackson's first thought was a kitchen fire. 'Do they have a gas range?'

'La Cornue, top of the line,' Simeon confirmed. 'Ninety thousand euros.'

'So maybe a gas pipe sprung a leak. An open back door could have funneled the force away from the front windows. The fire consumed everything flammable and went out. The security system failed. It happens.'

'Which was exactly my first thought as well,' Simeon said. 'And
it is wrong. Incorrect from start to finish.'

'You know this how?'

'Because I have never met a fire that has learned how to jump
against gravity and ignore an entire floor.' Simeon turned to the
stairs. 'Come, Jackson. Let me introduce you to the real mystery.'

The stairs encircled a steel and concrete monolith, perhaps fifteen
feet to a side, that served as the lone support column for the entire
house. Simeon took Jackson upstairs, where the only ash on the
white wool carpet came from the footprints of other investigators.
All the upstairs rooms were empty of clothing or furniture or
personal items of any kind.

Simeon returned to the stairwell and led Jackson down into the
cellar. The odor of smoke and ash was thicker there, but Jackson
found no evidence of a fire in the landing or the wine cellar or what
he assumed was a maid's chamber. Every room was utterly bare,
all the closets empty.

Simeon then led Jackson across the hall and stepped through
the final door. '*Voilà.*'

The windowless office was carved from the hillside behind the
house and was almost as large as the upstairs parlor. The walls were
bare concrete. The room contained the one piece of furniture Jackson
had seen in the entire house: a massive desk of polished gray stone.

The ash here was almost two feet thick. Jackson reached down
and cupped a handful. It held the same treacly consistency as upstairs.
The investigators had plowed several furrows through the muck.
Where they had moved, an ash-stained carpet was visible. The ash
did not shift or fill in or float in the air. Which was why, Jackson
realized, Simeon had not offered him a face mask.

Jackson needed both hands to pull the door around so he could
inspect the interior face. The ash clung to the base like glue. The
door's veneer had been burned away, revealing solid steel. Jackson
ran his gloved fingers down the surface and asked, 'Who lived here?'

'Monsieur Bernard Bouchon ran one of Switzerland's largest
manufacturers of timepieces.' Simeon was lean and hardened by
sixteen years on the force. He was more or less the same age as
Jackson and carried himself with an unkempt grace. He spoke the
man's name with an acidic bite. 'Madame Bouchon owned a
successful interior design firm.'

'What aren't you telling me?'

'Bernard Bouchon has come to our attention before,' Simeon replied.

'He's been arrested?'

Simeon tch-tched. 'Arresting a man as powerful as Bouchon would require me to answer for my actions to the national government in Bern. He has been questioned. Three times. His homes have been searched twice.'

'The crime?'

'Dealing in forbidden texts. And artifacts.' Simeon started along the broadest of the channels through the ash. 'Come. There is more.'

The path led them past the desk and around what Jackson had assumed was the back wall. Instead, an alcove led to an open safe door that measured at least ten feet to a side. Simeon gestured Jackson inside. When he hesitated, Simeon said, 'When I said I needed your assistance, Jackson, I was being sincere.'

The vault's interior was twenty feet square. Floor-to-ceiling steel shelves lined three walls. They were coated with ash that clumped together like melted wax. The ash here was thigh-deep. The investigators had tracked around the sides while working the chamber and taking samples from the ash and dusting for prints. They had been careful to stay well clear of the room's center because of the imprints. Jackson did not know what else to call them. Three valleys were cut from the ash, as precise as sculptures.

'Monsieur Bouchon was married with two children,' Simeon told him. 'A boy aged eleven, and a daughter, four.'

The imprints formed the shapes of three bodies: one adult perhaps five and a half feet tall, a slender figure a foot or so shorter, and a child. All were frozen silhouettes, snapshots of people sleeping peacefully. All three indentations in the ash formed profiles of bodies half-curled on their sides.

Jackson followed the trail around to where he could grip the shelf and climb it like a ladder. From the higher position, he looked down into valleys so precisely carved he could make out the features on three faces that were no longer there.

The shapes reminded Jackson of a trip he had taken with his late wife to Pompeii. Sylvie had been a Talent specializing in healing herbs. She had brought Jackson to Italy in search of rare plants that only grew on the slopes of Mount Vesuvius and could only be identified in the light of a full moon. They had spent their days wandering the silent streets of the ancient city, both of them captivated by the shapes frozen in lava. None of the figures showed any sign of distress. Just like these.

Simeon led him back up the stairs, where they dumped their protective gear and exited the house. They stood on the front stoop, staring out over the mist-draped waters, breathing deeply. Jackson thought he smelled the sweet freshness of incoming rain.

'So, my friend. Tell me—' Simeon was halted by the chiming of his phone. He checked the read-out, then started down the stairs. 'Excuse me. The chief.' Three minutes later, Simeon turned and declared, 'We are ordered to withdraw immediately.'

'Who can take you off your own crime scene?'

'Precisely the question I asked my chief. And exactly what he asked the minister of the interior in Bern, who issued this order. The answer is no one seems to know. Or, rather, whoever knows is not talking.' But when Jackson started down the steps, Simeon continued, 'Not you, my friend. You are to stay.'

'I don't . . .' Jackson glanced at his car. 'Interesting.'

'You brought someone?'

'A new guy. Assigned from Brussels.'

'He arrives just in time for this?'

'Apparently so.'

Simeon frowned at Jackson's car, but all he said was, 'You will tell me what is going on, yes? The very instant you know.'

THREE

When Luca asked Jackson for a description of what he had discovered, Jackson responded with the terse sound bites he used in reporting to Brussels. Preparing top-secret accounts for HQ had once been part of his regular duties. As Jackson spoke, Luca's fingers ran lightly over the cane's surface, illuminating traces of half-seen script.

By the time Jackson went silent, rain speckled the car's windows. Lightning over the lake created diamond prisms on the windshield. When Luca did not speak, Jackson asked, 'Why isn't there thunder?'

Luca stirred. 'Where are the Geneva police?'

'They pulled back off the property. But you already know that, since you made the call, didn't you?'

'It was done for their safety,' Luca said.

'Aren't you going to answer my question?'

'You already know it is not lightning.' Luca opened his door. 'Let's go.'

Luca kept a light touch on Jackson's arm as they crossed the graveled forecourt. He weaved the cane in a tight arc, the tip trailing a faint glow that flickered in time to the lightning over the lake. Jackson asked, 'Are you the least bit worried about the Swiss ban on magic?'

'What you witness is merely a discharge,' Luca replied.

'You mean, everything we're seeing here is the result of magic that was used earlier?'

'Precisely.'

'Including what's happening out there on the lake?'

'Correct.' Luca climbed the stairs, entered the front portal, and halted in the granite-tiled foyer. He breathed deeply, then said, 'The cellar, yes?'

'That's where the bodies are located.'

'Careful. Do not jump to conclusions.'

'You didn't see the imprints of those bodies in the ash.'

'And you were the one who told me the investigators have found no trace of life anywhere in the house.' Luca motioned with his cane. 'Where are the stairs?'

'First, you need to put on a protective coverall.'

'No, Jackson. I do not.' He gestured with the cane, and this time the tip's illumination was as strong as a living flame. Where the staff touched, the ash rippled and flowed and moved aside, leaving them a clean furrow in which to walk. 'Lead me downstairs.'

Jackson took hold of Luca's arm and used the descent to make a closer inspection. Both of Luca's eye sockets were covered by scar tissue that was creased and wrinkled in the manner of well-healed wounds. Other than the empty sockets, Luca Tami was handsome in a sparse and rugged manner, with a muscular frame and square-jawed features.

When they reached the cellar, Luca's movements became as certain as those of a man with eyes. He walked with his nose aloft, inhaling long, slow breaths. He crossed the downstairs hall and entered the office. The tip of his staff kept weaving, and the ash kept slipping out of his way. Jackson followed in his path. The channel made by Luca's passage revealed an utterly spotless beige carpet. The ash banked up to either side of their track, as high as Jackson's waist.

Jackson had once thought he had a cop's ability to withstand any truth, however deadly. But that had been before he had retreated to the most boring Interpol assignment on earth. Where he had hoped he might hold on to some shred of his former existence and reknit what was left of his life. Jackson watched Luca cross in front of the desk and wondered if he was ready for whatever Luca was about to reveal. Because he was absolutely certain, beyond any shred of logical doubt, that the scarred steel portal opened to far more than an ash-filled office. Up ahead loomed his former world of scalding powers and impossible dilemmas.

Jackson stepped into the room.

Luca said, 'Tell me what you see.'

'Windowless office. Stone desk the size of a boat. Three walls are paneled, the one behind the desk is carpeted. Faint shadows where framed pictures once hung. Several floor-to-ceiling shelves, empty except for ash. The lights are embedded in the ceiling.'

'The desk is bare?'

'I don't know if the investigators removed anything. The Swiss detective, Simeon, didn't say—'

'No. I meant, is there any ash on its surface?'

Jackson was left feeling exposed by the question. The only piece of furniture in the entire house was utterly clean. He felt as if he had made a rookie's mistake, not noticing that before. 'No ash at all. Why is that?'

'The question is not why it is clean but why it still exists. And the answer is most likely because it was carved from the bedrock upon which the house stands.'

'You mean, like an altar?'

'Precisely.' Luca remained where he was. Light pulsed up the cane, from the tip to the hilt, brilliant enough to glow through his clenched fingers. 'Where is the vault?'

'Inside an alcove opening to your left.'

'Is there a position where you can observe both the vault's interior and the desk?'

'I guess . . . Hang on.' Jackson stepped off Luca's channel and felt the ash cling to his feet and legs, as if it was trying to prevent him from shifting position. 'This stuff is like wet cement.'

'The charge is growing. Hurry.'

Jackson forced his way to the corner opposite the desk. As soon as he stopped, the ash congealed around him. Slowly it began rising, clenching his knees, his thighs. 'I'm in position. But the ash—'

'Forget the ash. Watch closely.'

Luca moved around the carpeted wall and approached the open safe. The ash covering the floor shifted away from his cane. The motion caused ripples across the floor's covering. Jackson felt the tremors course through his lower limbs.

The staff's tip traced a smoldering line in the carpet as Luca stepped forward and halted in the safe's portal. Luca breathed again, nodded to himself, then asked, 'Where were the imprints of the three bodies?'

'The woman's is directly in front of you. The two children are to either side.'

Luca breathed again, then said, 'I detect no hint of death.'

Jackson found no reason to doubt the man. Which surprised him. He had a lifetime's experience in the illusions that magic could throw up. And yet he found himself trusting the blind stranger. 'So what happened to the family?'

'That is precisely the question.' Luca gripped his staff with both hands. 'Ready, Jackson?'

He wanted to ask, *For what?* He wanted to tell the man to wait, give him a chance to retreat to the safety of Interpol's boring office. Instead, he replied, 'Ready.'

FOUR

Luca lowered the staff to the floor by his feet. He intoned one long, slow word. Luca's voice was different now, low as a foghorn and carrying the sorrow of a hundred empty lives.

The ash rustled and muttered and rolled back to gather around the side walls. Luca asked, 'Does any imprint remain from the three?'

Jackson started forward. 'Not that I can see—'

'Stay where you are!'

But Jackson had already jerked back. His footstep had raised a spark as loud as a pistol shot.

'*Jackson.*'

'I'm good.' His shoe smoldered and the smoke stank of burned leather.

'Watch carefully. Tell me if anything changes.' Luca lifted his staff once again and spoke in that same rumbling cadence. His shoulders bunched, his neck, wrists, arms. His entire body arched as he lifted the staff to its pinnacle. A spark flashed between the floor and the tip, then continued to grow, whirling now around the entire staff.

Luca *slammed* the staff into the carpet.

For a pair of heartbeats, there was nothing save Luca's rasping breath. Then Jackson heard a faint drumbeat, far in the distance.

Jackson had once stood on the lip of an awakening volcano. The eruptions had produced rumbles so deep in cadence and tone he could not actually hear them. Instead, his bones had vibrated to the sound created by an angry earth.

Just like now.

The drumbeats grew in volume as they approached, the march of a vengeful giant. Each step shivered Jackson's every bone and sinew.

Luca yelled, '*Watch!*'

The sparks were a constant flood now, rippling across the floor, through the door to Jackson's right, out of the safe, a million angry snakes speeding towards Luca. The blind man stood at the heart of an electric maelstrom. The tempest grew until Jackson could no longer see anything except a fiery cocoon. The light was so fierce it shone through the hands Jackson used to shield his face.

Even Luca's voice carried the electric distortion. '*Watch!*'

Then, 'I see it!'

Luca lifted the staff. The electric snakes vanished, but the distortion kept its grip on the blind man's voice. 'Tell me.'

'Scrolls on the table. Like . . . shadows, but they glow . . .'

'How many?'

'I don't . . . Three. One on top, two more underneath. And the safe is rimmed by fire.'

'Never mind the safe!' Luca reached out a trembling arm. 'Help me!'

Jackson stepped forward and gripped the outstretched arm. The current shot through his hand as if he'd touched an open socket. Jackson grunted in pain.

'To the desk, hurry!'

Jackson kept his hold because he could tell Luca would have gone down if he had let go. By the time they reached the desk, his hand felt blistered. 'OK, we're there.'

The words came as hard as Luca's breath. 'Tell me what you see!'

The translucent sheets glowed and pulsed in tandem with the current blistering Jackson's palms. 'The top scroll is stretched out over the other two. Right across the whole desk.'

'Is there writing?'

'In places. But I can't read—'

'Put my hands on the script you can see. Hurry.'

As Luca traced his fingers across the surface that was not there, the words came alive beneath his touch. They changed. They writhed catlike upon the translucent surface, then stabilized once Luca's fingers had moved on. Luca muttered beneath his breath as his fingers traced the lines, faster and faster as the scrolls began to fade.

'No,' Luca moaned, his arms sweeping in a constant blur. 'Not yet.'

The office was filled with a vast groan as if the house itself regretted ever letting them past the front gate. Jackson felt as much as heard the rush of power beyond the wall. Luca appeared so caught up in the living script that he could neither hear nor give conscious thought to anything except the gradually fading images beneath his fingers.

Jackson watched the ash mash itself flatter and flatter, as though condensing into a second floor. He could walk across it now, though the sparks continued to rise about him and the odor of burning shoe leather tracked his progress back to where he could look around the partial wall.

The vault was rimmed by fire. Only this was unlike any flame he had ever seen before. The blaze was *alive*. It framed the safe and consumed the door. But there was no heat. Nor did it attack or give off any sense of danger.

Luca had said the vault didn't matter. Yet Jackson felt drawn toward the fire enveloping the vault's entire frame, flowing in a brilliant rhythmic pattern. Faster and faster, as though Jackson's approach *excited* it. As though it *saw* him. Jackson knew the thoughts were ridiculous even before they were fully formed. And yet that was how it seemed.

The three imprints of the missing family members were gone, along with every hint of the ash. The vault now contained nothing but shadows and the faint image of stairs leading down, down . . . But even as Jackson peered more closely, he could see the stairs begin to fade.

Behind him, Luca cried, '*No, no. Not yet!*'

The roaring rush of an electric waterfall filled the vault. The fire dimmed, the stairs vanished, and even the shadows began to retreat.

'More time,' Luca moaned.

The safe was just that once more. Only the ash was no longer there, nor the bodies' imprints. It was as though they had never existed.

Jackson heard the thud of a body going down hard. When he raced around the dividing wall, he found Luca slumped on the carpet. His face was creased in the agony of utter, inconsolable defeat. He moaned one word that sounded to Jackson like *Lost*.

FIVE

Interpol's commander ordered, 'Make your report.'

Jackson was very comfortable with the brusque format required by Brussels. Interpol's agents hailed from forty-one different countries. Less than a third had English as a first language. Jackson's report took seven minutes, start to finish.

Two faces glared at him from the laptop opened on the hospital conference table. The computer belonged to Detective Simeon Baehr, who was seated next to Jackson. The laptop's screen showed the chief of the Geneva station seated beside Commandant Bev Barker, head of Interpol. Barker had seen duty as the chief of Philadelphia's police, and before that as deputy chief in Toronto. If her own PR was to be believed, Bev Barker had been aiming for Interpol all her life. Jackson had worked with her on two other occasions. He thought Barker was an excellent officer, so long as the investigation did not endanger her ambitions. Then she became just another political piranha, devouring anything that stood in her way.

Jackson's station chief, Zoe Meyer, was the physical opposite to the woman seated beside her. Zoe's snow-white hair framed a rather plump face. She was short and pleasantly overweight, while Bev Barker was pared down to muscle and fire. But the two women shared identical gazes, piercing and highly intelligent and utterly merciless. Zoe asked, 'Any word on Luca Tami?'

'His vitals are strong,' Jackson replied. 'But he hasn't been conscious since the incident.'

Commandant Barker asked, 'What can you tell us about this script Tami read?'

'The words unfurled as Luca touched them.'

'What do you mean by that?'

Jackson replied slowly, 'I think you know.'

'Nonetheless, I want your assessment.'

'They changed shape. They had been written in a format that was not the way they were intended to be read.' Jackson glanced at Simeon, who responded with a fractional nod. Clearly, he agreed with Jackson that the question itself was curious. Jackson continued, 'I don't understand, Commandant. We all know this is the primary method for identifying an authentic scroll of the Ancients.'

Barker asked, 'Have you ever seen such a scroll before?'

'You have access to my file,' Jackson replied.

'Answer the question.'

'I just did.' Jackson looked from one woman to the other. He would hate to play poker with these two. 'The real issue isn't what we're talking about. Luca Tami showed the ability to unravel the Ancient script. This is an ability limited to a handful of senior Talents. And in this case, Tami did so on a scroll that wasn't actually there.'

Jackson and Simeon Baehr were seated in the hospital's smallest conference room. The oval table and fabric-covered chairs were the same off-white coloring as the walls. Some interior designer probably assumed the effect would be soothing. Commandant Barker said, 'Perhaps we might ask Detective Baehr to give us a moment.'

Up to this point, Simeon had remained silent and motionless, his chair shifted back so he could observe the two women over Jackson's right shoulder. Simeon smiled at the screen and replied, 'Then again, perhaps not.'

'Sir, our agency strives to maintain close liaison with all local forces. But there are times when—'

'My city. My murder investigation. My rules.' Simeon gave a very Gallic wave. 'Please, Commandant. Do feel free to continue.'

The commandant gave Jackson a hard look, clearly wanting him to stand up for the team. But it so happened that he agreed with Simeon. Jackson leaned back, crossed his arms, and waited.

Finally, Barker said, 'Stay where you are. We will get back to you.'

She reached toward the terminal and the screen went blank.

Simeon used the phone on the conference table to speak with the duty nurse, enquiring about Luca Tami. He cupped the phone and said to Jackson, 'There is no change. He remains unconscious. Vitals are stable. You would like tea?'

'Coffee. Black.'

'After an all-night ordeal, tea is better for your stomach.'

'Coffee.'

Simeon said into the phone, 'Two teas, if you would. Milk and three sugars in both.' Simeon cut the connection and declared, 'Your stomach will thank me. How is your hand?'

Jackson glanced down. The palm and three fingers were dotted with pale blisters, like tiny burns. The duty nurse had rubbed on a salve and told him to keep it open to the air for faster healing. 'It hurts.'

'This is a hospital. They have a rainbow assortment of tablets for pain. You should try one. Or several. They can't be worse for you than coffee after a night with much action and no rest.'

'When I'm done with the boss.' Jackson studied the detective. Despite the sleepless night and his evident exhaustion, Simeon Baehr remained a striking figure. His hair looked fashionably unkempt. Even his two-day growth suited him. Jackson suspected many women found him irresistible. 'You're married?'

'Nineteen years next month. My mother claims Noemi is an angelic being sent to make me behave. My mother says this is the only reason a woman as lovely as Noemi continues to put up with me. I never mention any argument I might have with Noemi to my mother. She would merely order me to crawl on my hands and knees and beg forgiveness from the angelic being.'

When the door behind them opened, Simeon dredged up a weary smile and a few flirtatious words, enough to leave the young nurse flushed and glad she had done them this service. Simeon pushed one cup over in front of Jackson, peeled off the lid of his own, slurped, sighed, slurped again. When the door closed once more, he continued, 'I have two boys. The elder is fifteen and looks like me and will soon be locked up for felonious disobedience. The younger is twelve and is a clone of his mother.' He drank more tea. 'You and Sylvie did not have children?'

'No.'

'How long were you married, Jackson?'

'Three and a half years.'

'She was Swiss, yes?'

'From Lausanne.' He sipped his tea. 'This is awful.'

'It is medicine. Drink. You wish for me to stop with the questions?'

Jackson did and he didn't, which was very odd. He rarely allowed himself to reflect on his former life, much less speak about it. But this off-white conference room was already lined with dread secrets. Jackson's past fit comfortably into all the former dilemmas and impossible moments.

Simeon took his silence as permission and said, 'When you first arrived, I made inquiries. After all, we were going to be working together, you and I. Our laws against magic mean we Swiss have become vulnerable. When something like this happens, we must rely on the strength and experience of others.'

Jackson sipped again and studied the man seated beside him. 'That's smart.'

'Tonight was inevitable. Sooner or later an event like tonight's would happen; I was certain of this. Just as I was sure we would be unable to meet the challenge alone.' Simeon set his cup on the table and turned it slowly, pretending to inspect the contents. 'When I heard about how this highly decorated agent was being sent to Geneva, I was very glad, Jackson. Of course, I was sorry to learn about your late wife. But I was glad just the same.'

The laptop's ping saved Jackson from needing to respond. When the screen came back to life, Chief Meyer was alone. 'The Commandant has been called away.'

The Swiss detective responded with a surprisingly cheery smile. 'We will miss her enormously, I'm sure.'

'Can anyone hear us?'

'We are alone,' Jackson replied.

'I have personally disabled the room's monitoring devices,' Simeon said.

Zoe Meyer said, 'We need to go off the record.'

'With respect, madame, that is not your decision to make,' Simeon replied. 'Or mine.'

'It is the only way I am able to discuss this situation.'

Simeon rose to his feet. 'One moment.' He punched a number

into his phone and took it to the room's far corner. A few moments later, he returned and asked the woman on the screen, 'May I have your assurance that you will be completely candid, Chief Meyer?'

'You have my word.'

Simeon turned away, spoke softly, then slipped the phone into his pocket. 'We confirm that Interpol will not be linked in any way to whatever intel you are able to share with us.'

Chief Meyer leaned back. 'Jackson, I assume you have questions.'

'Affirmative.'

'Why don't you start us off? Let's see where it takes us.'

'This morning at five I received your call, sending me to observe what appears to be a multiple homicide and arson attack. For company, I'm given a ride-along who defies description. Now I'm locked in a hospital conference room, addressing the chief of the station about an incident that should be raising global alarms. Except for one thing. Nobody outside the house witnessed a thing.'

Zoe Meyer asked Simeon, 'You noticed no change?'

'A mist rose over the lake. It rained. My men waited on the street. Jackson came out and requested an ambulance. I followed them to the hospital. We settled Luca into a room for observation. Jackson used my computer to place this call.' Simeon smiled once more, an expression that had disarmed many a suspect during interrogation. 'My men report the ash has vanished from the house. Whatever else happened, the residence is not just cleaned. It has been rendered sterile.'

Jackson said, 'Let's back up for a second. You ordered me to remain on duty in case a raid happened tonight. But Simeon checked. There's no record of any action.'

'All the way to Bern my inquiries went,' Simeon agreed. 'All the way to national intelligence agencies. No raid.'

Jackson went on, 'Did you know in advance this attack was going to take place?'

Simeon said, 'I am asking myself the very same thing.'

Jackson said, 'It's the only thing that makes sense of the timing. You had some indication of an attack. You sent Tami here from headquarters. But why keep us in the dark? Why order me to participate and not tell me the truth about what's happening?'

She waited until she was certain Jackson had finished, then began, 'For the past four years, Luca Tami has been assigned to our headquarters as a researcher. His remit is the investigation of stolen documents and artifacts.'

'These documents,' Simeon said, 'they are related to magic?'

'The ancient arts,' Meyer confirmed. 'Of course, most of what we recover is bogus. But a certain number of artifacts are genuine. Or so Tami claims. And we have to take his word for this because, as you said, only a handful of specialists can read the ancient scrolls or ascertain the power contained within genuine articles.'

'And none of these others have clearance,' Jackson guessed. 'Why didn't I hear about Luca's status last night?'

Chief Meyer nodded. 'A valid question. Jackson, do you trust me?'

Even after the previous night, he did not need to think that one over. 'Absolutely. You're a good cop and a better station chief.'

'The answer is that I told you what I was ordered to say. Those orders stood until Barker sent me back in here alone.'

Jackson and Simeon exchanged baffled glances. 'Why?'

'I won't deal in suppositions. All I know for certain is that international agencies are watching our every move on this one.'

'Politics,' Simeon said.

But Jackson heard something else. 'Luca's research has uncovered some very worrisome evidence.'

'No one has said for certain. But yes, I agree with your assessment.'

'Will you tell us what you *think* is happening?'

Meyer leaned her elbows on the table. 'Interpol has two primary objectives. The public knows just one of them, which is to identify and help detain Talents who break a nation's laws. But there is a second aim, one that some say holds even greater importance. We must help maintain the global order. Neither magic nor the seven global Institutes of Magic may ever threaten nations or governments. Which is why I think Luca's discoveries have raised so many red flags.'

'What has he uncovered?'

'I have no idea. I'm not even sure Barker knows. But whatever it is holds the power to topple power structures on a global scale. There is no other reason for such a furor as we're facing right now.' She stabbed the air between them. 'As far as the outside world is concerned, you are investigating a multiple homicide. Nothing more. This is for your own good, gentlemen. We learned yesterday that other agencies previously launched their own probes. Everyone involved is dead. Luca Tami is the only survivor. We must identify what precisely happened and do so with all possible haste.'

SIX

When Chief Meyer cut the connection, Jackson said to Simeon, 'The lady seemed awfully eager to finish with us.'

'I am thinking the same,' Simeon replied. 'It is rather curious that Interpol would grant this level of access to an outsider like Tami.'

'Not for a day or a week,' Jackson agreed. 'For years.'

'Has this ever happened before?'

'Not that I know of.'

'Which suggests Luca Tami arrived in Brussels with some interesting allies.'

'Powerful enough to force the upholder of international law to bend their own rules,' Jackson agreed.

Simeon's chair complained as he leaned back and laced his fingers across his middle. 'Who might those allies be, I wonder.'

'That's the first question,' Jackson said. 'Question two is, why didn't these allies keep their investigation in-house?'

Simeon's enigmatic smile returned. 'You have a theory, I suppose.'

'Maybe.' He sipped his tea, which was even worse cold. 'Let's say the CIA is involved—'

'Or Sûreté, or MI6.'

'—And they catch wind of something so bad they don't even want to make an official in-house record of its existence. So they tell their agents, "Check this out, but discreetly." Or maybe they don't even tell their agents what the real target is.'

Simeon nodded in time to Jackson's words. 'Then they assign a lone wolf—'

'A blind one.'

'—To Brussels. Where he hunts quietly and stays safe . . .'

'While their own agents go out and get wasted.' Jackson drank the rest of his awful brew. 'This situation remained the status quo until the day before yesterday.'

'Which is when everything goes into high gear,' Simeon said. 'Because one of the possible connections to this awful whatever it is happens to be murdered. Along with his family. In a safe that is larger than my front parlor.'

Jackson's response was cut off by a knock on the door. The young nurse who had served tea rattled the lever, then knocked again. When Simeon unlocked the door, she burst in and announced, 'The patient is awake and asking for you. He says it is urgent!'

SEVEN

When Jackson entered the room, a nurse was using her considerable strength to hold Luca in the bed. The nurse was massively built and had the grim ugliness of a battlefield vet. She yelled, 'Sir, you must *stay down!*'

Luca responded just as loudly, 'Tell Jackson Burnett it is vital he come—'

'I'm here.'

The nurse had arms as big as Jackson's thighs and used them to keep Luca from stripping away the heart monitor's wires. Luca swiveled his head from side to side, the veins standing out on his neck. 'Jackson, get her out of here!'

Jackson said in passable French, 'Please, madame, if you will allow, I will settle him.'

The nurse was red-faced from the exertion. 'Either he behaves or the doctor will sedate him!'

'Of course, of course.' Jackson stepped up beside him. 'If I could just have one private word with your patient.'

When the door sighed shut, Luca asked, 'Are we alone?'

'For the moment. What's the matter with you?'

Luca tore the monitor cables from his chest. 'How long was I out?'

Simeon checked his watch. 'It is three hours and seven minutes since the ambulance arrived at the Bouchon residence.'

Luca's head resumed its frantic swiveling. 'You said we were alone!'

'This is Inspector Simeon Baehr. A friend.'

'You're absolutely certain of that?'

'I trust him, and you should, too.' Jackson watched the head motions accelerate and realized where he had seen them before. It was the nervous movement of a bird of prey, hunting in all directions for game or threats. 'You sense something?'

'Jackson,' Simeon asked, 'what precisely is happening here?'

Luca said, 'We have to *leave. Now.*'

Jackson turned to Simeon. 'Check the hall.'

The detective shot him another doubtful glance but did as he asked. 'Everything appears normal.'

Jackson asked Simeon, 'Do you have any backup on hand?'

'Actually, no. I stationed a guard at the Bouchon residence and sent the others home.'

Jackson watched the head on the bed, saw now how Luca was constantly tasting the air. 'Luca, how much time do we have?'

As if in response, Luca froze, his sightless eyes turned towards the open door. 'Too late. They are here.'

EIGHT

There was a certain type of bureaucrat that Jackson had detested since his first day on the job. Jackson's response had been instantaneous, like a guard dog growling at the scent of a guy it knows is bad. Such officials did not live by the rules; they were *defined* by them. They were rigid in their views and arrogant in their attitude to all outsiders. Their dress, their speech, even the way they moved was constipated. Their entire world was black or white. Us or them. And not one possessed a sense of humor.

The doctor who entered was exactly like that. He demanded in German-accented French, 'Who are you?'

'Detective Simeon Baehr, Doctor, at your service.'

'I do not care for your service. In fact, I do not care for your presence at all. Surely you are aware of the hospital code.'

Simeon shrugged. 'So many rules, no?'

'Only immediate family! Even a policeman can understand this.' The doctor's white coat was so starched the shoulders shone blue in the fluorescents. His name was meticulously sewn into the pocket containing a plastic pen holder. His creases held a military edge. 'Now get out!'

'Most certainly, sir.' Simeon did his best to pretend at meekness.

Jackson thought he gave a valiant effort. 'I will just gather my things and be on my way.'

The doctor dismissed him with a sniff. 'Nurse, what was so urgent that I was pulled from my duties?' He pulled Luca's file from the slot at the end of the bed. The nurse stepped in close behind.

Only it was not the same nurse.

The woman who entered the room behind the doctor wore a mockery of a nurse's uniform. The outfit was tailored to accentuate her curves, which were impressive indeed. Her skirt was too high, her stockings palest cream. Her raven hair was thrown back as if tossed by a professional wind. She positively radiated sexual heat.

Simeon did not quite turn his back on the scene as he pretended to rummage inside the patient's closet. Jackson watched from his cover, his vision somewhat hampered. But he could see enough to know the fingers of Simeon's right hand hovered by his weapon.

The doctor was so intent on the file that he remained blind to the woman standing behind him. Jackson watched as the woman's heat gradually increased, rising from a magnetic allure to something far more deadly.

The woman's skin roiled as if angry beasts burrowed just under the surface. Knotted humps flitted across her face, causing her features to writhe.

The doctor said, 'Step back, Nurse.'

The nurse growled.

'You are crowding . . .' The doctor glanced up then and gasped.

The nurse was building in size. Especially her eyes, which now glowed with ravenous fury.

The patient's records clattered to the floor. The doctor tried to back up, but he rammed into the foot of Luca's bed.

The only reason the doctor survived was that the nurse scarcely noticed him at all. Her gesture was a casual act, as if she flicked aside a gnat. But the strike catapulted the doctor off his feet. He slammed into the wall beside the exit and slumped to the floor.

The nurse's hands grew talons. Jackson watched her claw at the covers draped over Luca's bed. She flung the blanket aside . . .

Revealing Jackson lying there in Luca's place.

He grinned at the beast that the nurse had become. She appeared utterly flummoxed. Despite the danger, her astonishment held a comic edge. Jackson gave a three-finger wave. 'Well, hi there.'

The nurse responded with a vulture's scream.

Simeon's Taser hit a fraction of a second before Jackson's. But the two strikes were so close together that they probably felt like one. Simeon's darts stabbed the nurse's rear left shoulder just as Jackson's Taser struck her gut.

The nurse's body rippled again, tight spasms that shredded the scream. On and on the sound went, impossibly long, as though the beast was capable of yelling without the need to draw breath.

The nurse expanded further as it convulsed, and a second being was formed from the scream.

This new entity possessed no physical body, just the shimmering figure of a gargoyle, shaped from electric ferocity.

The roar was no longer anything that resembled a human sound. The shriek was almost metallic. Its claws reached towards Jackson, and the talons grew across the distance, snakes that hissed with a force all their own.

Then Simeon's Taser pinged ready, and he shot a second time.

When the darts struck, the beast became surrounded by a yellow swarm. The clanging screech grew higher still, right to the edge of hearing. Jackson knew it would have shattered his brain if he had remained the target, but the beast convulsed to the left, and its claws tore a jagged hole in the wall.

Daylight punched in with the dust. The beast ripped the darts from its back and leaped through the opening.

Simeon opened the bathroom door. The blind man remained crouched on the floor where they had deposited him. 'How is our patient today?'

NINE

They spent an hour and a half with the local police, pretending to inspect the crime scene and answering questions about the terrorists who somehow slipped past the hospital guards. The doctor and nurse recalled nothing and grew angry when the police continued to demand answers neither had. When the press arrived, Jackson retreated to the ER cubicle where they were holding Luca. As a rule, Interpol officers never appeared in the public eye. They had no powers of arrest. They were present in an advisory capacity only. A good Interpol officer was a specialist at remaining invisible.

Luca kneaded the handle of his ever-present cane and waited until the nurse slid the curtain shut to ask quietly, 'Are we alone?'

'For the moment.'

'Where is the Swiss officer?'

'Right now, Simeon is being thanked in front of the television cameras by Geneva's deputy chief,' Jackson replied. 'For saving your sorry hide.'

'We need to leave,' Luca said. 'Immediately.'

This time, Jackson did not object. 'Any idea where we can keep you safe?'

'This is not about safety.' Luca's hands ran across the steel rails of his portable bed. 'This is about *timing*. We must travel to a village in the north Rhone and return before midnight.'

The Rhone was a picturesque valley that opened at the lake's other end. It was a two-hour journey each way, even with traffic. 'What about the fiend that attacked us?'

'That particular enemy has tracked me for years. She saw my moment of great weakness as a long-awaited opportunity. She will not try again.'

'So . . . we're good.'

'I did not say that. I said this specific enemy will not risk decades of secrecy and clandestine acts on a second attack. Especially now that I am no longer unconscious.' Luca clutched his cane, and his knuckles shone white. 'Please, Jackson. It is vital we leave *now*.'

Jackson checked his watch. It was just after one in the afternoon. 'The drive there and back shouldn't take more than four hours.'

Luca snorted. 'You are still thinking that the forces against us can be seen.'

Jackson found no need to argue. 'Why the Rhone, and why do we need to return before midnight?'

'If you will arrange this one journey, I hope everything will become clear to us both.' When Jackson did not respond, Luca's face twisted with the same desperate urgency he had shown before the attack. 'Please. This is the only way we will *ever* confirm what I fear has taken place.'

Simeon pulled some strings and obtained a black Mercedes S500 from the diplomatic corps. Geneva was home to the United Nations'

European headquarters. Black Mercedes were almost as common as taxis.

They settled Luca into the rear seat. Jackson then placed Luca's right hand on the door-controls that adjusted the seat's position. Luca's hand was distinctly warm, which surprised him. Jackson had assumed that when not playing the human lightning rod, Luca would possess all the circulatory heat of a mushroom.

Simeon insisted on driving, which was fine by Jackson. He liked being able to settle into the luxurious leather, stretch out his legs, and work on digesting recent events.

Simeon waited until they had slipped through the city traffic and were flying down the lakeside highway to ask, 'Will you tell us what happened back there?'

'I will tell you everything you want to know,' Luca said. 'The time for subterfuge is over. Our success depends upon total clarity.'

Simeon glanced at Jackson and lifted his eyebrows. Jackson nodded in response. This was new.

Luca went on, 'But I would ask you to wait until we arrive at our destination.'

'Why is that?'

'Because only then can I speak with any certainty of being right,' Luca replied. 'And if my assessment is correct, it is also the only way you will believe what this case is truly all about.'

Simeon was unimpressed. 'I would have thought that surviving a magical blast would be enough for anyone to dispel doubt.'

Luca's only response was to turn and face the side window.

Simeon adjusted the rearview mirror to look at the man seated behind him. 'So tell me. We are going to Bouchon's home village, correct?'

'Yes, Detective.'

'You think there will be something so potent hidden there that we will accept whatever mystery you refuse to reveal? A trove of illegal documents, perhaps?'

Luca did not respond.

Simeon glanced at Jackson. 'Am I asking an improper question, Jackson?'

'Not as far as I can tell.'

'You tell us that you are going to be open. And yet—'

'We do not travel north to discover evidence,' Luca replied. 'We go so we can confirm for ourselves the new definition of reality.'

*   *   *

The Rhone River entered Lake Leman at Aigle, a nondescript farming community that served as a transit point for the luxury ski resorts of Chamonix and Leysin. The town had no view of the lake itself. The river at this point was slow and sullen and largely encased in concrete; in the distant past, Aigle had been mostly marshland. Aigle was flat and boring and quite possibly the least attractive town in Switzerland.

The Rhone Valley had been carved by glaciers. These ancient beasts of ice and snow had deposited a rich blanket of topsoil upon their departure. Now the valley served as the nation's breadbasket. The surrounding terrain was a verdant springtime green, dotted with Swiss farming villages. The Alpine slopes rising to either side were flecked with the skeleton branches of vineyards, and above that glistened sharp-edged peaks and snows that defied the lowland seasons.

The road ran straight down the valley's heart. As they drove away from the lake, the flatland narrowed and the mountains closed in. When they finally arrived in the village of Fuern, the place was already locked in shadows.

Simeon remarked, 'This strikes me as an excellent town to leave behind.'

Jackson said, 'I thought you told me Bouchon was rich.'

'Bernard Bouchon was born to the farming branch of a powerful family. A distant relative owned and ran the watch company. The company owner saw potential in Bernard and promoted him over the heads of his own three sons.' Simeon showed Jackson a humorless smile. 'Not all was harmony and triumph in the Bouchon realm.'

Luca spoke for the first time since Geneva. 'I sense a presence.'

Simeon hit the brakes. Jackson gripped the dashboard and reached for the gun he was not permitted to carry.

But there was nothing. No living thing. Theirs was the only car on the village road.

Luca leaned forward. 'Roll down your windows.'

When they did so, the only sound came from the local watering trough. All Swiss towns had at least one, a throwback to the country's agricultural heritage. Every settlement, no matter how small, was legally required to offer strangers and locals alike fresh water. Water spilled from a pipe forged in the shape of a dragon's mouth. The sound was constant, gentle.

Luca turned sightless eyes to Simeon. 'You have been to Bouchon's home before?'

'Twice.'

'Drive us there.' Luca settled back in his seat. 'If you can.'

TEN

Half an hour later, Simeon had no choice but admit defeat. 'I don't understand!'

Jackson agreed. 'This village only has six streets.'

'And yet we remain more lost than I was my first time in Paris!' Simeon hit the brakes and demanded. 'Tell us what is happening!'

'Explanations mean nothing,' Luca replied. 'That is why we came. Events founded upon Ancient magic can only be revealed. Now that we have confirmed its aftermath, I must use magic for us to proceed.'

Simeon showed no surprise. 'You are asking me to go against our country's constitution.'

'Look around you, Detective. The laws are already broken. We have no choice now but—'

'All right, all right, do what you must!' Simeon softly pounded the wheel. 'I require answers!'

'Very well.' Luca lifted his cane so that the handle met with his forehead. The white stick glowed like steel drawn from the forge as he pushed it out between the seats. 'You may drive to the Bouchon home now.'

Which was precisely what they did.

Like many of the old Swiss clans, the original home had been expanded into a sprawling manor, part chalet and part working farm. As youngsters grew up and opted to remain on the family land, what once had been stables and cottages for farmhands were turned into proper homes. Simeon parked in front of the main house and cut the motor. 'What are we doing here?'

'Speak with the clan elder,' Luca replied. 'Ask about his son.'

But when Simeon and Jackson rose from the car, Luca made no move to join them. Simeon asked, 'You're not coming?'

'It would only complicate matters for him to see me, Detective. And bring us no closer to realizing the truths we all seek.'

As they crossed the cobblestone forecourt, Jackson asked, 'You know this elder?'

'We have met twice, Monsieur Bouchon and I. The first time, he denied his son would ever do anything improper. The second time, I arrived with a search warrant. We had words. Quite a few of them.' Simeon used the heavy iron knocker. 'He will not be happy to see me.'

But the elderly gentleman who answered the door showed no recognition whatsoever. 'Yes?'

'Monsieur Bouchon, I am Detective Simeon Baehr.'

To Jackson's eye, the man could not have looked more Swiss if he had been leading a cow by the bell. His iron-gray sideburns almost met at his chin. His rumpled corduroys were held up by suspenders decorated with the national flag. His eyes had the unfiltered blue of Alpine ice at dawn. 'A detective? Here? What on earth for?'

'Sir, we have spoken before.'

'Really? Where was that?'

'Actually . . . it was right here.'

The farmer settled one meaty hand on the doorjamb. 'Are you sure it was me?'

'Completely. We argued.'

'No, no, that's not possible. I am old, but I am not addled. I don't forget a quarrel.'

When Simeon seemed unable to continue, Jackson said, 'Sir, my name is Jackson Burnett. We wanted to ask you about your son.'

'Burnett is not a Swiss name. Where are you from, young man?'

'Originally, the United States. But I live in Geneva.'

'There are so many foreigners in Geneva. My son, you say. Which one?'

'Bernard.'

The name seemed to catch the old man off guard. His eyes clouded over, not in grief but rather in total confusion.

There was an instant, scarcely longer than a single heartbeat, when the world was rocked by the sound of an unseen wind. It rushed at Jackson from all sides, a great moaning agony of transition. But the air did not shift, nor did the old man seem to hear anything at all. But Simeon most certainly did, for he cast about with an alarmed gaze.

Then it was gone, and everything was exactly as before. Or so Jackson thought.

The old man said, 'I . . . have no son by that name.'

'Sir, that's not possible—'

'No, no, Bernard left here when he was fifteen. He claimed he was going to Sardinia, and we were not to seek him. He said he was changing his name and becoming an Acolyte at the Institute of Magic. Bernard cast aside his family and his nation's heritage. My late wife begged me to find him when she neared her end. I tried. I failed. Bernard is lost to us.'

Jackson searched the man's face for some indication he was lying. But all he saw was the remnants of old pain, the scars of a long-healed wound.

The elder Bouchon demanded, 'You have news of one who claims he is my son?'

'Sir . . .' Simeon swallowed. 'There was a report. But now . . .'

'We need to go back and confirm some things,' Jackson said.

'I am not sure I want to hear more. My own son, studying magic! If that is so, I am glad he has taken a new name. You hear me? Glad!'

'Bernard Bouchon,' Simeon said. 'A Talent.'

'We are good Swiss! We have no truck with any such outlawed actions! If this is indeed true, we are well rid of him!'

After the elder Bouchon shut the door, Jackson asked, 'Are you sure that was the same guy you met before?'

'When I showed him the search warrant, he threatened me with a shotgun. I cuffed him and left him to stew in the squad car for almost two hours. It is the same man.'

'Maybe he's got a twin.'

'He is the lone cousin of the wealthy Bouchon.' Simeon scowled. 'I think he is telling the truth.'

'He sure looked that way to me,' Jackson said. 'Is any of this making sense to you?

'Not yet.' Simeon glanced back at the car. 'We have much to discuss, that blind agent and I.'

ELEVEN

But after they returned to the car and Jackson reported what had transpired, no one seemed eager to break the silence. Simeon drove them back down the empty Rhone highway.

The afternoon shadows were stronger now, drawing the valley into an early dusk. The sunset was sliced cleanly by the Alpine cliffs, shooting great swaths of gold across the sky directly overhead. Strangely enough, it only added to the lowland gloom. Jackson had skied the neighboring resorts several times, but never before visited the Rhone plains. He had no intention of ever returning.

To Jackson's surprise, it was Luca who finally broke the silence. When the car passed through Aigle and accelerated on to the lakefront highway, Luca touched the face of his watch and said, 'It is twenty past four?'

Jackson checked the clock set in the dash. 'Right.'

'Then we have time for one more stop. Could you please drive to a jewelry store in Vevey?'

Simeon snorted softly but did not speak. He took the next turnoff and entered the lakeside resort. As they drove along Vevey's main shopping avenue, Jackson asked, 'Any store in particular?'

'An expensive one,' Luca replied.

Simeon angled into a parking space and cut the motor. He made no further move. He just sat there, blind to the pedestrians and the scene beyond the car's windscreen. Jackson understood the detective's silence. They were supposed to be professionals, able to break down a crime scene's chaos into definable fragments. But this maelstrom of confusion left him unable to identify the first question he needed to ask.

Luca must have read in the silence their need for answers, for he said, 'Your conversation with Monsieur Bouchon is the evidence I required. Gentlemen, there were no murders. There was no crime.'

Simeon swiveled in his seat. But he did not stare at Luca. Instead, his gaze rested on Jackson.

Jackson repeated, 'No crime.'

'Correct.' Luca kneaded the cane, briefly illuminating the carved surface. 'Bernard Bouchon did not kill his family. He did not commit suicide.'

'No crime,' Jackson said once more. 'What about the stolen documents?'

'How could Bernard Bouchon possess anything,' Luca replied, 'when the man we hunt never existed?'

'Bernard Bouchon spent years on a personal quest,' Luca said. 'The result carried enormous, life-changing power. But it is not enough for one to hold such scrolls. They do not give up their knowledge to anyone.'

'The hidden script,' Jackson said.

'Exactly. Bernard must have had quite considerable magical abilities. But he never studied as a Talent. On this point, I am certain. Everything else is pure conjecture, so please—'

Simeon spoke for the first time since leaving the Rhone. 'Tell us what you suspect.'

'Very well.' Luca gripped the cane with both hands, much as he might have reached for the edge of a lectern. Preparing himself before launching in. And that was how Jackson thought the man spoke. 'Bernard Bouchon probably became aware of his magical abilities later in life. At that point, he was already set upon his life's course.'

Simeon said, 'I thought magic revealed itself to the young.'

'In most cases, that is certainly true. But there are exceptions. Some Talents do not realize their potential until they are in their twenties, sometimes even older. It is very rare, but it happens. If I am correct, this occurred with Bernard. And when the discovery was made, Bernard decided to keep it a secret. Why? Because he was ambitious. His uncle owned one of the largest watchmaking conglomerates in Switzerland. Bernard did not want to be a Talent. He wanted to rule the clan's fiefdom. So he hid his magic from everyone. No doubt it proved a powerful asset in gaining control of the Bouchon empire.

'But once he obtained his prize, Bernard Bouchon found only strife and struggle. My research indicates that Bernard was far from being a happy man. He divorced his first wife and was estranged from his first three children. He married a much younger woman and had two more children. But the problems within the Bouchon clan continued to plague him. His second wife recently filed for divorce. What is more, the company has fallen into financial disarray. Profits have been declining for four straight years. Many of the senior employees loathed Bernard. The board was talking of dismissing him. Bernard's triumph was empty. He hated his life.'

Jackson tried to find a logical pattern but failed. 'So he decided to use magic for . . . what?'

'He elected to *try*. He had identified something that offered hope of a genuine transformative event. That much is certain. And he pursued this magical ambition for years. Remember, for Bernard to have learned the elements required to unfold the true message of an Ancient scroll signifies that he was a Talent of some measure. He used this and his fortune to seek out texts and artifacts that have been lost for centuries. He spent years of his life and millions of his fortune.'

'The question still stands,' Simeon insisted. 'What was he after?'

Luca's fingers played over the top of his staff, igniting fire and mystery. 'I have a theory. If I am right, we should receive confirmation at midnight. What I think is this. Bernard Bouchon sought a means to start over. He wanted to revisit a crucial juncture in his previous life. In so doing, he erased the man we encountered from human existence.'

Simeon said, 'What about the bodies in the safe?'

'You are still thinking in the straight lines of a magic-free universe,' Luca replied. 'Remember what I said.'

'There was no murder,' Jackson said softly. 'Because they never existed.'

'The wife never met the man who did not take this course through human existence,' Luca confirmed. 'How could there be children? All we witnessed was the eradication of what is now myth.'

Simeon shifted in his seat. 'And the father?'

'Bernard's father . . . now, that is why we made this journey. So we could witness for ourselves the truth. Bernard Bouchon's former life is already being erased.'

The Mercedes was so well insulated that the passing traffic was reduced to a soft murmur. Jackson listened to the dashboard clock's soft ticking. He felt his heart beating. The soft leather anchored him to reality.

Luca went on, 'Step by step, all signs that Bernard ever existed will vanish. The wife and children of his second marriage are already gone. His first wife will not recall him – if indeed you can even track her down. His cousin will take over the business, and within a few hours, no one will even remember that Bernard was ever associated with the firm. The home on Rue Gambord will be acquired by someone else, and soon they will feel as though they have lived there for years.'

Jackson asked, 'What about our investigation?'

'You will make no progress. People will appear confused when you speak of the case. Records will evaporate. Your own files will soon disappear. Before long, no one will remember anything about the event. Why should they, since it never happened? You will be reassigned. The next case will occupy you completely.'

Softly, Simeon protested, 'But I remember everything.'

Jackson saw the answer illuminated in the car's luxurious interior. 'Luca is making this happen.'

'Exactly. And that is why we have stopped.' He leaned to his left and pulled a worn wallet from his back pocket. He extracted a credit card and reached forward. 'I need you to both go inside and buy Bouchon watches for yourselves. They must be as close to solid gold as the store offers.'

Jackson accepted the card. It was in the name of Luca Tami and issued by the Julius Brothers Bank, one of the ultra-private concerns in Geneva. Jackson knew very little about them, other than that their clients were required to maintain a minimum balance of several million dollars.

Luca added, 'Diamonds embedded in the face would be helpful.'

'No diamonds,' Simeon said.

'Diamonds would help,' Luca insisted. 'But more importantly, the watches must be gold. And no crystal movement. Which should not be a problem. The Bouchon group remains traditionalist in its watchmaking.'

Jackson said, 'Two gold Bouchon watches will cost a fortune.'

'I am very rich,' Luca said. 'The card's PIN is four nines. Hurry. We must be back in Geneva well before midnight.'

TWELVE

Simeon remained locked inside his internal debate, so Jackson selected a jewelry shop with fabulously ornate display windows. The security guard stationed inside the bulletproof door admitted them one at a time. The portico between the exterior door and the second was an airless coffin, made bearable only because both doors were glass. When the outer door clicked shut, the guard opened the interior and asked Jackson's business. Jackson fully understood the guard's apprehension. He had worn the same clothes since starting his midnight shift the previous evening. He had been through a hospital blast and a very long day. But when Jackson said

they wanted to buy matching gold watches, the guard pointed him
towards a smiling sales clerk and released the outer door for Simeon
to enter.

The Swiss detective showed no real interest in the selection process,
so Jackson chose a classical design, rectangular and slim with an
alligator band. The watches were yellow gold, as were the Roman
numerals marking the face. When Jackson pointed to the cabochon
sapphires adorning the winding stem and asked if they could be
replaced with diamonds, the clerk offered to insert additional diamonds
on the face, above the twelfth Roman numeral. Jackson gave Simeon
a chance to object, and when the detective remained silent, he agreed.
What the young man thought of two hard-bitten and weary men
buying matching watches that cost over ten thousand dollars each,
he did not show. The Swiss were nothing if not discreet.

The clerk ran their purchase through Luca's credit card, then
excused himself to change the gemstones. The guard remained
stationed by the door, staring at the world beyond his bulletproof
cage. The other sales clerk asked if they wanted coffee, then vanished
into the store's interior.

Simeon murmured, 'How will these watches keep our memories
alive?'

Jackson did not feel any need to respond. He could already see
where this was headed.

Simeon sighed, 'Luca will cast another of his spells.'

Jackson waited.

Simeon said, 'I cannot begin to count the laws I have broken.'

Jackson did not respond.

'If I choose not to wear this watch, it would mean that I could
resume the life that I call normal,' Simeon said. 'Arresting normal
crooks for committing normal crimes. All of this would vanish.'

'It would,' Jackson agreed.

'My biggest concern would once again be my delinquent son,'
Simeon went on. 'I could love my wife in peace. I could once again
assume that my beloved country remains free of all magical design.'

'Probably within a matter of hours,' Jackson said.

'I must think about this very seriously. Most likely I will discuss
it with my wife.' He glanced at Jackson. 'You will not think less
of me for declining to proceed?'

'In your circumstances,' Jackson replied, 'I would be tempted to
do the same.'

'Tempted,' Simeon repeated. 'But what would you actually do?'

Jackson shook his head. 'My path and yours are so wide apart that it is impossible for me to say.'

'Your path. Your path.' Simeon found a bitter taste in the words. 'What path will you take now, Jackson?'

'I think you know.'

'Even if it means you might be swallowed as well? Even if one day I might forget that I once had a friend named Jackson Burnett?'

'You are tied to your homeland and your family,' Jackson pointed out.

'And you?'

The sales clerk emerged then, bearing the two watches in gold-embossed leather cases. Jackson accepted them both and let the guard seal him once more in the bulletproof portico. Only then, in the still air and the tight confines, did Jackson silently release the truth. The hazards and mysteries and risks enshrouding this case actually sounded rather appealing.

When Jackson offered to drive them back, Simeon responded by slipping into the passenger seat. Jackson handed the two watches to Luca and watched as the blind man took them both, compressed them between his hands, and lifted them to his forehead. Then he simply sat there. After a time, Luca handed them back. The watches felt intensely hot, almost scalding. Jackson let his cool slightly, then strapped it to his wrist. Simeon accepted his and slipped it into his pocket.

Jackson had a growing number of questions for Luca, but he had no problem with waiting. In fact, he liked the silence. He needed time to come to terms with the new situation. Far more was involved than recalling a series of events. Jackson knew he was resuming a pattern of action from his past. He had rarely permitted himself the luxury of dwelling on those lost years. The memories of the period leading up to his wife's death remained a wound that was very slow to heal. And yet now, as he drove the powerful vehicle along the lakefront highway, he found he did not mind this new direction. The truth was, he felt exhilarated.

While they were mired in Geneva's evening traffic, Simeon asked to be dropped off at his home. Jackson was mildly disappointed but not surprised. He halted before the detective's house and watched Simeon tread wearily up the front walk. When the front door closed behind him, Jackson said, 'He isn't wearing the watch.'

'He still has time to change his mind. Midnight – perhaps an hour or so later.'

'After that?'

'You know the answer, Jackson.'

'No, I mean, about this investigation.'

'We will make other arrangements.' Luca's fingers traced over his watch face. 'There is still time. We must eat something.'

'I am not hungry.'

'You will be. We should hurry.'

'Midnight is still hours away,' Jackson pointed out.

'We must be in place well before then. If I'm right, the closer we come to midnight, the more time will congeal.'

'If you are *right*,' Jackson repeated. 'You mean, you still don't know?'

'The evidence we gathered in the Rhone Valley merely serves as a compass heading,' Luca replied. 'Tonight we find the true direction of our quest.'

Jackson slipped the car into gear. 'And here I was thinking this was about an investigation.'

'An investigation requires a crime,' Luca reminded him. 'The authorities will accept that we must hunt for scrolls of the Ancients, nothing more. And that, my friend, defines a quest.'

Jackson found himself sniffing the air, much like Luca had, only more softly. Trying to decide how it felt to be called this strange man's friend. 'So where do we need to get to?'

'Back to the Bouchon residence,' Luca said. 'As quickly as possible.'

'The vanished crime scene,' Jackson said. When Luca did not respond, he asked, 'Does takeout work for you?'

THIRTEEN

B ut as he started towards his favorite sandwich bar, Jackson found the reality hovering above the lake's rose-tinted waters. 'This investigation is going to take us far from Geneva.'

'That would be my assumption.'

'In that case, Simeon won't be joining us. Even if he wears the watch. He is a detective on the Geneva force. It's all he's ever wanted.'

'That is my impression as well,' Luca replied.

'I need a partner in this.' When the rear seat remained silent, Jackson added, 'A partner who can see. A partner who's a cop.'

'I am not objecting, Jackson. There could well be instances when my presence would create additional danger. You have someone in mind?'

Jackson was already reaching for his phone. He had all the Interpol officers in his address book. 'I do.'

'Should we discuss this?'

Jackson hesitated. The question was valid. Even so, he was reluctant to take that step. 'I don't like setting a precedent.'

Luca did not respond.

'I think this is a good person to bring in. She is someone I think I can trust. Too many of the agents assigned to the Geneva station operate at half speed. But that's not the real issue. Once we start moving, I need the freedom of independent action. I can't keep coming back to you for approval of my decisions.'

Luca nodded slowly. 'I understand.'

'In that case, her name is Krys Duprey.'

'We have met. Briefly.' Luca kneaded his cane. 'She may object to my participation.'

'Either you both agree to work together or we find someone else.'

'Very well.'

Jackson found the name and hit speed dial. When Krys Duprey answered, Jackson asked, 'Would you like to help me with a new investigation?'

'Is this a joke?'

'I have a case. It's been given the green light by Brussels. I need . . .'

'What?'

'Someone I can trust.'

Krys huffed a very hard breath, a sound Jackson recognized from his own injured time. She asked, 'Where do I meet you?'

'I'm coming by.' He checked the phone's read-out. 'You live on Rue Champéry?'

'The old building on the corner, by the plaza.'

He gunned through a light and took a sharp right inland. 'Meet me out front. I'm inbound in five.'

*   *   *

Any excitement Krys Duprey might have felt over Jackson's call evaporated the instant she opened the passenger door and spotted the man in the back seat. 'What's this about?'

'This is Luca Tami. He's—'

'I know who he is.' She made no move to enter the vehicle. 'I asked you a question.'

'Luca's presence is essential to this investigation.' When she remained standing on the sidewalk, Jackson said, 'Get in or shut the door. It's your call.'

Krys shot Luca a very hard glare, then settled into the passenger seat. And slammed the door.

When they stopped at Jackson's favorite takeout, a corner shop selling astonishingly good Lebanese, Krys remained immobile, silent. Jackson ordered three falafel-and-salad flatbreads and three with roast lamb and spring onions, then selected three soft drinks and three fresh juices. The Lebanese matriarch was seated behind the cash register. As usual, she chided Jackson for not letting her find him a nice girl, someone who would help him start living healthy for a change. She complained that he looked exhausted, demanded to know when he last slept, looked genuinely insulted when he replied that the days had started to swim together. He caught a fleeting glimpse of his reflection, saw feverish energy in his hollowed gaze, and assumed Luca was holding the exhaustion at bay. The matron accepted his money and said, 'Even criminals must find time to sleep, *monsieur*. Even the heroes.'

The fragrances filled the car upon his return. Jackson handed a falafel to Luca, set another on the divider between the seats, and took a lamb for himself. 'Do we have time to eat here?'

'The night is congealing,' Luca replied. 'We should go.'

Traffic was moving slowly enough for Jackson to drive and eat in relative comfort. He did not feel the least bit hungry. Even so, he ate three of the flatbreads and then motioned to the one still resting on the divider. He asked Krys, 'You want that?'

'No, thank you, Jackson.'

It was only then that he noticed the change. The hard-edged cop was gone. Passing headlights illuminated a face creased with old sorrow. He wished he felt close enough to Krys to offer comfort, but there was nothing to suggest she was willing to lower her barriers. So he said, 'When we started this morning, Luca said the only way we would understand was if we followed his lead. He was right. We've seen things . . .'

Krys did not look his way. But he knew she was listening because she asked, 'Who is "we"?'

'Simeon Baehr. A detective with the Geneva force.'

'He is off the case?'

'If it's OK, I'll wait and answer that tomorrow.' When she did not respond, Jackson went on, 'I asked you to join us now because we're entering a new phase of the investigation. And my gut tells me you won't really understand unless you see it for yourself.'

Luca said, 'This is good thinking, Jackson.'

They crawled forward another hundred meters, then Krys asked, 'Understand what?'

Jackson took another bite, swallowed, and replied, 'I have no idea.'

They did not reach the house on Rue Gambon until after eleven.

If Jackson had needed any confirmation that they were entering far more than just another night, it was how a drive that normally took less than ten minutes required over an hour. The closer they came to the house, the more the traffic slowed. The average Genevoise was far from polite or patient when behind the wheel. But there was not a single horn, not an angry shout, nor a car that sought to move out of line. The people inside the cars Jackson could see were stationary. Staring straight ahead. Silent.

Finally, Krys asked, 'What is happening?'

'Like Luca said, the night is congealing.'

'What is that supposed to mean?'

'I'm not certain. But my guess is, the only reason we notice anything at all is because of the man in the back seat.'

Krys shifted slightly. 'You're using magic?'

'I have been constantly since the assault in the hospital,' Luca replied.

She asked Jackson, 'That explosion on the news was your fault?'

'We were attacked,' Jackson said. 'We escaped.'

Krys turned back to the windscreen. 'I should have known.'

'Luca, can't you do something to speed things up?'

'I am trying, Jackson.'

Even the clock in the dash seemed to slow. Jackson watched the second hand, trying to see if it ticked forward at all. He also checked his new wristwatch. But focusing on both caused his head and neck to ache. As if he was trying to fight a mental battle he had already lost.

Luca leaned forward and set a hand on Jackson's shoulder. The touch was fiery. Luca said, 'Do you see it?'

A tight ribbon of asphalt, scarcely as wide as the car, abruptly opened between the frozen lanes. It meant crossing over the central lines, and the diplomatic car did not have a siren or police lights. Jackson put on his flasher and gunned the motor. 'Hang on.'

As soon as he started moving, horns blared from all sides. Despite the car's soundproofing, the noise was astonishingly loud. Jackson felt as if he was being physically assaulted. Which only made him drive faster still.

Rue Gambon opened abruptly on his right. One moment there was nothing but the angry horns and the solid lines of flashing headlights. The next, a space was there and the road as well, appearing like, well . . .

Magic.

He rammed the big car up the rise. Ahead of him, the tall metal gates stood open. Jackson powered through the entry and spewed gravel as he braked.

Luca said, 'Park as far from the obelisk as you can.'

Jackson let the car's four-wheel slide carry them up beside the house. Krys's door was jammed tight to the stone wall. She waited until she had climbed over the divide and stood beside the car to demand, 'Tell me what is going on, Jackson.'

Jackson leaned down and asked through the open door, 'OK if I take her inside?'

Luca felt the hands of his watch. 'You have eighteen minutes. Not an instant longer.'

FOURTEEN

The Bouchon residence was not just cleaned; it shone and even smelled like a new home. The police crime-scene tape was gone, along with any indication that criminologists had ever been inside. Jackson could find no evidence of either smoke damage or ash. None of this disturbed him nearly as much as he might have expected.

Jackson walked Krys through the house, describing what had happened. He kept glancing at his watch, but here time seemed to be moving at a normal pace. He pretended not to notice Krys's response. Even so, he found her a continual mystery. The longer he talked, the more vulnerable she seemed to become.

Jackson led her downstairs and described the events that took place both here and during their drive into the Rhone. He decided the hospital and the decision facing Simeon could wait. When he was done, he just stopped. He watched her move slowly around the office. She inspected the desk, tracing her fingers over the cool surface as if she was searching for the fiery script Luca had read. She asked, 'Did Luca tell you what the scroll contained?'

'Not yet. Too much, too fast. I assume he will. He says there are to be no more secrets between us.'

'And you believe him?'

Jackson did not find any reason to reply.

She nodded, as though his silence was the proper response. She walked into the safe, studied the empty structure, and said, 'Where were the bodies?'

He stood in the same spot from which he had experienced the transformation, where both the office and the safe were visible. 'About five feet in front of where you're standing. The adult was in the middle. The younger child was to the left. All positioned on their left sides. Sort of spoon-shaped, but there were a couple of feet between each of them.'

Krys turned and walked past him. Jackson followed her out of the office and up the stairs that wound around the massive central pillar. Their footsteps were muted by the plush ivory carpet. To Jackson's eye, it appeared that no one had ever before set foot in this home.

When they reached the front door, she stopped and crossed her arms, her shoulders bunched against her jacket. 'I need to tell you what happened.'

'Krys, we've got time for that tomorrow—'

'You need to know now.'

Her quiet voice carried the subtle hint of suppressed rage, like fresh gunpowder with the fuse lit. Jackson checked his watch. 'We have four minutes.'

'This won't take long.' Her breath came in tight pants, fracturing the sentences. 'I was based in Cairo, then Malta. I was fast-tracked for senior status, so they decided I needed a stint in Brussels. But you know all that.'

'Most of it,' Jackson replied. 'I read your file.'

'Three days after I arrived, the deputy chief of the Brussels police force assaulted me. I was working late. I thought inside our offices we were safe . . . What can I say?'

'You thought you could trust your colleagues,' Jackson said.

'The official report claims I overreacted to his advances. He didn't *advance* anything. He *attacked* me.'

'You managed to fight him off,' Jackson said.

'No, Jackson.'

'Then what . . .'

The impact of her unspoken message crackled in the air around them. Krys said it anyway. 'I used magic.'

Jackson nodded. Everything was clear now. Why she had come straight into Interpol, how she had been targeted for fieldwork, her stations, then Brussels, everything. Talents did not serve with Interpol. It was an unbreakable code.

The seven global Institutes of Magic were constantly pressing to have Interpol disbanded. They accused Interpol field agents of overstepping their boundaries, of harassing their members, of seeking to restrict the lawful use of magic. The Institutes supposedly policed their own ranks and fought against any interference from outsiders. Like most agents, Jackson assumed their real motive was to hide dark practitioners.

To have a Talent serving as an agent was astounding.

Krys went on, 'I pinned him to the wall. Actually, I slammed him so hard it creased the wood. I should have stopped there. I should have . . .' She shook her head. 'You don't know how many times I've relived that night.'

Jackson stood there, waiting. Trying to figure out why this was important now. But he came up empty.

'I was so *angry*. I knew this was going to be trouble, and it wasn't my fault. I had a Taser in my purse. I zapped him six times.'

'Wow.'

'The jolts burned right through his uniform and his shirt. It was impossible to pretend I hadn't gone too far. The official review board wanted me prosecuted for malicious assault. I threatened to go public with my side of the story. Their idea of a compromise was to post me here and put a black mark on my record.'

Jackson resisted the urge to check his watch again. 'Krys, I'm really sorry, but I'm not sure why we need—'

'Luca was there.'

'What?'

'In the offices. I saw him hiding in the coffee alcove, just down the hall from the bullpen. When this blew up, I asked him to testify on my behalf. I *begged*. Know what he said?'

Jackson nodded. 'That he hadn't seen anything.'

The bitter fury was cold now, the beautiful gaze shattered. 'I know you think you can trust him. I get the impression you think he's your friend. But you need to remember this: Luca has his own agenda. I have no idea what it is. But there is nothing and no one he will not destroy to get whatever he's really after.'

FIFTEEN

Together they descended the front steps and crossed the fore-court to the car. Jackson tried to determine how he felt about Krys's warning. He already had his concerns about Luca. The man was one huge inscrutability. Luca's lack of eyes was a symbol of his character. Krys might be entirely correct. Luca might have an agenda that at some point in their investigation could prove dangerous. But every case involving magic that Jackson had ever led had, at one point or another, revealed an impossible link to the unseen.

Before the loss of his wife had driven him to Geneva, Jackson had held one of the highest solve rates at Interpol. He had learned to live with the murkiness of cases involving magic, when the bounds of reality were rearranged. The accompanying danger was simply part of getting the job done.

He opened Luca's door and said, 'OK, we're back. What now?'

For the second time, Luca asked Jackson to guide him.

It felt strange to have Luca take hold of his arm. The man's strength was unmistakable. But the closer they came to the fore-court's central fountain, the more unsteady his movements became.

'What's the matter?'

'There is a gathering of forces. It leaves me . . .' Luca stumbled and almost went down.

Jackson caught the man and held him upright. 'Where are we going?'

'We need to be touching the obelisk.'

'It's in the middle of a fountain,' Jackson pointed out. 'Water looks pretty deep.'

'There should be a path. Hurry.'

Krys turned on her phone's flashlight app, illuminating a series of black stones hidden just beneath the water's surface. Steps were also sculpted into the fountain's waist-high perimeter. But climbing them proved impossible for Luca. When his foot touched the outer wall, his movements became spastic, uncontrolled.

Jackson mounted the fountain's rim, tossed Luca's staff to the ground, slipped Luca's arm around his shoulders, took a firm grip on the man's chest, and maneuvered him forward. Luca's breath became increasingly labored. When he started for the pool's first step, Luca froze.

Krys stood at the fountain's base and asked, 'What now?'

'Fireman's carry.'

In response, Luca slipped around in spastic jerks until he could grip Jackson from behind. The man seemed surprisingly light, which Jackson assumed meant Luca had magically relieved him of the burden.

Krys steadied them with one hand while illuminating the steps with the other. The water covering the square stones was half an inch deep and very cold when it filtered through Jackson's shoes.

Then he touched the obelisk.

It felt to Jackson as though they entered the eye of a tornado.

Even when Luca released his grip and stood with his arms wrapped around the obelisk, the sensation did not diminish. Unseen forces whipped about them. The fact that he could neither hear nor see anything only heightened their power. When his breath steadied, he asked Luca, 'You OK?'

'Yes, Jackson.' The man's voice resumed its flat monotone. 'Thank you.'

He helped Krys find footing by the stone tower, waited until her hands made contact, then asked, 'Do you feel it?'

In reply, she spoke to Luca directly for the first time. 'What is going on?'

'Bernard Bouchon unleashed forces that have not been witnessed for centuries.' Luca used the black stone for support and slowly drew himself upright. 'My investigation uncovered documents that speak of these after-effects. If I am correct, we will now witness confirmation of all my suspicions. Bernard Bouchon uncovered missing scrolls that date back to the Ancients. His desperate quest unleashed powers capable of rearranging events and lives that already existed.' Luca lifted his chin and sniffed the air. 'It is almost time. Maintain your hold of the obelisk.'

Jackson gripped one corner of the stone with his left hand. He wanted to keep his right free. It was the natural reaction of a man who had trained for years with firearms. Even when there was nothing visible to shoot.

The obelisk was slick and cold to the touch. Jackson stood listening to the tight breaths of his two companions, waiting. 'What are we looking for?'

Luca lifted his head and sniffed again, then replied, 'There are ancient legends that speak of a hidden island.'

'In the lake?'

'At this end. Supposedly, this was why Geneva was situated here, in the bowels of the worst weather in Europe. And why still today this city produces the world's most precise timepieces. The legends refer to it as the Island of Time.'

'Never heard of it.'

'Many such tales are little more than folklore, the cultural legacy of dark eras. But this one holds at least a fragment of truth. I have discovered references to it in too many different places. Scholars at the seven Institutes also insist it is true.'

'Again, what are we looking for?' Jackson persisted.

'Seven hundred years ago, before magic was outlawed, Geneva was frequented by adventurers in search of this island.' Luca shifted around to face the lake and settled the back of his head upon the obelisk. 'No one can say for certain where it is, or even if it exists, because no one who finds the island ever returns.'

'Doesn't sound appealing to me – an island that makes you vanish.'

Luca's sightless eyes peered out over the lake. 'If you could have the chance to undo one mistake, relive one segment of your life . . .

Knowing what you do now. Moving forward through life a second time, only equipped with all the knowledge you possess from this journey.'

Krys demanded, 'The island does that?'

'Supposedly. It is the quest that Bouchon was on, if my evidence is correct. To reassemble the spells required to create the bridge. Cross to this island. And revisit the crucial juncture in his earlier life.'

Jackson asked, 'And the obelisk?'

'There is no clear understanding of what purpose the obelisk serves. But it plays some role in every account I have come across.' Luca lifted his chin and sniffed. 'Pay careful attention.'

Jackson started to ask, *To what?* Then the night answered his question.

SIXTEEN

The air was filled with a grinding noise, like two mountains clenched in a fist the size of Switzerland. The air around Jackson shuddered from the impact. But he still could feel nothing. Without thinking, he lifted his hand from the obelisk to rub his eyes, and instantly the noise and the sense of surrounding power vanished.

'Keep hold of the stone!'

Jackson reconnected with the obelisk, and immediately the grinding action resumed. He could feel the crushing force in his chest.

Luca said, 'The instant anything becomes visible, you must tell me.'

Jackson asked, 'Are we in danger?'

'I don't think so, but I can't say for certain.'

Krys announced, 'I see something.'

'Where?'

'Far down to your right. Over the water. Something . . .'

Jackson saw it then. 'A fog is forming over the water. Same as before. Looks like lightning in the mist, or big sparks. Same tall pillars.'

Krys said, 'You didn't tell me anything about that.'

'At the time, Luca just called it a discharge. And we had other things to—'

'Later,' Luca snapped. 'Describe what you see!'

'It's moving fast. Staying low to the water, mostly. But the pillars are tall, several hundred feet, maybe higher. And they're . . .'

'Tell me.'

Krys said, 'It looks like they're walking.'

Luca sighed. Jackson glanced over. The man's face was illuminated by the headlights frozen along the lakefront road. He could have been in agony or ecstasy; Jackson could not tell.

Krys asked, 'Is it alive?'

'We retain very few remnants of the Ancients. But from what I have gleaned, this is not life as we know it,' Luca replied. 'We witness a final release of primeval force.'

'The pillars are drawing together,' Jackson said.

'You must tell me *exactly* where this happens,' Luca said.

'OK, the fog has completely covered the lake. The lightning or whatever is streaking the entire length, end to end.'

Krys said, 'The obelisk is glowing.'

Jackson felt the heat build beneath his fingers. But he kept his eyes on the lake. The sight was mesmerizing. 'It isn't lightning. It's more like . . .'

'What?'

'Rivers of fire. They come and gather and then they vanish.'

'Gather how?'

'Like a lot of little streams joining together. At first, the juncture was pointing at Geneva, where the Rhone flows out. Now it's angled . . . OK, the force is shifting towards where the pillars are combining.'

As they congregated, the pillars elongated into a parody of the Geneva fountain. Jackson found that astonishing. He had wondered for years where the idea for that fountain came from. Nowadays it served as a symbol for the city, this man-made geyser that continuously blew a spout of water four hundred and twenty-two feet in the air. But no one could ever tell him why it had been built in the first place. When he had asked about it, people had treated his question as silly, an uncertainty raised by a detective who did not know when to turn off his investigative mind. And now before him was the answer. The massive column was filled with a constantly flowing, shifting fire. Jackson had no way of measuring it, but he suspected it was precisely the same height as the city's waterspout. To the centimeter.

Then it vanished. The fog, the river of fire, the pillar, gone.

But Luca kept them exactly where they were, with just the one word: 'Wait.'

The fire reformed, in the same position as the vanished column, a bundle of energy that grew out of the lake and took on form . . .

'It's an island,' Jackson said.

Luca groaned, an involuntary noise. He swallowed hard and said, 'Is there a bridge?'

'Is there . . . Yes! Three humps, maybe two hundred meters in length total.'

'Where does it touch land?'

'It's hard to see.' The light was almost blinding in its brilliance. The island was tiny, less than fifty feet across and shaped like a camel's back. At its heart was an obelisk, identical to the one he touched. 'It looks like it connects to the eastern side of the Rhone's mouth. But I can't be certain . . . Wait! There's somebody on the island!'

A man became fashioned by the same fire that formed the island and the bridge. He reached out a hand toward the obelisk. At least, Jackson thought it was a man.

The night exploded.

The roar was deafening, a massive rush of force that blasted all three of them off their stone perch. Jackson fell into the fountain's icy water, then reached up to catch Luca. 'Krys!'

She came up sputtering. 'I'm OK.'

'Luca?'

The man gripped his wet sleeve and muttered, 'I was right. I was right.'

Jackson looked out at the lake. The waters were moonlit silver, the air calm. Below him, the traffic flowed in a sibilant nighttime rush.

SEVENTEEN

Jackson slept nine hours and woke up sore from head to foot. He showered and stretched and sat at the kitchen counter for over an hour, allowing himself to ease into the day. His apartment was under the eaves in a centuries-old structure above Geneva's medieval center. The studio was cramped and cluttered, and the heating tended to break down in the middle of frigid winter nights. There was scarcely enough room for a single bed, his weights and workout bench, and his desk. When he wanted to watch the wall-mounted television, which was seldom, Jackson swiveled around his office chair. The place was ridiculously cramped for a man who topped out at six-three. But Jackson had arrived in Geneva with the sole aim of shrinking his life down, retreating into a cave of his own making, and trying to reknit the tattered remnants. The few leftovers from his marriage that Jackson had been unable to discard were locked in Sylvie's favorite case, a vintage Hermès, that was hidden in the back of his closet. On nights when sleep was demolished by dreams, Jackson often crouched in the doorway and stroked the case. Sometimes Sylvie felt close enough to whisper comfort.

An hour later, Jackson left his building and drove to a cemetery midway between Geneva and Lausanne. Jackson climbed the slope behind the village and opened the wrought-iron gate. The graveyard contained five centuries of Sylvie's family. Jackson had once considered her burial site a bitter irony, since her family had disowned Sylvie when she left Switzerland to study magic. Now he could look back and almost thank the family that had wanted nothing to do with this amazing woman. Their cold rejection had only knitted the two of them more intimately together. The Talent and the Interpol agent. Not even the Institutes' perpetual rage at her choice of spouse could touch them.

He visited her grave once or twice each season. Here was his one safe island, where he could revisit their three wonderful years together. Jackson knelt and removed the dry stalks from the stone urn and replaced them with a new bouquet. Sylvie had always loved wildflowers. She had specialized in Europe's natural herbs, binding and enforcing their qualities with her special brand of healing magic. Talents could not use their force directly to heal the human body. But those gifted in the related arts could magnify the curative powers of herbs and other natural remedies. Sylvie could walk through a meadow of springtime blossoms and name the therapeutic qualities with each indrawn breath.

Jackson had often wondered how such a gifted and ambitious Talent could damage her career by marrying an Interpol agent. He had asked her only twice, however, because both times she had responded with an almost tragic sorrow. As though his questions released tightly repressed emotions, those for which she had no ready answer save love. But he could ask the silent meadow now, and listen to the wind's vague murmurs, and wonder if perhaps Sylvie's love for him had been anchored in the same defiance and internal conflicts that had forced her to flee her family and her homeland.

The cemetery occupied a saddle of land reached via granite steps bowed and weathered by the centuries. Jackson turned around and stared past the village roofs, out to where the lake glistened in the afternoon breeze. It was as fine a resting place as he could ever imagine.

Jackson had been with Interpol for twenty-nine months when they met, fresh from a successful career with the Magic Squad of the Denver police. His own superiors had also frowned upon their relationship. But Jackson had defied them and married her, and his career had thrived despite this down-check. He was a good agent. He knew that. But his primary target had been the very same Institutes of Magic that had licensed his wife. The Institutes' Directors never let Sylvie forget her crime of loving the wrong man.

Jackson patted the headstone and started back down to the parking lot. They had known some wonderful days, he and Sylvie. Nights of wild passion, days of wine and laughter, and hopes bigger than the forces aligned against them.

But as he opened his car door and slipped behind the wheel, he cast a final glance back up the slope and wondered if he would ever find an answer to the question that plagued him still: Did the Institutes have a hand in Sylvie's demise?

When he was ready, he checked his messages. There were three from the station chief and four from Luca. Jackson was disappointed that Simeon had not been in touch, but not surprised. His first call was to Krys. 'How are you?'

'I'm okay, I guess . . . Where are you?'

'Finishing up an errand. How are you doing, Krys?'

'Coping.'

'Do you want to talk about it?'

'I want to try, but not now. I'm in the bullpen.'

'Has anyone asked for me?'

'The chief called before I got in. She didn't leave any message except for you to get in touch.' She went quiet, then, 'Luca phoned me.'

Jackson nodded to the glistening lake. 'For us to move forward, you and Luca have to work together.' When Krys did not respond, he added, 'Luca's been involved in this investigation for years. We don't have time to relearn the basics. The scrolls are already out there. You understand what I'm saying?'

She paced out each word very carefully, her voice muffled from cupping the phone. 'I don't think I can ever forgive him for what he did to me.'

'That's your decision. But it doesn't change what I said.' Jackson started to add that a measure of distrust might actually be healthy. Then he decided that he probably didn't need to add to her smoldering cauldron.

Krys asked, 'Are you coming in?'

'Later. Call me if something comes up.' Jackson cut the connection and sat staring out over the rooftops. When he was ready, he placed the call to the station chief. The instant she answered, he jumped in with, 'This is Jackson. Are you certain you are genuinely safe?'

The question was part of their tradecraft. It was intended to break the flow, alert the other party to potential incoming fire. Chief Meyer hesitated only a second, then said, 'I'm on the train. Wait one moment.'

There was the sound of rustling, then a low steady drumming came through the speaker. Jackson knew she had stepped into the passageway. Meyer said, 'I couldn't fly. There's been some bad weather down your way.'

'It wasn't weather,' Jackson replied. 'Not like you think, anyway.'

This time her pause lasted longer. 'Perhaps we should delay this conversation.'

'I definitely agree.'

'You think Swiss laws have been broken?'

'I know it,' Jackson replied. 'I witnessed it. Repeatedly.'

The Geneva station chief asked carefully, 'Are there potential repercussions I need to discuss with Brussels?'

'Most definitely yes.'

'Can it wait?'

'I think it has to. A couple of hours one way or the other won't matter.'

'Very well.'

'I need to ask you one question now,' Jackson went on. 'What specifically was the duty you gave me earlier?'

The train's rumbling marked time's passage. Meyer finally replied, 'We are speaking of the scrolls.'

Jackson watched a gull soar past his window. 'So we are not dealing with a multiple homicide.'

'Not that I am aware.'

'No fire at a private Geneva residence. No suspicious events of any kind.'

'I'm not clear on what you mean by that statement,' Meyer replied. 'You have evidence that connects Interpol's hunt to some local crime?'

He nodded to the gull's passage. Her response was a clear tell. Meyer did not know what she had told him about the previous night. 'I'm going to write up two reports before I head into the office.'

Meyer repeated, 'Two reports.'

'Right. One for the official records. The other you may want to read in complete privacy, then send it by courier to Barker. Marked "eyes only".'

Zoe Meyer might have been headed for retirement, but she retained a lifetime's experience of reading between the lines. 'Perhaps it would be best if you dropped both your reports by my home.'

'That was my thinking. Also, I'm going to need a partner on this. The case is growing, and time has become an issue.'

'Do you have someone in mind?'

'Krys Duprey.'

'Jackson . . . There are some questions being raised over Agent Duprey's future with Interpol.'

'I think she's the right agent for this. Maybe essential.'

Meyer's voice dropped. 'She told you what happened?'

'She did.'

'Did she also—'

'Describe how she restrained the assailant. Yes.'

'"Restrained" is hardly the word I would use. And he is not officially considered an assailant.'

'The guy should be the one brought up on charges,' Jackson said. 'And you know it.'

'It would be extremely inappropriate of me to agree, even off the record. Very well. I'll try and clear this with Brussels. Make sure Krys understands this assignment is provisional, pending final approval.'

Jackson cut the connection, rose to his feet, and saluted the day with, 'Well, all right.'

EIGHTEEN

Writing the two reports took Jackson into the early afternoon. He knew Chief Meyer assumed he was working on them at home because the reports contained highly sensitive material. And this was at least partly true. But more importantly, Jackson needed time to prepare his next steps.

Every now and then, Jackson found himself mentally repeating the word Luca had used. *Quest.* He thought it was probably the right term for where he suspected they were headed. But he was just not ready yet to make the sort of commitment that word signified. He was a case officer. He investigated. Such definitions might seem trifling to an outsider. But Jackson was gradually coming to terms with the fact that he was returning to full-action status. Words mattered. They shaped boundaries. They helped keep him alert to incoming danger, both seen and unseen.

When the two reports were completed, he ate a late lunch standing at his stubby kitchen counter, then phoned Luca, who complained, 'Being out of touch like this is dangerous.'

'I needed to get something done. Have you heard from Simeon?'

'Nothing.'

Jackson grimaced. Simeon's continued support was essential to his plan. 'I have an idea I want to run by you. Not in the office. And Krys needs to be there.'

'My home is the upper floor of the Julius Brothers Bank. You know it?'

'Of course.' The building was a dark steel monolith that shadowed the lakefront. The local Genevoise hated it worse than winter. They called it the Giant Wart.

'My entrance is between the café and the newsstand.'

'I'll be there in an hour.' Jackson phoned Krys and asked her to meet him in the café, then drove to the chief's home and slipped both reports into her mailbox.

Krys was seated at one of the café's outside tables when he arrived. Jackson remained in the car, studying her from the vantage point of being unseen. Without shifting his gaze, Jackson reached for his phone. He could put off the call no longer.

Simeon answered with, 'I was wondering when I would hear from you.'

Jackson felt the fear he had carried all day ease slightly. 'Does this mean . . .'

'I am wearing the watch. For now.'

Jackson leaned his head back and shut his eyes. 'You don't know, you can't imagine, how much that means.'

'Which is exactly what my wife said when I told her of my dilemma. That I could not leave you out there alone.'

'Your wife,' Jackson said, 'is a saint.'

'She is indeed.'

'And I am in her debt.'

'Careful. Such a conversation may result in your taking custody of a certain delinquent son.'

'I don't owe her that much.'

'I will not take an active role in your investigation, Jackson. You understand me, my friend? I cannot abandon you. I will continue to offer all the support I possibly can. But only within the boundaries of my nation's laws and constitution.'

'That is more than enough,' Jackson assured him. 'I have an idea.'

'Tell me.'

'Actually, it's only the first part of an idea.' Jackson ran through what he had in mind.

Simeon replied, 'This could work.'

'I need your help.'

'Of course you do. Let me make a couple of calls.'

'Simeon, thank you.'

'You are welcome, and my delinquent son will be ready to move in with you tomorrow.'

Jackson cut the connection, rose from the car, crossed the street, and slipped into the chair opposite Krys. He said, 'I want to run something by you. This is not a demand. It's a request. And a choice.'

Explaining what he had in mind took fifteen minutes. The waitress came, took his order, returned with a double espresso, left, and Krys neither spoke nor shifted her gaze one inch from his face. He liked the intensity of her gaze. He felt as though it was the first time she had ever seen him without the filter of past mistakes.

When he was done, she responded with, 'It's a good plan, Jackson.'

'You think?'

'I do. Excellent, in fact.'

'But there's a risk.'

'Of course there is.'

'I mean, personal. To you.'

'I understand that.'

But Jackson said it aloud anyway, just to be totally clear. 'This is basically forcing Brussels' hand. For you to achieve this assignment, they have to move past whatever pressure they're facing to dismiss you. They might decide it's not worth it. If we wait, you can still participate in a secondary—'

'No. I want in. I want in *now.*' She rapped the table with her knuckles. 'Two nights ago, I decided I couldn't take it. They had already won. I was going to resign. Do you see, Jackson? Either they let me back into the action or I'm done. I have nothing to lose anymore.'

He saw how much the confession cost her, how bitter her regret. 'Interpol would be losing their second-best agent.'

Fans of the Julius Brothers Bank building, and there were some, insisted that the structure represented the new concept of living art. They called it unique, bold, and distinctive. And it certainly was all of that.

Jackson thought the building looked like a dark gray mushroom. The upper floor extended out in a series of curved angles from the stumpy base. There were no sharp edges. The glass was tinted the exact same shade as the steel. The eye tended to slide off the structure. He had walked past the narrow alcove separating the café from the street-front newsstand any number of times. Even now, when he was following Luca's instructions, he could see no sign of a knob or handle. But as they approached, a light appeared at eye level. A second light shone above his head and ran laser-fast over his body, then did the same to Krys. A lock pinged softly, and the door clicked open.

When they stepped into the alcove, Jackson found himself facing the same double-fronted foyer as in the jewelry store. The space was scarcely large enough for the two of them to stand without touching.

As they waited for the outer door to sigh shut and lock, Jackson watched a woman flitter across his restricted field of vision. But the single glance was enough.

She moved from right to left. She was only visible for a second, perhaps two. The first alert Jackson had of her passage was how every male he could see turned and stared. Then she appeared: the nurse who attacked them in Luca's hospital room. Raven hair spilled over a crimson jacket and short tight skirt. Her every step was a liquid shift of her entire body. She tossed her hair in the manner of a woman who used every motion as a lure, but in so doing she turned and stared directly at him. Jackson had no idea if the glass door was mirrored, if she could see him at all. But the sensation was one of having been trapped in the amber-like force of her gaze.

Then she was gone.

The inner door clicked open. Luca's voice came through an unseen speaker. 'Come up the stairs.'

Luca's apartment was astonishingly white. It was a home designed for a man who lived without color. There was artwork on every interior wall, but all of it tactile. Jackson ran a hand over a framed imprint of ancient scrolls, the embossed lettering a subtle pattern under his fingertips. The exterior walls were all glass, but so heavily tinted the sunlight was a muted glow. Luca sat in a white straight-back chair pulled away from his white dining table and listened intently as Jackson ran through his idea. By this third telling, a number of the basic flaws were becoming clear to him. He adapted his concept a bit, but mostly held to the original flow. He was not after details at this point. All that would come later.

Part of his mind remained locked on the single glimpse of the woman in red. Jackson felt an element of doubt creep into his assumption that Luca was a man to be trusted. Confusion and deceit were at the heart of every investigation revolving around magic. One of the reasons Jackson had known such a high solve rate was because he could cut through the mystery and fix himself firmly upon the concrete, the real. Only now he felt unable to decide on a crucial element of moving forward. Should he trust Luca?

Every good Interpol agent relied on such gut instincts when it came to operating in the magical realms. The station chief and the head of Jackson's agency both vouched for this man. And yet, as he completed outlining his idea, Jackson found himself pulling back. Studying this strange, pale, eyeless man anew. Perhaps he had been too swift in accepting him as a trusted accomplice. Perhaps he should revisit the entire issue with his chief. Perhaps . . .

Luca interrupted his deliberations with, 'This plan has potential.'

'I think it is far better than that,' Krys said.

'You are probably correct.' Luca took a slender box from his pocket and held it out. The blue leather was embossed with the Bouchon name and logo. 'Jackson told you about the need for protection of awareness and memories regarding this case?'

'I . . . Yes.' She accepted the box, opened the top, and sat studying the elegant gold watch with its diamond-embossed face.

Luca said, 'You must wear this at all times.'

Jackson started to tell them about the sighting. But indecision gripped him with talons of very real fear. Jackson could not say exactly why this sighting seemed so pivotal, nor what left him convinced that it needed to remain his secret. But in the end, what he asked was, 'Where's your cane?'

'I do not require it here.'

'You're not talking about using it for getting around.'

'Of course not. I secretly maintain wards around this building. Which is why the Julius brothers lease me this space.'

Jackson saw Krys fasten the watch, study it a moment, then cover it with her other hand. He asked, 'You use magic to shield a Swiss bank?'

'The authorities turn a blind eye to certain activities out of necessity. Every financial transaction with any international connection must be shielded against magical interference. The national government treats this as a component of the global reach. Not national law.' Luca's fingers played along the table's edge. 'You will be reporting to Brussels?'

'I've written two reports,' Jackson replied. 'One for the local records, the other a more comprehensive run-down. I'm leaving it to my chief to alert Brussels when she thinks the time is right.'

'Your commandant should know the obelisk was mentioned, as it has been in every related document I have found. Also, the segment I managed to read did not deal with the manipulation of time. That top scroll, the only one I could access, was a spell of opening. Or unlocking. Or building a link.'

'A bridge to the island,' Jackson said.

'That is my thinking as well. But I can't be certain. The wording of the Ancients' spell-scrolls can be vague and misleading, even when unraveled.' Luca turned to a window he could not see. 'So much of the lore regarding the Ancients and their powers is mired in fable and outright lies. My approach is to only accept as real what has been proven in the here and now. What I read also confirmed two other points I have seen before. The Island of Time's appearance is linked to a blue moon, the second full moon in the same month. Very rare. That night, the bridge is open to whoever casts the spell. This same opening reappears for one night only, during the very next full moon. A blue moon occurred the day Bernard vanished.'

Jackson studied the blind wizard. There was so much about the world of magic he simply could not fathom. 'Why is this important to Brussels?'

'I think we should assume he is still out there. Which means we risk Bernard learning of our investigation.'

'The chief mentioned other agents who were murdered.'

Luca nodded. 'Which is why I am hesitant to ask my superiors for help locating him. It could potentially stir the hornet's nest.'

'Let me handle it.'

'Discreetly. Our lives may depend upon it.'

'Quietly or not at all,' Jackson agreed. 'You said, two points.'

'Indeed so. The scrolls confirmed the bridge can only be crossed once. We must assume this means no Talent can repeatedly access the past.'

Jackson was trying to determine how that impacted their investigation when his phone rang. He checked the read-out and said, 'It's Simeon.'

'He is with us?'

'Partly. At least he's wearing the watch.' Jackson hit the connection. 'Go.'

Simeon announced, 'I have received official permission from my superiors to assist in your plan. They, of course, want to speak with your chief.'

'She's on her way back from Brussels. Call her cell.' Jackson gave him the number.

'Once this communication has taken place, we will need to have things happen quite swiftly,' Simeon said. 'Any wasted minute raises the risk of our opponents stepping in.'

'What are you talking about?'

'You will soon see, *mon ami*. How fast can you get here?'

NINETEEN

Jackson drove back by his house, retrieved the Mercedes, and had Krys follow in his Jeep as he returned the vehicle to the diplomatic compound. They continued out past the airport to Simeon's office. Geneva's central police building was a bland concrete structure in the eastern industrial zone. The only adornment was a large ceramic shield by the glass entry. Police headquarters had previously been in a stately structure downtown, but the interior had been an outdated maze. No officer Jackson knew had ever expressed regret over the move.

Jackson called ahead, and Simeon was waiting outside the front entrance when he pulled up. When the Swiss detective opened the rear door, Jackson said, 'Inspector Krys Duprey, Detective Simeon Baehr.'

'A pleasure, *madame*.' Then he noticed her watch. 'Is that . . .'

'A gift from Luca.'

Simeon slid inside and shut his door. 'She knows?'

'Everything,' Jackson replied. 'Where are we headed?'

Their destination was an industrial zone on the airport's other side. Simeon directed Jackson along a central avenue sandwiched between vast freight warehouses, then told him to stop in front of a gated entrance. Jackson had passed the compound any number of times. The complex occupied a full city block and was surrounded by triple fencing topped with razor wire. He had always assumed it belonged to the Swiss military. As Jackson pulled up to the reinforced barricade, Simeon said, 'Give me your badges and IDs.' He rose from the car and entered the guardhouse.

Krys asked, 'What is this place?'

Jackson shook his head. He watched as the guardhouse duty officer carefully inspected a sheaf of documents Simeon produced, then lifted the phone and placed a call.

Krys pointed to the street behind them. 'Check out the posse.'

Jackson shifted around as a trio of police vehicles parked on the street's opposite side. He was drawn back around by his phone ringing. Jackson hit the button on the steering wheel and said, 'Burnett.'

Luca's voice emerged from the vehicle's eight speakers. 'Where do you live?'

'I have a studio apartment on the Boulevard Henri.'

'That will not do. Is the apartment in your name?'

'No. It's on a long lease to the office. The official line is, I'm using it until I locate something suitable.'

'That is now being arranged,' Luca said. 'I need your full name.'

'Jackson Edward Burnett. Why?'

'I have acquired the house on Rue Gambord and am assigning you the title. What do you drive?'

'A Jeep Grand Cherokee.' Jackson turned and stared at Krys, who was frowning at the sound system. 'Say that again about what you're buying.'

'You need a residence that is suitable for the tactics you outlined in my apartment. And you will require a new car. I am supplying both. Where are you now?'

'Police compound by the airport. Luca—'

'I have spoken with your chief, and she has approved. In case anyone checks, the records now show you paid cash for both.' He cut the connection.

Krys demanded, 'What just happened?'

Jackson did not respond. He was busy sorting through the news. He half expected to feel some sense of outrage over Luca taking such an action straight to Jackson's boss. But he decided Luca had been right. Jackson had sensed the same time pressure that morning. If the scrolls were indeed out there, they had to move fast.

When he remained silent, Krys demanded, 'The guy just bought you a *house*?'

Jackson looked at her. 'We are entering a two-tier investigation. That is, assuming the chief and Brussels both back us. Our official remit is to locate and obtain and probably destroy any outlawed magical documents. Clear?'

'Of course, but—'

'To make this happen, we are going undercover.'

'You already said that.'

'You will be serving as aide to a major buyer, one Jackson Burnett. Your ties to Interpol are now severed.'

'I thought . . . you know, fake IDs.'

'There isn't time to set up a proper history. And we'll be checked. Documents will be structured to reveal that I have recently been dismissed for questionable dealings, which includes taking bribes. An internal investigation has uncovered that I gradually went rogue after my wife died. And you . . .'

Her expression turned bitter.

Jackson said it anyway. 'Everything you've been fighting against will now become reality.' He pointed to where Simeon emerged from the guardhouse and waved. 'Heads up. We're on.'

Krys was still sorting through Jackson's comments when Simeon slipped into the back seat. Through the rearview mirror, Jackson watched the Swiss detective roll down his window and offer the parked police convoy a cheery wave. Jackson asked, 'What's with the Swiss assault troops?'

Simeon tch-tched. 'You Americans with your cowboy attitude. This is Switzerland. We Swiss make excellent chocolate and we yodel and we tuck our children in bed at night with pleasant stories. No assault troops on city streets. We leave such things for the cinema.'

Jackson could see the detective was smiling. 'I hear the words but I completely miss the meaning.'

'Drive through the gate and park by the building's front entrance. All will be made clear.'

The central structure was far too small for the compound. It sat like a square cement island in the middle of an asphalt sea. Seven civilian vehicles and four armored vans were clustered in the south-east corner. When Jackson cut the engine, Simeon said, 'This place is run by one Herr Horst Gaynor. He is everything I despise in the Swiss bureaucracy. Do you understand what I am saying, Jackson?'

'I've got a pretty good idea.'

'Gaynor has worked here for thirty-two years. He runs this place like a military prison. His underlings despise him. They beg for reassignment. If Switzerland had an outpost in Patagonia, they would prefer it to here.'

Krys asked, 'What is this place?'

'A repository for illegal materials,' Simeon replied.

'As in, magical items,' Jackson said.

'*The* repository,' Simeon confirmed. 'It has existed since our constitution outlawed magic. The building you see is merely the cork in the bottle. Everything except administration is housed in caves that predate our nation. We have had our little run-ins, Herr Gaynor and I.'

Krys said, 'He tried to keep us out?'

'He is still trying,' Simeon replied. 'Herr Gaynor is in there right now, working every contact he has in Bern, trying to overturn my remit.'

Jackson asked again, 'Why the backup?'

'You'll see.' Simeon flashed another impish smile. 'This is going to be fun.'

TWENTY

T he building was a windowless concrete cube with fluorescent lighting and cheap linoleum floors. The cheerless foyer stank of industrial cleaner. The reception cubicle was fronted by thick bulletproof glass. A young man with a practiced blank expression made careful note of their badges and IDs, then had them stand in front of the glass so he could take their picture. He slipped visitor badges bearing their photographs through the slot and said they must wear them at all times. Throughout the entire process, Jackson could hear someone shouting in the background. When the armored door was buzzed open, the yelling became much louder. An unseen man was using Swiss German, which Jackson did not speak. But he did not need to understand the words to know the man was beside himself with rage.

A nervous young woman stood before a pair of armored elevators. She introduced herself as Edna Koch. Every time Herr Gaynor hit a high note, Edna winced. She flashed a badge before the scanner, then ushered them inside the elevator. Even when the doors slid shut, they could hear the man shouting.

Edna asked Simeon a question in Swiss German, and he replied in French, 'We wish to descend to your lowest level.'

The woman's hand hovered over the buttons. 'Herr Gaynor . . .'

'Your director is not with us. In fact, he has been expressly forbidden to impede our work in any way. Which is why you serve as escort, and not him.' Simeon's standard brand of mocking good humor did nothing to ease the young woman's nerves. 'Be so kind as to escort us to the deepest portion of your keep.'

A tight shudder passed through Edna's slender frame. She pushed

the bottom button, which was rimmed in red. A bell sounded overhead. Beyond the steel doors, Jackson could hear Herr Gaynor's
voice hit a new pitch.

The elevator began to descend. Herr Gaynor's irate tone gradually
vanished into the distance. Simeon bounced on his toes and hummed
a soft tune. The woman kept her back to them. The elevator clanked
noisily as they passed each floor. From the machine's tight vibra-
tions Jackson had the impression they were descending at a rapid
pace. Even so, the distance between these clanks was considerable,
suggesting that the cave network was both massive and quite deep.

Simeon said, 'When I was a young policeman, I was assigned duty
with the federal prosecutor's office. One of my early cases involved
a murder by magical means. A knife from the crime scene had been
brought here because it was covered with strange markings that shifted
whenever the blade was touched. Herr Gaynor refused our request to
bring in experts. For months he delayed, he fought, he argued.
Eventually, the case against our murderer was dismissed, and the
suspect was released. When my team was finally able to inspect
the item, we found the suspect's fingerprints on the hilt. A new arrest
warrant was issued, but the suspect had vanished. The case is still
open.' The elevator clanked and slowed. 'Ah. Here we are.'

The elevator foyer was a tomblike chamber with an ancient mosaic
embedded in the floor. Illumination was supplied by fluorescent
lights strung from the distant ceiling. A ratty desk was positioned
to catch as much of the meager light as possible. A young man rose
uncertainly to his feet and peered at them myopically.

'They call these lowest levels the dungeons,' Simeon said. He
waved a cheery greeting at the young man. 'You must have done
something truly awful to be assigned this duty.'

The young man flapped his hands in frantic protest. 'You are not
permitted here!'

'Ah, but, you see, Herr Gaynor now possesses a directive that
arrived from Bern this very morning. In it, the minister himself says
otherwise. Is that not correct, Fräulein Koch?' When the young
woman nodded uncertainly, Simeon pointed at the ancient vault
door. 'Be so good as to open that, will you?'

The series of caverns was unlike anything Jackson had ever seen
or heard of. In fact, something about them left Jackson extremely
unsettled, as though he was about to enter a forbidden realm. The

chambers were definitely sculpted; no natural occurrence could have resulted in anything so regular. But from Jackson's first glimpse beyond the security portal, he was certain they had not been carved by man.

Each cave was oval in shape, about forty feet long and twenty wide. The floors and ceilings and walls rippled in odd formations, like grooves shaped to mimic waves on a stone sea. They opened end on end, connected by a pattern of curved steps too narrow for Jackson's feet. From where Jackson stood, in the opening that led into the first chamber, it appeared as if he stood inside a petrified beast whose stone shell extended in lumpish regularity far into the distance. The ceiling lights and their connecting cables struck him as a desecration.

Simeon said, 'Rumors abound of such places scattered about the country.'

Jackson's voice bounced softly through the chamber. 'Who built them?'

'No one knows. Nor are we likely to ever find out. Officially, the Swiss government ignores all evidence that ties our past to magic.' Simeon turned back to Jackson. 'What precisely do you need?'

'A few items valuable enough to turn heads,' Jackson replied. They had been through this on the phone, but nothing could have prepared him for the sheer volume of items on murky display. 'Old enough to have no public record that they came from here.'

Simeon pointed at the vast array of goods stacked on the stone shelves that rose floor to ceiling, lining every cavern Jackson could see. 'These items were collected during our civil war. Seven centuries ago, as each canton was declared magic-free, all of the condemned artifacts were brought here. You will need to be more specific, Jackson. There are dozens of caves crammed with such relics. Because of people like Herr Gaynor, the only records are maintained by junior staffers who have no magical abilities . . .'

Simeon stopped talking because Krys slipped past them and descended the narrow stairs and entered the first cavern. She walked down the line of narrow shelves carved into the right-hand wall, like oval cupboards about five feet long. Stone partitions held the same rippling pattern as the floor. Krys moved slowly, tracing one hand over the air by the central shelves.

Jackson watched her, uncertain what was happening. He entered the cave and shifted over to the left, so he could see her face. Her features were tight, concentrated, focused. Her eyes held a distant intensity. As though having taken aim at something she could not yet identify.

A tiny spark joined Krys to one of the objects half-hidden in the shadows. Krys said, 'Here.'

Jackson stepped forward and withdrew a box carved from what appeared to be solid gold. He turned to Simeon and asked, 'Any chance of a handcart?'

'I will ask.' But he remained where he was, his gaze wide with astonishment. Krys had just overturned a cop's lifetime assumptions. Tilting the earth on its axis. Simeon asked, 'Can this be? She is a Talent?'

'No,' Jackson replied. 'She is an agent of Interpol.'

TWENTY-ONE

Jackson followed Krys as she proceeded slowly through the warren of oval caves. Simeon remained at the main opening, there to ensure they were not halted by the young man or his boss. Edna Koch located a flat-bed pushcart and tracked Krys and Jackson from chamber to chamber, making careful note of each article Krys uncovered and carrying it back to the small pile. Jackson was fascinated by the way Krys interacted with each item. The power did not spark from her fingers, as Jackson first thought. Rather, a force reached out from the shelves as she passed. He wondered if Krys somehow attracted energy from these magical objects, or if perhaps she woke these inanimate articles from their sleep of centuries.

Then it happened.

Jackson felt a rippling current impact him at gut level. 'Whoa.'

Krys turned around. 'What is it?'

'You didn't feel that?'

'Feel what?'

Jackson had no idea what to say. But her eyes remained steady on him, so he said, 'This place is spooky.'

'You OK?'

'I think so.'

'I can handle this alone.'

'No, I'm good.' Which he was. The sensation was with him still, but there was nothing unpleasant about it. 'Does it hurt when the spark strikes you?'

She held up her right hand, showing unblemished fingers. 'Actually, it's kind of exciting.'

Which was how Jackson felt. Thrilled without understanding why or what was causing it. Krys turned back and continued moving forward, each step a slow dance across the rippling stones. Her right hand moved up and down the shelves, not quite grazing the outer edge.

They arrived at the next passage, where two caverns opened up. Krys hesitated, then went right. But when Jackson arrived at the same point, he felt an unmistakable draw to his left. Which shifted the experience to an entirely new level. Up to that point, Jackson had assumed he was tracking some run-off from Krys.

As he entered the left-hand cavern, Jackson inspected the sensation more carefully. It was very pleasant, like a spice applied to a fragrant dish. Jackson walked to the center and did a slow circle. The room was somewhat larger than the others, maybe fifty feet long and twenty wide. Krys's voice echoed from a distance. 'Jackson?'

'Give me a minute.' He had no idea where to search, or what he was looking for. The cavern was lined with the same oblong shelves, dozens of them, all stuffed to overflowing.

Jackson sensed that the place held no danger for him. Actually, it was much stronger than mere supposition. The magnetic appeal or whatever it was carried an unmistakable form of unspoken communication. He was *absolutely certain* that he was safe.

Jackson followed the magnetic pull to the left-hand wall, stood on his toes, and reached into the highest shelf.

But all he touched was stone. The shelf was empty.

He could not understand it. He was *positive* the thing that called to him was there.

Jackson used the lower shelves to climb up to where he could look inside. What he found was another mystery.

Of all the shelves he had passed, this was the only one that held nothing at all.

He heard footsteps and dropped down to the floor.

Krys entered the chamber and demanded, 'What are you doing in here?'

'I thought . . .'

'What?'

Jackson was unable to come up with anything to say. But the connection remained intact, filling him now with a distinct need to keep this *private*.

Krys seemed to find nothing wrong with his silence. She began her slow circuit of the room. There was no spark, no sense of connection. At least, none directed at Krys. The staffer joined them and remained in the doorway while Krys completed her course and returned to the opening. Krys asked, 'You coming?'

'Not just yet. I need . . .'

Krys nodded as though she understood him completely. 'You feel it, too.'

Jackson looked at her. 'Feel what?'

She smiled. 'I have no idea.'

Edna Koch volunteered, 'Most aides refuse to come down here. They say . . .'

'Tell us,' Jackson demanded.

'They have dreams,' the staffer replied. 'For weeks.'

Krys said, 'I can well imagine.'

Jackson asked the staffer, 'That doesn't bother you?'

Edna hesitated, then confessed, 'Herr Gaynor refuses to enter the lower realms. I feel . . . safe here.'

Krys asked, 'How many chambers haven't I visited?'

'Just three.'

'OK, let's get to it.'

'I'll be just another minute,' Jackson said, then waited as their footsteps faded.

He reclimbed the shelves and inspected the empty space. Standing there in the chilled cavern, his right hand touching the rear wall, he was filled with a sensation as strong as his own breath. He *knew* something was there. Something that called . . .

He had no idea what drew him around. Perhaps it was another impression from beyond the reach of his physical senses. Jackson turned, his hand still resting on the stone, and saw a different world.

It was the same cavern, only now the bland gray stone rippled with waves of color. The walls and floor and ceiling and shelves all supplied a light that was *everywhere*. The longer Jackson watched, the more certain he became that the light formed a distinct pattern. It seemed to Jackson as though the cavern actually *breathed*.

Then he saw the people.

Or, rather, he saw their silhouettes. It was like watching shimmering images through water. A light streamed off them, forming illuminated currents behind and masking all but their bare outlines. They were small figures, with heads that appeared utterly flat and two stubby arms and two short legs. Even so, they moved in poised elegance, flitting about with astonishing speed. The cavern and these half-seen beings lived in constant synch. It was beyond beautiful.

He withdrew the hand touching the rear wall so he could clear his eyes without losing his grip. Instantly, the image was replaced by a gray cavern lit by the cold fluorescents screwed into the blank stone ceiling.

Jackson clamped his hand back in place.

Gradually, the scene clarified, the colors returned, the lights rippled, the small figures shifted and flowed.

Then one broke away and scampered up the stone that separated one set of shelves from the next. The light streaked about it, leaving Jackson unable to see anything clearly except the streaming colors. The figure reached into the empty shelf where Jackson was poised, and touched the stone wall in a certain place, thumb and fingers formed in a double V, and where it touched, the stone became alive. The wall flowed like liquid, revealing a second shelf. The figure set a small object inside, then turned its hand in the opposite direction, resealing the stone wall.

As soon as the being touched the floor, the vision ended. For that was what Jackson considered it now. A brief glimpse offered of a different realm. One from the far, far distance. A domain from before the time of man.

He fitted his hand into the same positions and turned.

The wall became liquid, flowing away from his hand in silky silence.

The item was there, waiting for him.

TWENTY-TWO

Jackson exited the cavern just as Krys and the staffer reappeared. Both women carried items. Krys's forehead was streaked with grime. 'Where have you been?'

He knew he was going to tell her. But for the moment he was willing to follow the simple urge to keep this secret. Which went against the grain. Staying safe in an investigation of magic required partners to move in synch. Confidentiality was absolutely necessary, especially when dealing with departmental superiors. Leaks were constant. But between partners, openness was the rule. Yet here he was, convicted now by secrets he did not share. What was more, Jackson had no logical explanation for his actions. All he said was, 'Trying to come to terms with what this means.'

To his surprise, Edna Koch said, 'I often feel the same way down here.'

Krys asked, 'And?'

'Sometimes I sense the place wants to communicate with me.'

'Like the sparks flying from my fingertips,' Krys said.

Jackson asked, 'How did you make that happen?'

'I didn't.' Krys shrugged. 'I just felt drawn forward. I walked. The sparks formed a sort of connection to these things.' She lifted the final two artifacts that she held. 'What they are, I have no idea.'

As the elevator clanked its way back towards the surface, Edna Koch confided how Herr Gaynor followed a pattern set in place decades ago. No outside examiner had been permitted entry to the lower levels for almost a century. Back then, an interior minister had so loathed Talents that he had enacted the law making magic a capital offense. The minister had assigned the role of custodian to a man who shared his zeal. Since then, the position had been passed down from one enemy of magic to the next.

Edna Koch softly confided how she had three months left of her two-year stint. She hoped she would be able to forget the misery she had endured here. She hoped she would be rewarded with a posting that actually mattered . . .

The pushcart was a simple steel slab on wheels. A chest-high handle ran across the back. Krys had connected with seventeen items in all. They formed a small pile in the center of the cart. Simeon listened to Edna Koch with an alert and sympathetic air. Jackson had never had the chance to observe Simeon interrogate a suspect. He decided the detective would prove very adept at drawing out the most intimate of confessions.

When the elevator clanked up to surface level, Edna Koch stepped away from the doors, compressing herself into a small space against the side wall. Jackson saw the expression of genuine fear crease her young features and shared Simeon's anger at the man responsible.

The elevator doors opened, and Jackson pushed the trolley forward. Edna Koch remained where she was, clutching the wall. As Simeon left the elevator, he murmured, 'You may wish to observe what happens next, *mademoiselle*.'

The man who barred the hall leading to the exit could only have been Herr Gaynor. He was tall and big-boned and clearly used to shoving his way through life. The director's size and brutish force made his graying toothbrush mustache appear utterly misplaced, as if an aging caterpillar had somehow gotten lost on his face.

When Gaynor spotted what was clustered on the trolley, he grew so enraged his eyes actually bulged. '*Das ist strengstens verboten*!'

Simeon actually seemed to find pleasure in the moment. 'Get out of my way, you . . .' He turned and smiled at Jackson. 'Forgive me, *mon ami*, what is the proper translation for *crapaud*?'

'Toad,' Jackson offered.

'Of course.' Simeon turned back to the massive custodian. 'You corpulent toad.'

Gaynor bellowed and rushed at Simeon.

Simeon moved with a lithe grace, slipping under the roundhouse punch. He snagged the man's wrist and flicked it up, compressing the pressure point over the nerve ganglion. It was as smooth a move as Jackson had ever seen, and he had trained with the best.

Gaynor's bellow was cut off as cleanly as if Simeon had taken him in a chokehold. Gaynor hiccupped from the unexpected pains – three of them, actually. His wrist was now trapped in an impossible angle, the nerves of his hand were shrieking, and his forward momentum threatened to pull his arm out of its socket.

Simeon stabbed his other thumb into the point where the man's skull met his spine. Gaynor's head snapped fully back, trying to protect this sudden fourth vulnerability.

Simeon then redirected the man's massive bulk into the side wall.

Jackson felt the impact through his shoes.

Gaynor's emitted a strangled, 'Ack'.

Simeon released his hold and stepped in closer. His hands only seemed to move a fraction of a degree: three quick stabs, to both kidneys and then to the point at the top of the spine where his thumb had been. The punches were blindingly fast.

Gaynor 'acked' a second time, then slid slowly down the wall and slumped on to the floor.

Simeon smiled with genuine satisfaction. 'You realize, of course, Herr Gaynor, that it is a criminal offense to obstruct a police officer in the course of his lawful duties. And another to try to strike said officer.' He reached to the leather holder attached to his belt and extracted a pair of handcuffs. 'Which is why I am obliged to place you under arrest.'

TWENTY-THREE

When they emerged from the building, the police cars had been joined by an armored van. Simeon waved to where they now idled in front of the gate. The compound's security guards were clearly overwhelmed by the sheer size of the opposing force. Not to mention how their boss was being trundled outside on a pushcart, atop a pile of the treasures he was assigned to keep permanently underground. The entire staff emerged, clutching one another in stunned disbelief.

It would have been wrong of Jackson to suggest that the police were unnecessarily rough in how they handled the Swiss bureaucrat. But Jackson could most definitely say that Simeon was not the only policeman smiling.

Simeon accepted the return of his handcuffs, then watched as Gaynor was shoved into the rear seat of the armored transport. His wrists and ankles were then bound by chains linked to the van's floor. Gaynor was coming around now and protesting loudly over his treatment.

Simeon stepped up to the rear door and said, 'Look at me.'

The man growled and snapped and protested. Then he realized he was surrounded by uniformed officers who were not moving. The message finally got through that he had no choice. He spoke in heavily accented French, 'I will *crush* you and everyone involved in this *travesty—*'

'Be quiet.' Simeon waited until the man was silent, then went on, 'Perhaps you recall an instance where your objections forced us to release the prime suspect in a murder case? It was some time

ago, and you have caused our department so many other obstruc-
tions since then. But that was my first contact with you, and it left
quite an impression. Particularly since DNA has tied that suspect
to five further murders in Rome and Athens.'

Simeon shut the door and tapped his knuckles on the car roof.

A senior officer whose uniform was adorned with gold braid
snapped off a military salute. '*Merci*, Simeon.'

Simeon remained standing there as the cavalcade drove slowly
away. He then walked over to Jackson and said, 'I am far from the
only officer who has suffered at the hands of Herr Gaynor.'

Jackson said, 'I'd say that guy is in for quite a long journey to
headquarters.'

'Indeed. It is remarkable how easy it is to become lost in this
city.' Simeon sighed with genuine pleasure. 'There certainly are
compensations to being involved in your investigation, Jackson. I
must return to headquarters and assist with Gaynor's arrest warrant.
But I will assign you a police escort.'

'Simeon, one thing can't wait.' He stepped in closer. 'Bernard
Bouchon.'

'Yes?'

'We need to know more about him in this new situation. Where
he is, what he's doing . . . Most important of all, is he a threat to
our investigation?'

Simeon lost all traces of his former good humor. 'I should have
thought of this.'

'If I go through Interpol, it has to be in the form of an official inquiry.
Having Interpol check on a Talent is like poking the angry bear.'

'No, no, that is unacceptable.'

'Can you be discreet?'

'I am Swiss. I am a master of discretion.' Simeon pondered, then
said, 'Our tax authorities are notoriously thorough. They are, after
all, Swiss.'

'But magic is outlawed. If Bernard is now a Talent—'

'Where he lives and works does not matter to the taxman. He is
still Swiss, unless, of course, he has renounced his citizenship. In
either case, they will have a record. And if he has failed to declare
his income from these magical pursuits, my allies in the tax division
will make his present existence a misery.'

'A current photograph would help. And one more thing. Can you
check through the records for the house on Rue Gambord?'

'That is a much simpler task.'

'Who commissioned it, who built it? Who owned the property before? What structure was there? I assume they tore down something and built that house in its place.'

'Most certainly.' Simeon started away. 'I should have something for you tomorrow. Two days at the most.'

They made the return journey to Rue Gambon in nineteen minutes. The garage door was open, so Jackson pulled inside, then walked back out to thank his guides. The officers responded in easy cheerfulness. They clearly had accepted Jackson into their ranks, at least temporarily. It was a rare and unexpected reception from the clannish Swiss force. Jackson remained standing in the forecourt as they drove away, the only fitting gesture he could come up with.

When he and Krys opened the door connecting them to the kitchen, they entered a house transformed.

Gone was the hollow emptiness that made even the newest of homes a challenge. In its place was an ornate elegance.

Luca entered the kitchen through the portal leading to the dining alcove. 'Did you succeed in identifying an artifact you can use?'

'Several, thanks to Krys.' Jackson sketched a look through the framed doorway into the living area. 'You did this?'

'I told you, Jackson. You are now a man of means.'

'Give me a second.' He made a slow sweep of the ground floor. Krys walked beside him. He waited for her to make some comment about Luca's actions, but she seemed as stunned as he felt.

The furnishings were definitely not to his taste. The decor was mostly French Empire. The furniture's spindly legs were adorned with ornate carvings and gold leaf. The sideboards and coffee tables were finished in ormolu, as were the dining table and cabinetry. The carpet in the marble-tiled front foyer appeared to be vintage Persian. He was fairly certain the oils on the walls were original. He saw Krys gaping at the parlor's new crystal chandelier and said, 'Luca mentioned he was rich.'

'This goes way beyond wealth,' Krys said. 'He did all this in a *day*.'

Jackson was saved from needing to come up with a reply by the ringing of his phone. He checked the read-out and said, 'It's the chief.'

When he made the connection, Zoe Meyer asked, 'Where are you?'

'Rue Gambon. Luca has arranged for me to live—'

'I know all that. Is this phone secure?'

'Definitely not.'

'You need to arrange for a new one. Home also. And daily sweeps.'

'Understood.'

'I've just heard from the Geneva chief of police. He seems to be quite satisfied with today's events. He actually thanked me for the role you played. I thought you were just going to collect a few artifacts.'

'Things got complicated,' Jackson replied. 'Maybe we should wait and discuss this in person.'

'The office is now off-limits,' Meyer ordered. 'My home. One hour.'

TWENTY-FOUR

When Jackson told the others that he had to leave for a meeting with the chief, Luca asked Krys to help him inspect the new artifacts. Luca explained he would assess them in the downstairs office, one at a time. When he was done, Krys would set the item in the vault before bringing the next one downstairs. This meant each initial examination would be as free as possible from the energies and influences of the other artifacts. Luca made it sound like a request, but it was still enough for Krys to fume. Jackson watched Krys follow him down the stairs carrying an artifact, her face a sullen mask.

The internal debate was enough to effectively split him. One side said he needed to address this friction. But to do so meant confessing his suspicions and discussing the woman he suspected was tracking them. Not to mention . . .

The artifact he had removed from the caves.

Jackson touched the item in his pocket. He had broken a dozen Swiss laws by taking it and not making an official declaration. He was effectively placing his career on the line. And over what?

He entered the garage and selected a second artifact at random. When he reached the bottom of the stairs, he discovered that Luca stood very close to Krys, his face almost touching hers. His voice was soft, insistent. Krys's sullen expression was gone. In its place was a hollow distress. She glanced at Jackson, then looked away.

Jackson set the item by the bottom step and returned upstairs. He unloaded the Jeep and piled the remaining artifacts on the garage floor. He then made a quick inspection of the kitchen cabinets, preparing a mental list of items he would bring over from his old apartment and another list for groceries. All the while, his internal debate seethed and roiled.

Krys entered the kitchen behind him and said, 'Luca is ready for the next item.'

'They're all waiting for you in the garage.'

'Don't you want to know what he told me?'

'I can guess.' Jackson turned back around. 'What is he, MI6? French Sûreté?'

'CIA.'

'It had to be something like that.' Jackson leaned on the doorjamb and filled in the blanks. 'He was probably placed in Interpol head-quarters with a strict remit to observe only. No direct involvement in any case, no matter how critical. Witnessing your assault put Luca in a terrible quandary. If he took part in an official inquiry, it would have jeopardized four years of work.'

'He told me that he took his request all the way to the agency's director and was turned down.' She stared blindly out of the kitchen window. 'Maybe I believe him. But that doesn't mean I trust him. And I don't think you should either.'

Jackson knew the time had come to relate his concerns. How, on the one hand, everything Luca had told them appeared to be valid. How he was operating as one of their team. How any number of Jackson's superiors kept a hidden agenda; that this was in many cases part of the job. Working within an international organization like Interpol required juggling many political balls. Conflict and secrecy were inevitable.

And then there was the other side. How just standing here allowed him to feed on her distrust. The tension radiating from Krys was a palpable force. He needed to tell her. Even so . . .

Jackson left her standing in the middle of the kitchen, arms gripped across her middle, staring at the floor. He eased the Jeep out of the garage, swung around the forecourt, and departed.

* * *

Geneva's station chief lived in a home she had inherited from a great-aunt. It was located in a quiet suburb north of the UN head-quarters and would have fetched a small fortune on the open market. Zoe Meyer's husband was a professor of sociology at the university, and neither of them was particularly interested in housework. Jackson had been there on several occasions. The house showed both age and disrepair. Meyer greeted him in slippers and a cashmere sweater, then led him through a dining room where every flat surface held open books. 'My husband is finishing up a paper. His office can't contain everything he requires. I allow him use of our living space under protest, and with strict time limitations.'

Her study was exactly what Jackson would have expected of a senior officer: neat and laid out with an eye to military precision. Once he had declined her offer of coffee, she settled into the chair next to Jackson and opened her laptop. 'Barker wants in on this conversation.'

When Interpol's commander came on the screen, Jackson updated them in the terse manner both women preferred. He left out any mention of the artifact resting in his pocket. The internal pressure to keep things private remained very strong. Jackson knew it would all come out, sooner rather than later. But for the moment, he told himself to hold back. See where this was headed. Pretend he had a choice.

The commandant told Jackson, 'There is still considerable pressure to dismiss Krys Duprey outright. I have resisted the demands because I don't want to lose a good agent.'

'Especially a Talent,' Jackson agreed.

'Even so, Krys Duprey used her top-secret abilities on a senior police official. She then Tasered him six times. The only factor in Duprey's favor is that this is not the first time the deputy chief has shown such aggressive behavior. Yesterday I met with a lieutenant from the Brussels internal affairs. He has gathered testimonies from two other women, both of whom are willing to describe the events in court. But the pressure remains. Our agency has received complaints from the regional government over how one of their own was physically assaulted and publicly shamed.'

Jackson understood where this was headed. 'It will be easy for you to say you bowed to the pressure and invited her to resign.'

Barker asked the Geneva chief, 'What do you think of Jackson going undercover?'

Meyer did not hesitate. 'No one at our office is carrying anywhere near a full caseload. We could easily backdate his records, show there have been rumors of black-market dealings that we have only recently confirmed. And because of his wife's death and previous record, we were trying to keep it quiet. And then use trusted sources to reveal he's been let go.'

'Jackson, are you OK with that?'

'Do it,' he said.

'It will be set in place this afternoon,' Barker said. She settled her hands upon the desk in front of her. 'Interpol's lower levels contain a secret vault that is magically protected. It holds a select group of files, artifacts, and an evidence locker. You understand what I am saying?'

'Cases that remain unknown to the outside world,' Jackson said. 'Cases that never existed.'

'Your second file regarding Bernard Bouchon is now part of these records. We will hand-deliver a copy to the director of each national security agency with whom we coordinate.'

Jackson felt impacted by the solemnity of this moment. Even so, he had to ask, 'Are you certain I can trust Luca Tami?'

Both women gave him the stonelike expression of leaders with years of experience fighting political battles. Barker demanded, 'What evidence do you have to the contrary?'

He knew his response needed to start with the hospital attack and the fake nurse. Then relate how he had again spotted the woman outside Luca's apartment. Describe the potential threat she represented. Conclude with the simple fact that if Luca's participation added an additional risk, he needed to be reassigned back to headquarters.

'Jackson?'

Jackson felt as though he was being torn in two. His concerns were in direct contrast to the positive impact Luca was having, the steps that were only possible because of the blind researcher's input.

The doubt and confusion and turmoil threatened to rip him apart.

Finally he said, 'I don't have enough concrete evidence to make a case. Just the same, I have concerns.'

Barker said, 'The pressures we face to include him are immense.'

Meyer agreed. 'We need very real substantiation to withdraw him from the investigation.'

Bev Barker then took a long moment to examine him. Jackson

could feel her gaze probe beneath the surface. He waited for her to demand to know what created his internal tempest. He had no idea what to say or even if he could speak at all.

But all the director said was, 'It's good to have you back.'

TWENTY-FIVE

Throughout a solitary dinner, Jackson toyed with the artifact he had found in the cavern. The memory of those swiftly moving figures filled him with a sense of pleasant mystery. He was still holding it as he prepared for bed. He lay down and turned it over and over in his hands, wondering at the connection he felt. Logic said such an item held huge and unknown dangers. But logic played no role in this visceral bonding. Jackson fell asleep with it still in his grasp.

For much of the night, illuminated silhouettes danced a silent ballet, choreographed by shimmering rainbow lights. An hour or so before dawn, however, the dreams took a drastic shift.

The colors faded so swiftly that it would have been possible to forget they had ever existed. In the same instant, Jackson's reverie took on a crystalline intensity. He stood alone in a desolate cavern, carved in the rippling pattern but lifeless as a tomb. The air in his dream tasted dusty, like old bones. The stone cast a grim light, barely enough for him to see that he was alone and trapped.

Then he realized it was no longer a dream.

The turmoil and distress that had swamped him the previous day now clenched him with an impossible force. He was pulled into a hole so desolate he could not even scream for help.

He was drawn forward with ever-increasing speed. Until the woman appeared there before him. The nurse. The lady in red. The temptress.

The cavern where she waited glowed with a crimson heat. It reflected upon her body and upon him. Jackson drowned in her sexual lure, a magnetic force that trapped him in the amber of his own desire.

'What a lovely surprise. Who do we have here?' She leaned in tight, probing, stripping. 'Jackson, what a lovely name. And how handsome. You'll make a splendid addition to my collection.'

Jackson knew now that her name was Riyanna. But the knowledge brought no comfort. He could neither speak nor escape. Her power was an electric lust, and he was already captured. The enticement wrapped itself around him and dragged him to his doom.

Then Riyanna hesitated. She took in her surroundings and declared, 'Where is it you've chosen for our first tryst, my new darling?'

Her uncertainty brought Jackson a brief flash of clarity. He knew he should call upon the implement he had recovered. So that he could shield himself from her insidious control and flee.

Only the implement was not there. The attachment had been lost.

'You naughty boy.' Riyanna seemed positively delighted with her location. 'You have brought me to the forbidden realm. And you . . . What are you, an untrained Renegade? Wait! You're Interpol! Can that be? Oh, the sisters will have fun with you, they will.'

Then a second figure lumbered into view. A red behemoth similar to the form Riyanna had taken in the hospital. But different in the sense that he was still half man. As if he had remained in this state so long he had morphed into a being that would never fully be human again.

He drew in close to Jackson, and his probing was done with the brutal swiftness of a cleaver. 'He's no Renegade. He's Interpol.'

'I know that. Now get away!'

'We're forbidden to be down here. Kill him and be done with it.' He swept out one claw and would have raked off Jackson's skull had Riyanna not caught the arm.

'He's mine!' She shoved him violently away. 'Now go away and leave me to my pleasures!'

In the instant Riyanna's attention was turned away, Jackson sensed a fractional opening. He wrenched and convulsed, and in so doing managed to draw enough breath to scream.

The force of his yell punched at the two of them. That granted him just enough space to break free entirely.

'Wait! I *claim* you! You can't—'

Jackson woke up standing beside his bed, his lungs gasping for air. His entire body felt bruised by the grip of her talons.

Then he looked down, and there it was. The artifact lay on the carpet where he had dropped it.

Why it held such importance now that he was awake, Jackson could not say. Only that he had to reestablish the bond.

Jackson pulled out his gym bag and slipped a sweatband around his wrist. He fitted the artifact inside the band.

He pulled his chair over to the windows and sat there, watching the night, until he was certain it was safe to go back to bed.

TWENTY-SIX

The next morning Jackson showered and shaved and placed his first phone call. When Luca answered, Jackson asked, 'Where are you?'

'The downstairs office on Rue Gambord. I am inspecting the articles Krys brought us a second time. More importantly, where are you?'

'My apartment.'

'The idea,' Luca said, 'was to make this villa your home.'

'When I arrived back here last night, I was so tired I struggled to get my clothes off.'

'You will move today?'

'Tomorrow. Right now, I need to travel to Strasbourg.'

'Without me,' Luca said. 'My analysis of these artifacts will require most of today.'

Jackson lifted the artifact with the hand not holding his phone. Standing there in the morning light, the subtle bond between him and this mystery item felt even stronger than the night before. He knew he needed to tell Luca about his midnight confrontation with Riyanna. And yet . . .

'Jackson?'

'Give me a minute.'

The barrier that kept him silent was subtle, a faint whisper of force that urged without controlling. It was his choice. He could easily have broken through. And yet . . .

He turned from the window and said, 'I have something I want to try.'

When Jackson finished outlining his idea, Luca said, 'I should have thought of this.'

'Have you ever worked a case before?'

'You already know the answer to that.'

Jackson said, 'Procedure and investigative patterning is a world apart from research.'

'Stop by when you are ready,' Luca said. 'I will select an article for you to use.'

Jackson's coffee maker was vintage Italian and remarkably ugly. He screwed off the stubby top, filled the bottom with water, inserted the tin sieve, and spooned in the coffee. He screwed the top on tightly, then set it on the stove to brew. The laborious process produced three espresso-sized cups that were almost glutinous.

As he drank his first cup, Jackson placed the morning's second call. Once his ally in Strasbourg had agreed to meet that afternoon, Jackson phoned Krys. She answered with, 'I was just getting ready to call you.'

'What's up?'

'I was wondering about protocol. I've never been involved in an operation like this before.'

'What do you need to know?'

'For starters, what do I call it?'

'Off the books will do. Undercover. Whichever you prefer.'

'What happens if, you know, things go south?'

'We'll be receiving one or more phone numbers, only to be used in case of emergency. It will be manned twenty-four/seven. You will be instructed how to respond.' He waited. 'Is that it?'

'No.' A hard breath, then, 'I need to know how much of what I tell you will get back to HQ.' Another breath. 'And to Luca.'

Jackson answered very slowly. Not because he needed to think out his reply. But because in her question was confirmation that he had been right to place this call. 'You're my partner. If you tell me that something needs to stay between us, then it will. Unless it has a direct impact on the investigation. In that case, I'll give you a heads-up. If I can. But the decision must rest with me. You need to understand that going in. If I think the implications might impact our case, timing will depend on circumstances. Not on any hesitation or sense of privacy you might feel.'

'I can live with that.' Her voice had gone very soft. 'Jackson . . .'

'What?'

'Nothing. It can wait.'

'I need to travel to Strasbourg. That's why I called. Are you up for a trip?'

'Will Luca be coming?'

'Not today.'

'Outstanding.' Then, 'Sorry, that slipped out.'

'Pack a bag,' Jackson said. 'We'll stay overnight and come back tomorrow.'

When Jackson entered the forecourt on Rue Gambord, he found the left-hand garage door was open. He pulled his Jeep into the empty space, cut the motor, then sat staring at the beast parked in the next bay.

The Bentley Flying Spur was, in Jackson's opinion, one of the finest machines ever designed for the road. The fact that it was also utterly impractical only added to its appeal. The car weighed in at just over three tons and was powered by two turbo-charged V-6 engines that were remolded into a single W-12. The Bentley could accelerate from zero to sixty in three and a half seconds. The interior was leather and burl and sterling silver. The ride defined luxurious, or so he had heard. Jackson had never actually sat in one before.

He opened the garage door and called, 'Luca?'

'Downstairs.'

When Jackson entered the downstairs office and found Luca seated behind a cluttered desk, he asked, 'The Bentley is mine? I mean . . .'

'It is registered in your name.'

'Wow.'

'You need to move in here, Jackson.'

'I told you. Tomorrow.'

'Very well.' Luca slid a gold-colored artifact across the desk. 'This should establish your credentials in Strasbourg. Your contact has access to the underworld?'

'Roger Valente has served me well in the past. But I haven't been in touch in a year and a half.' The artifact was about the size of his hand and looked like a misshaped saucer. The plate could have been unpolished gold but just as easily have been cheap brass. 'What does this thing do?'

'The original purpose has been lost. But it will serve your purpose just the same. If Valente is truly aware of an article's magical value, this will raise the flag, I assure you.'

Jackson pocketed the artifact. 'If you say so.'

'There is a briefcase upstairs in the front gallery. It contains documents regarding ownership of the car and house. There is also a new bank account in your name at the bank where I reside. You must sign all copies.' Luca began fingering the next article. He might as well have been talking about a shopping list. 'The case also contains a hundred thousand euros. And a debit card placing another eight hundred thousand at your disposal.'

Jackson took his time responding. He was in no hurry to go anywhere. His own artifact's power was very evident now. Standing here in front of the stone desk. And it was not merely in how he continued to be held back from speaking about the woman. Riyanna. The temptress who hunted them both. Because here in this moment he realized something else. He could not say how he knew this. Nor did it matter. Beyond the realm of logic and reasoning, without any concrete evidence to go on, Jackson was utterly certain that Riyanna sought to use him *now*. She worked spell after spell, striving to break through his artifact's protective shield and use him as a weapon. To murder Luca Tami.

Jackson watched as Luca reached for the next article, cupped it between his hands, and brought it to his forehead. The knowledge of a new and ongoing threat changed nothing, at least as far as telling Luca. The entire issue had to remain a secret. For now. He had no idea why. But it was true, nonetheless.

Luca set the artifact in the growing pile to his right and reached for another. 'Most of these articles Krys identified have no magical charge that I can discern.' He started to raise the piece to his forehead, then stopped. 'Another issue we must address. What are you wearing?'

'My standard gear. Jeans, polo shirt. They're clean, but—'

'Stop. Just stop. There is a men's shop on the Rue du Rhone. Henri's.'

'I've never been in there, but I've passed it.'

'Go. Now. Ask for Frederique. Do what he says. Was there something else?'

The sense of being attacked by Riyanna's spellwork grew more intense. She shrilled at him to do her bidding. Rid the world of this man. Her malevolent lust surrounded him like a crimson cloud. Jackson gripped the artifact more tightly still. He started to defy the protective force and tell Luca what was happening. Logic demanded nothing less.

But trying to speak left Jackson feeling as though he struck a wall.

The sensation was so real that he almost reached out and tried to touch it. The barrier was not a command. Rather, it was the sort of insistence that an ally might offer another, a hand planted in the chest, a silent warning. Do not step forward, do not drop over that cliff.

Jackson knew he was going to have to defy the caution, and sooner rather than later. But for the moment, all he said was, 'Why did you ask for me? I mean before you showed up in Geneva.'

'I cast the runes,' Luca replied. 'A proper casting merely identifies a bond that already exists. When the bond is not there, the stones are lifeless. Nothing but little carved rocks.'

'What happened this time?'

'I cast the stones, and instantly the answer pounced on me. The rocks were hot as lava when I touched them.'

Jackson thought that over. 'Because of me.'

'The hour of our meeting,' Luca confirmed. 'The place. The fact that you would be on the phone with your station chief when I arrived.'

'The murders?'

'The urgency,' Luca replied. 'The sense of finality was very great. Either we met and worked together or dire events would unfold in the world.'

'Are we successful in stopping these events?'

Luca nodded, as though he approved of the question. 'I asked that very question, and the stones went cold.'

'What does that mean?'

'I have no idea.'

Jackson liked Luca's manner of his response as much as the actual words. There was no sense of prying an answer from Luca. He talked freely. Like two agents properly handling a case. But Jackson could not respond in kind. He *could* not.

Luca must have sensed Jackson's tension, for he lifted his sightless gaze and asked, 'Yes?'

'Once Krys and I meet with Valente, we'll probably be under observation. So will we be safe carrying this artifact that you claim has value?'

'I have set wards around this house and your new vehicle.' Luca reached out one pale hand. 'Which reminds me. Give me your phone.'

When Jackson set it in his hand, Luca gripped it between his palms and touched it to his forehead. Jackson watched a red glow emerge between Luca's interlaced fingers.

When Luca passed it back, the heat was almost scalding. Luca resumed his inspection of the next article. 'This and your watch will now serve as wards against most magical assaults. Your phone is also now shielded against electronic monitoring. Tell Krys she needs to let me treat her phone the same way.'

'She's a Talent. Can't she set up her own protections?'

Luca paused in his inspection of the next item. 'You should let her answer that. After today, these phones need to be our only method of communication. If you hear a sharp pinging sound when you answer, be warned that the caller is trying to channel magic through the connection. Have a good trip.'

TWENTY-SEVEN

The best thing Jackson could say about his first-ever experience in shopping for top-of-the-line clothes was, Frederique wasted no time.

Nineteen minutes after he arrived, Jackson emerged wearing navy gabardines by Zegna, a sports jacket by Cerrutti, a pale-blue shirt with chalk stripes by Van Laack, black loafers by Ferragamo. Jackson had three more outfits on order.

The total bill was just under what he had paid for his Jeep.

Jackson parked by Krys's front door and called up to say he was there. While he waited, Jackson programmed his phone into the Bentley's sound system and transferred some of Luca's cash into his jacket pocket. Then Jackson called the chief.

Meyer came on the line just as his partner appeared on the building's doorstep. Jackson waved Krys over. She opened the door, heard the chief's voice, slipped inside, and dumped her satchel on the rear seat. Jackson told Meyer about his plans for the day, then said, 'We need to establish an emergency protocol.'

Zoe Meyer cleared her throat. 'We're working on that.'

Jackson caught the edge. 'Anything I need to know about?'

Meyer said carefully, 'Perhaps it would be best if we leave it for the moment.'

'Roger that.'

'As a matter of fact, I would suggest you take considerable care in how you and I communicate. You read me, Jackson?'

'Loud and clear.'

'I will be in touch.' The chief cut the connection.

Krys asked, 'What just happened?'

'High jingo,' Jackson replied.

'What is that supposed to mean?'

'There are other agencies involved. When that happens, we have to expect high-level politics and maneuvering. Meyer just warned us that there might be listening ears.'

'Agencies are spying on Interpol?'

'It happens.'

She studied him intently. 'Doesn't this bother you the tiniest bit?'

'Not if I trust my chief. And Barker. Which I do.' He put the car in gear and pulled smoothly from the curb. 'If you aim for a posting at headquarters, you'd better get used to this.'

She settled further into the leather. 'High jingo.'

'It comes with the job. A case like this, we need to focus on the straight ahead. Remember what the chief said. The trail behind us is littered with corpses.'

The Bentley drove magnificently, soothing and exhilarating at the same time. The leather and burl interior was a haven made for sharing secrets. Jackson confessed, 'I could get used to this.'

Krys slipped off her shoes and tucked her feet under her. It was an oddly intimate gesture for such a hard-edged woman. 'You know I never worked for a regular police force. Or national intelligence agency.'

'I've read your file,' Jackson confirmed. 'And wondered about that.'

'You know the answer now.'

'You're a Talent.'

'Completely untrained,' Krys said. 'Unregistered.'

'Off the grid.' Jackson glanced over. 'Interpol must have done backflips when you showed up.'

'I did a criminology degree at the University of Connecticut. After graduation, I applied online to Interpol, then flew to Brussels and requested a meeting with someone who could be trusted with secrets. The agent was a woman on desk duty, counting down to retirement. She was too old for backflips, but she was definitely pleased.'

'You aimed for Interpol all along?'

'Since I was a teenager. What did I miss, not jumping through the normal hoops?'

Jackson could reply because he had thought about the same issue. 'Police work is ruled by making the arrest and keeping your investigations between the lines. That means you're trained to deliver both the culprit and a case that can be taken to court.'

'A case you can win.'

'You deliver the case, and you walk away. Or try to. It's hard, especially when a perp you know is guilty goes free. Which happens all too often. There are a lot of reasons why cops lose their edge. The cases they make and then watch fall apart in court are one reason. Another is arresting a perp again, for repeating a similar crime, and seeing the pain they've caused. Because the first case wasn't good enough to put them away.'

There were two possible routes they could take from Geneva to Strasbourg. One took them along the lakefront highway to Lausanne, then up the E25 past Bern, across the border, and up the A35. Four hours plus or minus: 380 kilometers of bland cement and highway views.

Jackson opted for the other route.

After Lausanne, he took the regional highway that wound through the Jura hills, then entered France at a tiny border crossing east of Besançon. The Juras were the most ancient mountains in Europe, gentle slopes that in springtime formed artworks in green. The three-lane highway was empty enough for Jackson to release the beast beneath the Bentley hood. He knew he was acting like a teen, taking the winding road at high speed and reveling in the combination of steady control and breathtaking power. Krys's only response was to lean her head against the seat and watch the road unfurl before them.

Twice he started to tell her about Riyanna. Both times, however, the same gentle pressure halted him. Sooner or later, he was going to have to push on. He knew and accepted this as fact. For the moment, it felt good to let the journey and the car and the company grant him a momentary release.

After crossing the border, they stopped for sandwiches and coffee at a village café. Krys did not speak once. Jackson decided the only way to describe her skin coloring was Mediterranean. A warm café-au-lait mixture that the sunlight turned translucent, revealing freckles that he had not noticed until then. Her eyes were green and golden both. Her lips were full, a fact that was easily missed because normally she compressed them to a thin line. But for this quiet moment, her customary tension was gone.

When they returned to the car and the road, Krys said, 'I wonder how he got so much money. Luca, I mean.'

'I've asked myself the same thing.'

'I've met rich people,' Krys said. 'The one thing they all have in common is how they treat money. It's not a *thing*. It's not *out there*. It's as vital to them as their next breath. Luca treats money like it's pointless.'

They sped through the Vosges National Forest. The region was a throwback to a different epoch, when wolves as tall as a man's chest were harnessed by ogres who relished battle and feasted on the terror of forest hamlets. Witches scattered sweets along trails and led children to slavery and worse. Early in his career, Jackson had taken part in a raid on a moonlit gathering that had sought to reopen the earth's wounds. But today the sunlight cast emerald glows upon the forest floor, and the air through Jackson's open window was spiced by pine and spring blossoms.

But if Krys noticed the surrounding splendor, she gave no sign. She became locked in some internal argument, or so it seemed to Jackson. Finally, as they emerged from the forest and entered the farmland surrounding Strasbourg, she said, 'I have to tell you something.'

'I'm listening.'

'I took an article and didn't report it.' She sounded almost strangled from the effort it required to speak. 'When we were down in the caves, I . . .'

Krys stopped in mid-flow when Jackson slammed on the brakes and jerked the wheel over. The wheels skidded on the grass verge. The car shuddered and finally halted. Jackson remained as he was, the wheel gripped in a two-fisted clench. Digesting what he had just heard.

Krys revealed her internal agony. 'It's terrible, I know. I can't even say why—'

'Stop right there,' Jackson said.

'I'm sorry, I don't know what else—'

'Krys. Just. Stop.' He took a breath, determined to break through the wall no matter what. But for the first time there was no opposition to him speaking. He turned to face her, wondering if his features held the same tense fears as her own. 'I did the exact same thing.'

TWENTY-EIGHT

'Start at the very beginning. Take it step by step. Give me the full version. No, hang on a second.' Jackson pulled out his phone and called his Strasbourg contact. When Roger Valente came on the phone, Jackson said they were probably going to be late. Then he cut the connection and told Krys, 'From the top. Go.'

'It hit me the instant the elevator doors opened,' Krys began. 'I mean before I even took my first step into the caves. You and Simeon and the staffer – what was her name?'

'Edna Koch.'

'Right. You were all focused on the guy at the desk. So you didn't notice. But the sensation . . .'

'Rocked your world.'

'It *grabbed* me. I knew I could fight it. But I didn't want to.'

'Have you ever felt anything like this before? I mean, you're a Talent—'

'Jackson, OK, let's get this out in the open. I have had *no* training. I have hidden these abilities *my entire life*.' She puffed hard over the words. 'It was either that or . . . You can't imagine . . .'

'Take it easy. Big breath. Just tell me what happened in that vault. The rest can wait. Your secrets are your own. All I want to know is if other Talents feel this when they connect with an item.'

His tone probably had as much effect as his words. Krys calmed and went on, 'I have no idea. But I've never experienced or read anything about an inanimate object affecting a Talent like that.'

'Good. Thank you.' Jackson kept his tone steady, but the word she had just used left him reeling inside. *Talent*. He had been married to a highly trained practitioner of the healing arts. He had seen her move through a field of flowers, searching for the hidden treasure, the magical herb. And he had never, not once, felt a thing.

Talent.

Krys went on, 'Like I said, Simeon and Edna handled the guy on desk duty. Then one of you asked how we could possibly find what we need, and I heard it all, but mostly I was focused on this . . . I still don't know what to call it.'

Jackson had been mulling over the same issue. He suggested, 'An *event*.'

The term had special importance for Interpol field agents. It hearkened back to their training days, when their instructors continually referred to the *questionable event*. Interpol maintained a catalog of every official Talent residing in their district, with a precise description of their abilities. As long as these Talents operated within the laws of their country, they were granted special status. But the instant a Talent was linked to a questionable event, they simply became suspects. From that moment on, their abilities were viewed like any other lethal weapon in the hands of a potential criminal.

To refer to what they had experienced as events meant Jackson was uncertain what they signified. But he knew they were potentially explosive. Good or bad. It could go either way.

'I like that,' Krys decided. 'OK. So the *event* already dominated my awareness before I crossed the foyer. It felt . . . good, really. I knew I could cut it off. But I didn't *want* to.'

'So you started walking forward,' Jackson recalled. 'In front of us. Before we had figured out how to proceed. You were already moving.'

'Right. And then those articles started zapping me.'

'I was watching,' Jackson said. 'At first I couldn't decide whether the sparks originated from you or those things on the shelves.'

'Them. Definitely.'

'So we started taking the items,' Jackson said. 'Assuming they had significance. That we had shown up just for them. That they were the end result. But all the while . . .'

'I kept being drawn forward. I wasn't in any real hurry. I just knew I wasn't leaving the place until I got it. Whatever it was.'

'Describe finding it.'

Krys smiled, a gentle recollection of a special moment. Her voice was almost dreamlike. The compressed tightness to her lovely features was erased. 'It was on the top shelf in the last cavern but one. I waited until Edna had gone back with the next article I'd identified. The feeling at this point was . . . I don't know how to describe it. *Tight*. There wasn't room for anything else. You were off in that side room, and she was gone, so I reached up and touched it. That very instant, it . . .'

Jackson softly pressed, 'Tell me.'

'It was mine. Not like I claimed it. Like it had been mine *forever*. And I knew that it was very important I kept all that secret.'

'Then you came to find me.'

'Right. The staffer came back, and I knew she expected me to keep on. I figured why not, even though I had what I'd come for. But I realized you weren't with us, and that bothered me, so I called, and you answered.'

'There weren't any sparks in my cave,' Jackson recalled.

'I wondered about that. You know, a sort of idle interest. I thought maybe because I'd located the artifact, that ability or whatever was over and done. Then Edna and I went to the last caverns, and I got two more sparks.'

Jackson sorted through everything he was hearing and remembering, and asked, 'Why are you telling me . . .'

'Why now and not before? Right.' Krys showed him round-eyed candor. 'Last night I dialed your number – twice. But I couldn't . . . I don't know how to describe what it felt like. A wall. A brake. But it wasn't unpleasant.'

'I understand.'

'This morning, though, soon as I got into the car, that wall or whatever was gone. Poof. Like it had never been there. I was so scared. I hadn't been the least bit worried until then. I wanted to tell you because you needed to know. Until that moment I hadn't even *thought* about what I'd done from the legal perspective. It just didn't matter. Not at *all*. I know that sounds crazy. But that is exactly—'

'Krys, I read you.' Jackson scanned his own interior and found the barrier was still gone. He waited through a long moment. Studying her. She knew what was coming next. He wanted her to know it was her decision. 'Will you show me?'

'Yes.' But she did not move. 'Will you tell me what happened to you?'

'Of course I will. But let's take this one step at a time, all right? First, you show me. Then I'll tell you everything.'

She remained exactly as she was. Turned in her seat so she faced him. Hands in her lap. Still. Frozen. 'Are we in trouble?'

Jackson rocked his hand back and forth. 'Not at the moment. OK, yes, we have broken Swiss law. Not to mention Interpol regs. But there is something at work here.'

'Jackson, if we don't tell . . . There's no going back.'

'Right. Probably not.'

'Wait . . . Probably? You mean there's an out?'

'We insert this into our secret report. The one that is eyes-only for Meyer and Barker. How we both felt the same draw, the same obstacles to revealing what we had found, the same sense of safety. We use the report as an official but secret register.'

She asked, 'You felt it, too?'

'Krys, everything you described was the same for me. With a couple of extra added attractions. But let's finish with your event first. Just one last question. Before you picked up your article, did you see or sense anything . . . you know, different?'

'I was hurrying. I could hear Edna's approach. And the draw was so intense. But no. Nothing else.' She looked at him. 'What happens if . . . you know, the sense of safety and goodness and all . . .'

'Is a lie.' Jackson nodded. He'd been thinking the same thing.

'Right. What then?'

Jackson found it good to have a reason to smile. 'Then I guess the last thing we'll need to worry about is breaking Interpol regs.'

Krys smiled back. It was a different look from any she had shown him up to that point. Jackson realized she was excited about sharing this with him. Seated by a forest harboring some of Europe's darkest legends, in a car bought with money from some unknown source, drawn together by events that were sweeping them along. Faster and faster. Jackson knew Krys had only touched the surface of her secrets. He also knew it didn't really matter whether they informed the authorities about these semi-stolen articles. He was convinced at gut level that the turning had already been taken. Whatever happened, there was no going back. But just then, it did not matter nearly as much as the new level of openness in her gaze, and what he realized it meant.

She trusted him.

TWENTY-NINE

Krys reached into her pocket and drew out . . .

A baby's bracelet.

That was Jackson's first impression. The opening was about three inches wide. A full-grown woman with slender hands could have worn it on her wrist. But Jackson doubted any fashion-conscious lady would be interested. The bracelet was a bland gold in color, as if it had been fashioned from cheap plastic. Where the sunlight touched the surface, there was nothing to see. No adornment, no polish, no carvings. 'Is it heavy?'

'An ounce, two at the most, I'd say.' She started to hand it over, then jerked back. 'Sorry.'

'The barrier?'

'I slept with it in my hand. Woke up twice in sheer terror when it slipped out.' She looked from the bracelet to him and back. 'I don't get it. I can show you, but you can't touch it.'

Jackson said, 'I had a terrible nightmare when I dropped my article.'

'Do you feel anything now?'

'A definite rightness over how we're talking about it. I feel like it's waiting for me to do something. You?'

'Pretty much the same.' She sighed. 'Times like this, I really hate my ignorance about all things magic.'

Jackson studied her artifact a moment longer.

Krys asked, 'What are you thinking?'

'I was wondering whether we got hooked into this because we were the first people who walked in there.'

'That doesn't work,' she replied. 'Edna didn't feel a thing, remember?'

'They entered the foyer only. I doubt anybody has gotten past that duty desk for years. Longer.'

But Krys remained certain. 'I was drawn to it before I left the elevator.'

Jackson nodded. He knew Krys was right. But the result was a pair of questions that troubled him more than the article itself.

First, why were they selected?

And second, how was *he* connected? A guy with not a shred of magical abilities. Sitting there with a secret burning a hole in his life.

Krys asked softly, 'Will you tell me what happened?'

Jackson tasted the air, as he had so often before. This time, the invisible barrier was gone. He started the car, pulled back on to the road, and said, 'I'll tell you everything.'

Jackson talked as he drove. He found it easier to focus on the road and let the memories rise without needing to watch Krys's reaction. This became even more useful when he reached the point of the confrontation with Riyanna. The only hesitation came over trying to describe the sense of Riyanna working her spells, striving to force him to murder Luca Tami. Feeling exposed even while protected. And his inability to speak of it. Until now.

They entered Strasbourg, passed through the modern perimeter, crossed the bridge to the central island, and parked on the avenue fronting Roger Valente's gallery. Jackson cut the motor and sat. The clock read a quarter past the standard French closing time of six o'clock. He made no move to rush Krys, however. He was certain this conversation was far more important than the original reason for their journey.

Krys shifted in her seat. 'Two things. First, the little people.'

'I understand. But they weren't people.' He shut his eyes and instantly was back in the cavern, filled with the magnetic draw that had brought him to the artifact. 'I have no idea what I saw. But their size . . . The tallest stood maybe three feet high. But it wasn't just their height. They were not human. The totality was . . . alien.'

'That's what I thought when you described the caverns' illumination. Not human.'

'The light flowed from every surface. Almost like music.' He had said all this before. But he liked being able to help her absorb the events through repeating. He also enjoyed the recollections. 'There were patterns within patterns. The wave designs carved into the stone suddenly made sense. I had the feeling that the lights were communication of some kind. And more. It felt . . .'

She waited him out.

'They were *bonded*,' Jackson said. 'With the lights. And the caves. And each other. All of it.'

'So . . . my bracelet could have been made for them.'

He nodded. 'I thought of that.'

'And then one of the little people climbed the wall next to where you stood, crawled into the one empty shelf, and . . .'

'He opened the stone.'

Krys asked, 'Do you think he *meant* to show you how? Which, of course, means he was somehow aware of you . . .'

'Standing there, a few thousand years after his little dance.' Jackson also liked finishing her impossible thoughts. This level of sharing helped him digest as well. 'I have no idea. Maybe the real message was to go ahead and jump off the cliff into the bed of snakes.'

'Doubtful, given how you felt it could have protected you from that woman.'

'Riyanna.' The light-filled memory was instantly erased. 'It was an absolute certainty. Like I had been brought to that place to find the artifact that would shield me from her.'

'Which brings us to the second point. Riyanna's lure was that strong?'

'Lure isn't the right word for what happened. She commanded. I came.'

Krys frowned at the passing pedestrians. 'And then a second wizard showed up. They argued over killing you. And you escaped.'

Once again, Jackson was filled with the panic-fear of facing his doom. 'The guy was looking for somebody. That's why he showed up.'

'You didn't mention that before.'

'I only remembered it now.' He could hear his own tight breaths, the rise of fear. 'He dug into my head. Just brutal the way he hunted. Found out I was with Interpol. Told her to kill me. They argued. While her attention was on the guy, I escaped.'

She gave him a moment to recover, then continued, 'You've got the artifact now?'

'Every moment since waking. Even in the shower.'

She leaned in close. 'Will you show me?'

Jackson pulled the article from his breast pocket and held it out.

She leaned in close, studied it intently, and said, 'A block of wood.'

'Right.'

'Old wood.'

'Right again.'

The article was about five inches long and a little over an inch and a half thick. Like the bracelet, there was not a single sharp edge. The dark object was not exactly round, more of an oblong shape. It fit comfortably into his fist.

Krys asked, 'How does it feel?'

'Not wood or stone or glass. But a little like all of them.'

'Is it heavy?'

'About the same as yours.'

'So maybe it's petrified wood.'

'I thought about that.' Jackson gave her time to inspect it further, then slipped it back into his pocket. 'The artifact Luca told me to use in our meeting with Valente. It's as bland and uninteresting as our two items.'

'You think they're linked?'

'No. Well, not like you mean.'

Krys nodded. 'We're not seeing the real significance.'

'That's it, exactly,' Jackson said. He glanced at the gallery across the street. 'I think it's time to focus on why we came.'

Krys drew back. 'OK, so what now?'

'I met Roger Valente on a case I was working on about a year after I started with Interpol. Five tourists in Athens had been murdered. At first, the local authorities declared it was poisoning. They wanted to put it down to bad food and make it all go away. I proved it had a magical connection and traced the poisonous artifact back to Valente's shop. Valente dealt with legitimate items in the front room, but he also served as an agent for unlicensed magic. Same as today, only now he operates at a much higher level.'

'Is he a Talent?'

'Definitely not. And that was one of the reasons I cut him a break. He had no idea what the article he had sold could actually do. He had acquired it without knowing it originated from a user of the dark arts. Roger has been a solid asset ever since.' Jackson stared across the street. 'The problem is, I'm not coming to him as an Interpol agent. I'm not officially seeking his cooperation.'

'You don't know how much help he's going to be.'

'Right. We need to assume everything from this point on carries a potential threat.'

Strasbourg was one of a dozen or so European regions that liked to claim they were the original settlement of the Ancients. Twenty-two centuries earlier, the Romans under Nero had destroyed a powerful community of Druid wizards and then established the headquarters of the Germania legion on what was now the Grand Isle. The city that grew around the military fortress was known originally as Argentinia. When the Romans withdrew four hundred years later, the city was first ruled by the Alemanni tribe, then the Huns, before finally becoming a provincial outpost of the Franks. The first official document showing the current name of Strasbourg was the license granting it the status of a Free Imperial City in the thirteenth century.

Roger Valente's gallery was located on Rue des Hallebardes, one of the original Roman avenues that traversed the central island. The shop owner had used his considerable fortune to reinvent his past. Nowadays Valente liked to present himself as the last of a long line of Phoenician traders who had spread across Europe serving the Roman garrisons. In fact, Jackson knew that Valente had been born in the slums of Lyon and had used the French armed forces as his ticket out. He had served for nine years with the Paratroopers, the French equivalent of America's Delta Force. He was a waifish man with effeminate ways. He used a hair oil that smelled of lilies. He spoke English with a musical lilt. Rumors abounded over how Valente had amassed the funds required to establish his gallery. Jackson had always assumed the most venomous stories probably came closest to the truth.

Since moving from Greece back to France, Roger had run a legitimate business dealing in high-end art. Very expensive. Very cutting edge. And all containing some elements of magic.

Roger's shop only represented Talents. In most cases, these artists refused to divulge their identities. Institute training took a dozen very intense years. Young Acolytes were indoctrinated with the Institutes' worldview and values. Art was considered a pedestrian sort of hobby, something best left to those born without the real gift. Talents who were also artists hid behind galleries who could be trusted never to divulge their true names.

The item that greeted their entry was a very angry ogre trapped inside a glass vial shaped like a massive Aladdin's lamp. As Jackson passed the pedestal on which the vial stood, the ogre blew a bubble that contained a magnificently shaped nude woman. The miniature woman waved at Jackson and writhed enticingly. The ogre performed a parody of the woman's movements, then offered another bubble to Krys, this one containing a much smaller ogre. Both beasts then writhed like the woman. Krys gave no sign she noticed it at all.

When Roger approached, Jackson said, 'That isn't art.'

'For seven hundred and fifty thousand euros, my dear boy, you can take it home and call it whatever you like.' Roger showed Jackson a snake-oil salesman's smile. 'So, the recently fallen and his protégé. Have you found it difficult adjusting to not carrying a gun? Legally, that is.'

Jackson asked, 'What have you heard?'

Roger pirouetted and flicked a wrist over his shoulder, beckoning them to follow. They crossed a pair of antique silk carpets to a rosewood secretary. The artwork on the walls was brilliant, shocking, and far too dark for Jackson's taste. Roger waved them into a pair of high-backed Regency chairs, slipped behind the desk, and replied, 'Of course, I made inquiries. My dear friend calls after two years of silence—'

'Twenty-nine months.'

'Let's not quibble. Too long. Shame on you, by the way.'

'I didn't have any reason to contact you.'

Roger Valente sniffed. 'Whenever do friends need a reason? Will you and your angry little friend take something, Jackson?'

'We're good.'

'I attended Sylvie's funeral, by the way.'

'I noticed.'

Roger shifted his head so as to give Jackson a sideways look. 'All those people, all that tragedy. You couldn't possibly have seen me there at the back.'

'You wore a white carnation in your lapel.'

Roger sniffed with disdain. But Jackson thought the man was oddly touched just the same. 'Carnation? Please. It was a rose.'

'Your coming only made a phone call that much harder.'

Roger nodded acceptance. Jackson knew Valente did not care about Sylvie. Jackson doubted the man had ever felt much emotion for anything. Roger Valente was a consummate pretender. He affected a foppish demeanor because it suited him. The yellow foulard around his neck or the soft leather dancing slippers or the tight stove-pipe trousers all were intended to hide the fact that Roger carried two throwing knives and a double-barreled derringer. And would use them all with genuine pleasure.

'The world is remarkably silent about you, *mon ami*. A former Interpol agent who has been struck by tragedy decides to change his profession. On the day of his official resignation, he acquires a house and a rather beautiful car, both for cash. It bodes well for our meeting. I assume your items are available for purchase?'

'Not this time,' Jackson replied. 'I already have a buyer.'

'I searched rather thoroughly. Of course, I needed to confirm that you weren't just after doing an old friend wrong. All I heard was a few snippets here and there. About your walking away from a job that had lost meaning. And now seeking to reinvent for yourself a new life. A strategy I highly commend.' The gallery owner's gaze slithered over to Jackson's right. 'It is rather a different case for your lovely young companion. It appears she has departed under something of a cloud. Or should I say a spark?'

Krys gave no sign she heard any of the exchange. Her attention remained focused on the artwork covering much of the side wall. A volcanic mountain rose from the heart of a verdant island paradise. Then it erupted, showering the villagers below with fiery missiles, before lava poured down its sides and consumed the entire island. Faint screams filled the gallery as the canvas was blanketed by steam and ash. Then the painting cleared, and the island was calm and beautiful once more.

Jackson said, 'What happens here today must remain totally off the books.'

'But of course, my dear boy.' He tracked Krys as she rose from her chair and began a slow inspection of the gallery's other works. Jackson heard a squeak and turned to observe a pair of furry caterpillars race from Krys's approach. One was pale lavender, the other a fiery orange. Both were as long as his arm. They raced up the side wall and tangled together in a fuzzy wrestling match directly overhead. After an instant's mock fury, they lifted their heads and sang Krys a welcome. 'All right, my dears,' Roger said. 'That's enough.'

The caterpillars scurried back down and reformed as a multi-colored ball on the carpet. Jackson said, 'Interesting.'

'For a hundred and twenty thousand euros, I would hardly think "interesting" does them justice.' Roger smiled. 'Shall we get down to business?'

'Sure thing,' Jackson said. 'As I said, I need a valuation.'

'Percentage of sale price, I assume.'

'Flat rate,' Jackson replied. 'I told you. I already have a buyer.'

'And if I can bring a buyer who will pay more?'

'The sale is agreed,' Jackson replied. 'I am here to reconfirm their valuer's estimation.'

'In that case,' Roger said, 'the price is thirty thousand euros.'

'Ten.'

'Fifteen.'

'Done.'

'In advance.'

'Five now. Ten when we're finished.'

'Half now. My final offer.'

'Done.' Jackson waved Krys back and reached for his cash. 'Close your gallery, Roger. This needs to remain between us.'

THIRTY

He drew the palm-sized plate from his pocket and set it on the desk. Jackson felt mildly embarrassed, presenting such an object in Roger's beautiful gallery. The artifact was as bland and unattractive as those he and Krys carried. Four stubby points emerged from the perimeter, little triangles perhaps a quarter-inch long. The interior face was scratched and battered. If Jackson had seen the object on the sidewalk, he would not have bothered to pick it up.

Roger Valente's response was completely unexpected. In the almost seven years Jackson had dealt with the gallery owner, he had never once seen the man so exposed. Roger tried to hide it behind his standard oblique smile. But his fingers trembled. His dark eyes glittered with an almost feverish intensity. 'My dear friend, you are certainly full of surprises. No wonder you resigned your commission.'

Krys leaned forward. Jackson knew she was going to ask Roger what it was he held. He shifted slightly, closing the distance until he caught her eye. Jackson shook his head and mouthed the word. *No.*

When he was certain she understood, he turned back. Something about this item had stripped away Roger's protective facade. Jackson wanted to use the chance while he had it.

Jackson said as casually as he could manage, 'Something I've been wondering about.'

'Eh? Wondering?' Roger turned the object over and flicked a fingernail against the surface. There was no sound. 'About what?'

'Who exactly were the Ancients?'

'Ha. You and everyone else are wondering.' He opened a drawer, rummaged about, and drew out a magnifying glass. He dropped it, searched further back, and retrieved a much more powerful instrument on a heavy onyx handle. 'Lean back, dear lady, you're in my light. Wondering, yes, I'm sure Interpol has given you its standard propaganda.'

Krys said, 'The Ancients were a tribe, possibly the Phoenicians, who were defeated first by the Greeks and then utterly eradicated—'

'What utter rubbish. It suits Interpol's interest to feed you agents that sort of rot.'

'Why is that, Roger?'

'Why? Because they want you to do your job, is what. They don't want you frightened out of your little agent minds.'

'Agents no longer,' Jackson corrected.

'Lucky for us, given the item you've brought me.' His accent was stronger now. He opened another drawer and pulled out a leather bundle which he unraveled without taking his gaze from the magnifying glass.

'What does that mean—'

'My dear boy, no one has the least idea who the Ancients were, where they lived, even if they were human. Shall I tell you a secret?'

'Please.'

He pulled out what looked like a dentist's probe and began tracing along the outer rim. 'There is a debate at the highest level of the Institutes' Adepts. Very hush-hush. Whether their magical abilities are the direct result of some tiny component of alien life, dwelling inside a human body. If perhaps Talents are individuals carrying some non-earthly component, an unintended gift from a far older race. A tiny shard of what must have been a truly monumental power.'

Krys said, 'There has been no evidence of any genetic difference between a Talent and those who show no magical abilities.'

'Yes, yes, I know this, of course. And do you know what I say to that? Piffle and snuff, is what.' He dropped the probe and extracted a small surveyor's hammer. He tapped the perimeter, listened, tapped again. 'You know how these things are. What if it is something much smaller than a gene? A fragment of protein, perhaps. Or even tinier. A subatomic particle we have not even identified. That is what the Adepts are now suggesting. They like this concept, you see. It ties them to the Ancients, whoever they were. It grants these elitists a reason to lift themselves above people they refer to as the mundane.'

Jackson recalled how, on one of his last returns home, he had stepped through the door and interrupted a furious tirade between his late wife and a Talent he had never seen before. Jackson repeated the last phrase the Talent had shouted before they realized an Interpol agent was watching. He softly spoke the words, 'Blood of the Ancients.'

That shocked Roger out of his reverie. He dropped the hammer and demanded, 'Where did you hear that?'

'I overheard a meeting of two Talents.'

'Well, don't repeat it in their company if you know what's good for you. Especially now that you don't have Interpol to watch your back.'

'What does it mean?'

'It's the watchword of those Talents I mentioned. And curiosity about that particular group has cost several acquaintances their lives.' He waggled the magnifier at Jackson. 'There's no profit in death, my friend. Not if the death in question is your own.'

*   *   *

Roger Valente settled their artifact on his desk, rose, and entered a
rear alcove. A few minutes later, he returned carrying a silk purse
the color of his foulard. 'Would you permit me to borrow your
artifact for a few minutes?

'You know the answer to that.'

'No, I thought not.' Roger seated himself and balanced the little
sack in both his hands. 'I must insist that no mention is ever made
of this.'

'Agreed.'

'Do you trust this young lady, Jackson? I don't mean during an
afternoon jaunt to come trouble the waters in France. I mean with
two lives in the balance. Yours and mine.'

Jackson took his time responding. 'We have other items. The
next time Krys will probably come on her own.'

'More, you say?'

'Quite a few.'

Roger continued to study Jackson as he untied the catch-knot,
opened the purse, and spilled its contents into his hand.

The object was a duplicate of what Krys had shown him.

Roger observed their shocked response and demanded, 'You know
this?'

Jackson hated how he had been caught so unprepared. 'We've
been told to look for one of these.'

Roger's voice rose a full octave. 'The other articles you mentioned,
they come from the same epoch as what you've brought me?'

'I have no idea.'

'You will show them to me?'

'Roger, you have my word. If anybody sees those items, it will
be you.' The only difference between Roger's object and Krys's
bracelet was the color. This one was milky green. Jackson asked,
'What is it?'

'It is called an Ebenezer armlet.' Roger's eyes flickered from one
to the other. 'My dear boy, if there is even the slightest *hint* of
acquiring such items, well . . . you are either soon to become
extremely wealthy or swiftly counted among the deceased. You
know my history, yes?'

'Some of it.'

'If word were to emerge that I possessed an Ebenezer armlet, all
my hard-earned skills would not be enough to keep me alive. I was
not exaggerating when I said you now held my life in your hands.'

Krys softly demanded, 'What is it?'

'Who knows? The latest thinking is that either the Ancients were very small, in which case it served as a bracelet, or they were giants, and this was a ring.'

Jackson said, 'The Ancients.'

'Anything to do with them, any article that might be traced to their legacy, is a death sentence these days.'

Krys asked, 'Why now?'

'I have no idea, my dear young lady, and I assure you there is no one in the mundane world with contacts better than my own. But something has the Institutes and senior Talents in a foment. I've assumed there is some unseen threat to their magical domain. I've even heard reports of secret scrolls coming to light for the first time in centuries. And then there are the rumors of a new gathering of Renegade Talents. You know of what I speak, yes?'

'A secret army of unlicensed wizards ready to destroy the Institutes,' Jackson confirmed. 'There have been such stories for years.'

'Well, things have changed, and not for the better. I hear some vague snippet . . . Then nothing. My source is *gone*. And if I inquire over their whereabouts, I receive the most stringent of warnings.'

Krys asked, 'You're saying we brought you a genuine artifact of the Ancients?'

'There is only one way to tell.' The hand that reached for Jackson's article trembled slightly. Whether from excitement or dread, Jackson could not tell. Roger held the golden item in his left hand, the Ebenezer armlet in his right. 'Observe closely.'

THIRTY-ONE

R oger Valente lifted both hands, then brought the two items together. The action was like a percussionist clanging cymbals: a swift tap and just as swiftly drawing them away. The result was a rolling thunderclap. The sound was magnificent. A hundred crystal chimes rang with a force that resonated in Jackson's bones.

An elongated spark grew between the two articles in Roger's hands. The flash carried an almost blinding intensity.

The sound grew more beautiful still. A thousand bells. And voices. A harmonious roar.

Even the surging spark carried a musical lilt, a shout of electric joy. The light shone upon Roger's look of exquisite pleasure

Then it was over. The light vanished with the sound. The world resumed its normal course. Jackson felt as though he had been deflated. The air tasted flat.

Krys must have felt the same way, for she said, 'Do it again.'

'If only I could.' Roger's voice carried the regret of ages. 'It will be weeks before another contact is possible.' He clapped the two objects together. There was a tinny clink, nothing more. 'See?'

Jackson managed, 'That . . . was . . . amazing.'

'Only three times in my entire career have I held objects from the Ancients. The first I sold, and the proceeds bought me this gallery and this building, both of which I own outright. The second was my Ebenezer armlet.' Roger reached forward with the hand holding their artifact. 'Whatever they are offering . . . give me twenty-four hours; I will double it.'

'Sorry. I can't—'

'Treble their offer! My dear boy, you think driving a Bentley makes you rich? Let me sell this and you could buy your own jet!'

'It's not just the money.' Jackson reached forward and wrested the article from Roger's grasp. 'This one is pledged.'

Krys demanded, 'But what does it *do*?'

'I have no idea. And as far as its value is concerned, it really doesn't matter.' Roger leaned back. He looked exhausted. Emotionally and physically spent. 'You would need a special sort of Adept. You know who I mean, yes?'

'Sure,' Jackson replied.

But Roger said it anyway. 'A senior Talent with second sight. They would take this, cradle it in their two hands, and do the head-tap thing.' Roger lifted his hands to his forehead, still holding the Ebenezer armlet. Nothing happened. He sighed, as though he had allowed himself to hope otherwise. 'Presto-bingo-bongo, all is made clear. Or not. I have never spoken to an Adept who has identified an artifact's true nature. Items dating from the time of the Ancients are said to possess a character or nature. Much like you or I would describe an individual.'

Jackson slipped the artifact into his jacket pocket. Roger winced as the item disappeared from view. 'My dear boy, you are going to be cheated by your buyers. I can feel it in my bones.'

Jackson extracted the cash from his other pocket and counted out the remainder of Roger's payment. 'We will be back with more items.'

'Only if you survive,' Roger corrected. 'And I have my doubts about that. You are skilled. As am I. But you do not know what turmoil the Institutes are in just now. They are seven boiling hives!'

Jackson stood and lifted Krys with a motion of his chin. 'We'll see ourselves out.'

'I beg you to reconsider, save yourselves, and leave the item with me!' Roger followed them back across the gallery, his outstretched hand a frantic claw. 'My dear boy, I can make you rich!'

THIRTY-TWO

Originally, Jackson had planned on taking rooms in one of the old-city hotels. Instead, he drove back across the bridge and left the city entirely. He followed the route towards the Vosges until they were surrounded by fields as the sun set. He liked how Krys held to her customary silence, though her features were creased by all the confusion and unanswered questions he himself carried.

Ninety minutes outside Strasbourg, Jackson pulled into a roadside café and bought them sandwiches and coffee to go. He returned to the car and motioned for Krys to roll down her window. 'Milk and no sugar, right?'

'Thank you, Jackson.' She accepted her meal, then waited until he had seated himself behind the wheel to say, 'I'm thinking maybe we should leave our discussion about Luca and the woman until he's with us.'

'I've tried to tell him twice now. And hit a barrier just as you described when you tried to call me about the artifact,' Jackson replied.

'It's time,' Krys said. 'Luca needs to know.'

He nodded, both in agreement and approval of her change in attitude towards their blind asset. 'Agreed.'

'Right now, we've got a small window to focus on the artifacts.' She gave him a chance to object, then went on, '"Artifact" doesn't suit what I'm carrying. Or "item". Or "thing". It's too impersonal. That's why I like the idea of your word: *event*. It makes it ours.'

'So what do you want to call them?'

She replied softly, 'How about treasure?'

Jackson felt a flurry of disquiet. 'I don't think so.'

'Why not?'

'Treasure signifies a rare value. As in ownership. It invites thieves who want to force a change.'

She looked miffed. 'You want to come up with something better?'

'I'll try. Sure.' He could see she was disappointed. 'Hey, treasure works fine.'

'You just said it doesn't.'

'Krys, look—'

'Don't you *dare* patronize me.'

Jackson decided this was not the time to try to make things better. He finished his meal, then rolled his napkin into a tight ball. 'You know there's something we need to do here.'

'I know.' She met his gaze. 'Sorry.'

He pretended confusion. 'For what?'

'I have a pretty short fuse.'

'Really? I hadn't noticed.'

She grinned. 'Liar.'

And just like that, they were back in synch. Jackson asked, 'We need to try to see if we can raise a spark of our own. You want to do it?'

'Absolutely.' The excitement he was feeling shone in her gaze. 'There's no time better than now, right?'

Jackson drove until he spied a lonely country road burnished by the last light of day. He followed that for a couple of miles, then turned on to a dirt track that meandered through a field of alfalfa. At least, that's what Jackson called the plants when Krys asked. It could just as easily have been okra. Or carrots. His interest in botany had died with his wife.

The track ended fifty meters from a copse of elm bordering the field. The rising moon, a degree or so off full, was silhouetted by the branches. Fading dusk formed a gentle canopy over the car. Jackson rolled down all the windows. They sat there for a long moment, listening to the night sounds, savoring the fragrances of a new season.

Nothing like a hint of the unknown, Jackson reflected, to sharpen the senses.

Finally, Krys said, 'Are we doing this or what?'

He had to smile. 'I bet you were the first girl to leap out of the plane in that sky-diving lesson.'

'You'd better believe it.' She held out her bracelet. 'Now you show me yours.'

Jackson pulled the stick from his pocket and reached out.

They jerked away. At the exact same instant.

Krys said, 'This is *wrong*.'

Jackson did not speak. He had felt it, too. An acute mistake in the making.

'I don't understand!' She pounded the door with her free hand. 'What are we supposed to do with these things?'

Jackson knew her irritation was fueled by the same excitement he felt. Which was why he was smiling when he said, 'So now they're just things.'

She glared at him. 'OK, wise guy. I'm waiting.'

'What Roger said at the end. About touching it to our foreheads.'

'OK, first of all, I'm no Adept. But hey . . . what's the worst that can happen?'

'We blow our brains all over this beautiful car,' Jackson offered.

'I fail to share your twisted, bizarre, unhealthy sense of humor.' Krys straightened in her seat. 'I'll go first.'

'You sure?'

'I'm the one with magical abilities, remember.'

'OK.' In truth, Jackson was more than happy to wait his turn. Years, in fact.

Krys took a pair of long breaths, then cupped her hands around the bracelet. She shut her eyes, took another breath, and drew her hands to her forehead.

She dropped her hands. 'What a waste.'

'You didn't feel anything?'

'Zip. Nada.'

'But no barrier?'

'No.' She slipped the bracelet back into her pocket. 'You try.'

'What's the point?'

'I know. But just to be sure.' Krys noticed his hesitation, and her teeth flashed in the moonlight. 'Don't tell me you're scared.'

'Cautious, more like.'

'Hey. We're sitting here in the middle of nowhere, so you can show us how it's done. Go ahead, partner. Light up the world.'

'Hah. This is me not laughing.' Jackson cradled the stick and took a long breath. Out of the corner of his eye, he could see Krys grinning at him, ready with the next quip for when he failed. He wished he could have come up with something snide to shoot back, but just then . . .

Everything changed.

It began as a very subtle force, as insistent as his being drawn forward in the cavern. A power began swirling out from between his palms, spinning a brilliant web around his hands.

Krys breathed, 'Oh. Wow.'

Jackson wanted to agree with her, but he dared not speak. He knew this was another event. The word had never felt more right than now. He also knew the moment was *delicate*. A single wrong motion, a single *breath*, and he would break the energy growing inside his hands.

Jackson shut his eyes. The sense of communication was clear as a shout. He needed to close out everything but the internal portion of whatever this was.

The artifact served as a battery, or conduit, for the force that was continuing to emerge and spin about him. Jackson did not need to see it. He could *visualize* what was happening with crystal clarity. The web was an intense silver light, run through with brilliant violet streaks. It formed a union between his hands and his forehead.

As he raised the hands cradling the artifact, the light grew in intensity until he was almost blinded by the quick flashes that shot through his fluttering eyelids. Then he touched his joined thumbs to the center of his forehead, and . . .

BOOM.

THIRTY-THREE

Jackson had no idea how long he sat there before returning to full awareness. He realized Krys was speaking his name. The sound of her voice formed a path back from wherever he had gone. He took a long breath and sensed that Krys had been calling to him for quite some time.

She said again, 'Jackson?'

'I'm here.'

'Are you OK?'

'I think . . . Yes.'

'You sure?'

'Definitely.' He looked at her. Krys knelt on her seat, turned fully towards him. 'How long was I out?'

'Not long. Five minutes, maybe a little longer . . . Jackson, look at your hand.'

He glanced down. At first, he doubted his vision, as though some component of his brain was still out there, drifting in the night breeze.

He was holding a *wand*.

The original stick was reformed to fit his fingers. It reminded Jackson of a personalized pistol grip.

The wand was a little longer than his forearm and had no weight. The instrument itself was a soft violet silver. It was shaped like a wooden obelisk, the eight faces rising to join in a softly curved point. The entire length glowed softly, and every now and then a flicker ran down its form, a more intense brilliance spawning a strand of light that spun around and around, rising to the tip and then fading.

Krys said, 'Your forehead is glowing.'

Jackson reached with his free hand and turned the rearview mirror. An octagonal pattern glowed at the center of his forehead, the same color as his wand.

His wand.

Jackson said, 'I think we should try something here.'

Krys was already reaching for the bracelet in her pocket. 'Absolutely.'

But when he reached out with his wand, they both jerked back. The same moment. Just as before.

Only this time, before Krys could erupt, Jackson said, 'Hang on.'

'What is it?'

'I think . . . No. That's not . . .'

'Jackson. Talk to me.'

'I have this idea . . .' He disliked how difficult it was to find some way to get it out. 'That's not the right way to describe it.'

She offered, 'An insight.'

'Exactly that.' He settled deeper into the leather seat. His breath was a battle against a chest locked in tense excitement. 'Here goes.'

Jackson shut his eyes, lifted his wand, and touched the rounded tip to his forehead.

Instantly, he *understood.*

Krys whispered, 'This is wild.'

Jackson opened his eyes to find the wand's glow had become far stronger. Krys's gaze was focused on his forehead. He assumed it was glowing again. The *knowing* was focused upon the reason he had connected with the wand. But it extended *much* further. Everywhere he looked, he *saw.* Jackson said, 'I know what we're supposed to do here.'

Krys said, 'You realize what this means, don't you?'

Jackson looked at her and found himself drawing back. He fought against the urge to delve into everything that was revealed. Her secrets were her own. He dropped his gaze to the wand. 'Yes.'

The ability to fathom beyond mortal confines was the key defining trait of an Adept. Supposedly, it required a lifetime's training and was only granted to the most powerful and disciplined of Talents.

But he didn't want to think about that or allow his extended awareness to shift out that far. He could sense the ability, if he demanded. And the yearning was a swift hunger to go out, further and further, beyond his ability to find his way home.

Jackson focused on what Krys held out to him. He said, 'What you hold. It's not a bracelet. Not a band.'

'Then what . . .'

'Put it on your finger. Right hand. No, the middle one.'

Krys did as he instructed, then made a fist to keep it in place.

'OK. Here goes.'

Jackson reached out the wand. As he did so, the illumination *flamed.* A silver fire spun a brilliant spiral between his wand and the ring. Jackson squinted against the radiance. The entire car glowed like an overpowering lantern.

He touched the band.

The bland surface came alive. The silver flame coursed around the band, faster and faster, like the force that had surrounded the transformed safe.

The silver light illuminated Krys as her body formed a rigid straight line, until only her feet, the back of her thighs, and her neck were in contact with the car. Her right hand flamed like a silver torch. Jackson strained against the glare and watched as the ring shrank down and formed itself around her finger.

The fire stopped racing about the ring's exterior. The light dimmed, faded, and was gone.

The night breeze drifted in through his open window. A cricket sang its brief melody. A branch creaked.

Krys did not release her rigid stance. She also did not appear to be breathing.

Jackson's wand began to fade. The last strand of light spun itself around the glowing wood. He reached out to her with this new awareness and recognized that she was OK. He touched her neck, called her name, and watched her go limp. She gasped, then coughed. A shudder wracked her frame. Her eyes remained closed.

As Jackson's awareness faded back to human limits, in that final instant he realized two things.

First, the night was *too dark*.

Second, they were about to die.

THIRTY-FOUR

Jackson could not get Krys to wake up.

Finally he crawled over her, opened the passenger door, dropped to the earth, and dragged her inert form out with him. He paused long enough to shut the door, dousing the interior lights. He doubted whether a car's illumination would be a danger to them, not after the fireworks display they had just put on. But he preferred to work now by moonlight.

Krys moaned softly as he dragged her over the rough ground. He could probably have made better time using a fireman's lift, but he feared that it could take precious moments trying to heft her by himself. She was utterly limp, even when he gripped her wrists and hauled her backwards over the furrowed earth. She moaned again, so softly he could not make out the word she half formed. Even so, he took it as a very good sign.

He moved as fast as he could, twice almost falling in his haste to make the treeline. When he finally reached the glade, he settled her on the soft earth and took a careful look around. The night was utterly silent. Far in the distance, a lone pair of headlights rushed down the country lane. Jackson remained exactly where he was. Kneeling beside his inert partner. Hand on his gun. Waiting.

The glade was only about ten trees wide. The trunks were slender, not saplings by any measure, but none as thick as Jackson's torso. The congealing darkness kept him from seeing any further above his head than the top branches. Jackson scouted the perimeter, searching the empty field.

Then he looked up once more and knew he had been right to run.

A dark cloud, dense as smoke from a green-tinder fire, was descending overhead. The moon and the stars were gone.

Jackson could *feel* the cloud's approach. He crouched down further, filled with a dread certainty that if it grew much closer, it would cut off their air.

He could no longer see Krys clearly, just a faint outline of her face. But he could hear the soft whisper she gave with each breath, like a dreamer struggling to rise to the surface. Her head twitched slightly, up and down. He tapped her cheeks. One side, then the other. 'Krys. Come on, wake up.'

She moaned a response that might have been his name. He slapped her harder. 'Krys!'

She opened her eyes. He knew because they caught the last faint glow. 'Jackson.'

In the wash of relief over her return, Jackson had time to realize, 'I've lost my wand.'

Krys jerked to a sitting position. Then she needed Jackson's support to stay upright. She looked around. 'Where are we?'

'Woods. We're being hunted.'

But the words didn't register. 'Your wand . . . We need to go back.'

He gripped her more tightly. 'Krys, they're here.'

He could feel the strength surging beneath his hands. 'Who . . .'

The cloud overhead became flecked by a greenish glow. These internal lights were neither constant nor comforting. They flickered and raced about.

Jackson had the distinct impression the cloud was hunting.

A tendril emerged from its base, which was now scarcely higher than Jackson would have been if standing upright. The tentacle was shot through with a stronger version of the same gleam. It held a putrid luminescence, like light reflected from an open grave.

The tentacle made contact with the earth. The miniature funnel retreated, shifted towards them, touched again. Each link to the earth caused the undergrowth to wither and blacken. The air became filled with an acrid, poisonous stench.

Abruptly Jackson was filled with a sudden thought, an utter certainty, of their only way to survive. 'Krys, use your powers—'

The tentacle whipped about, alerted by the sound of his voice. The light strengthened as the end opened like a snake's mouth, revealing fiery green fangs.

The tentacle struck.

At the same instant, Krys straight-armed the space between them. A sizzling bolt blistered the air and seared Jackson's eyeballs. The tentacle was blasted to nothingness.

In response, the cloud sunk, faster now. The mass was so dense that Jackson heard the limbs and then the trunks groan and crack. The green light intensified and pulsed in angry beats. It coalesced at various points, growing a multitude of deadly tentacles. All fanged. All aimed at them.

As Krys struggled to her feet, her light became brilliant. The ring's fire coursed through her entire frame.

Gone was Jackson's partner. In her place was a warrior vixen.

She straightened and screamed a battle cry that shook Jackson's bones.

Krys stabbed the cloud with her fist.

Her light rushed through the entire putrid mass, filling it with a fire that ate the tentacles from within. There followed a rumbling rush, like a rocket finally released from its gravity stanchions. The cloud groaned and flamed. A quick rush of blinding fire, then it was gone.

THIRTY-FIVE

The moon cast its soft glow over an empty night. The stars glistened through the branches. A soft night breeze touched his face.

Jackson asked, 'What was *that*?'

Krys gripped the nearest tree for support. The light of her hand and ring diminished, then faded entirely. 'You tell me.'

The trees and the field rustled softly, as though whispering their astonishment over the night. Jackson asked, 'Can you walk?'

'I think maybe—'

Her response was chopped off in mid-sentence.

The enemy dropped down from the sky.

The two attackers were the same sort of electric figures that Jackson had last seen in the hospital room. The beasts glowed in the night, an enraged red.

The pair landed on his car.

One struck the roof, the other the front hood.

Jackson felt the *slam* of their impact in his gut.

They *flattened* the Bentley. The tires folded outwards like little limbs sprawled in abject defeat.

All Jackson could think was, *There goes the wand.*

The beasts were twice Jackson's size and shaped like stone gargoyles of old, minus the wings. Massive shoulders supported arms that grazed the car with their claws. Their talons were longer than Jackson's forearm. Spines sprouted blades down their backs.

One in particular held Jackson's attention. Something about the way he pounded the car, slamming it with his fists. Then he swung about, spied Jackson, and bellowed. Facing the beast square on, Jackson realized it was the second attacker in the cavern. The one who had argued with Riyanna.

As the attackers started towards them, Krys shrieked right back. A bit fainter, maybe, but she matched them for fury.

The electric gargoyles launched straight at them.

In response, Krys fired up her ring, then her body. She shot out a force that to Jackson appeared a lot like a gigantic fist. Of fire.

One of the gargoyles was just *gone.*

The other jerked away, the one Jackson had met before. He was clearly injured and fell like a wounded bird into the hills beyond the road.

Krys raced across the empty field. Still screaming her very own war cry. She stopped and shrieked and fired again. The flame seared a trough through the field and turned the first line of trees into burning beacons.

Of the second attacker there was no sign.

'They destroyed our *ride.*' Krys stomped back across the field. 'I had a dress in my case I'd never even worn.'

Jackson followed her back to the demolished Bentley. 'Nice

shooting,' he said, wishing he could put a little more weight to his words.

She kicked a deflated tire. 'I wish they'd come back so I could blast them again.' She must have noticed his morose state, for she turned to him and said, 'Maybe you dropped the wand out here.'

'It was in the car,' he replied. 'It must have slipped from my grasp when I panic-crawled over the seat. Before I opened your door. Otherwise, it would have gotten in the way, and I would have noticed.'

'Still, let's check the terrain – you know, just in case.' Krys turned on her phone's flashlight app. 'Where do we focus?'

'By your door. I pulled you out.'

Together they began scouring the rough terrain. The ground was littered with shattered glass, which made looking for a small black wooden object extremely difficult.

Jackson was about to suggest they hold off until dawn when the phone's light flashed on Krys. 'Check your hand.'

'What?' Then she saw where he was staring. Krys lifted her right hand into the light. '*My ring!*' She swept the light over the ground in a panic.

'Krys. Wait.'

'It could be *anywhere*! How could I not have noticed—'

'Just hold up for a minute!' The sharpness of his tone halted her. 'Bring your light back over here.'

'You found it?'

The part of his mind trained by years of fieldwork wanted to say that logic had brought him to this point. When he could realize that one might have dropped their artifact, but not both of them. But even now, in the aftermath of a threat on their lives, Jackson was filled with the certainty that here was yet another idea from beyond his thought processes. He lifted his hand and felt a growing awareness of what to do.

Jackson needed to anchor the next action in something familiar. So he reached and swung his hand up as if he was drawing his gun. Only his weapon remained holstered. At least, the firearm did.

As he brought his arm up, Jackson willed the wand into his hand.

Krys stood bathed in the silver-violet glow from his wand. She said for the third time that night, 'Oh. Wow.'

Jackson made the motion of holstering his weapon, and the wand and the light disappeared.

He turned to Krys. Her face shone in the moonlight. Jackson said, 'Now you try.'

THIRTY-SIX

S tandard Interpol protocol after any high-risk operation required the agents to report in immediately. Jackson had always considered this one of the most useful lessons he had gained from initial training. The adrenaline rush that accompanied gunpowder and the closeness of a final breath heightened the senses and often saved lives. But after, when the heart still pumped and the eyes popped, the thinking was far from clear. Reporting to someone removed from the front line, especially someone who had known action themselves, put thoughts and next steps into proper perspective.

But tonight Jackson was officially cut off.

He said the only thing that came to him. 'Maybe I should phone Luca.'

Jackson expected Krys to say something about him destroying a perfectly good moment. Instead, she replied, 'Hard as it is to admit, that's probably a good idea.'

Jackson pulled out his phone, then took a moment for internal inspection. He could still sense the faintest whisper of Riyanna's spellcasting, her rage lingering like a veil over the night. Which he took as a sign that Riyanna was not the gargoyle Krys had destroyed. And this meant the renegade mage was probably still out there, hunting. Even so, he remained unconcerned. The artifact's power continued to surround him.

Jackson coded Luca's number and offered the briefest of summaries. He gave their meeting with Roger less than thirty seconds. The Frenchman's bracelet, their artifacts, all that could wait. For the moment, he focused on this evening's attack. As for how they managed to survive, all he said was, 'We barely managed to escape.'

When he was done, Jackson half expected Luca to start pointing out all the holes in his story. Starting with how he and Krys were still standing. But all the blind man asked was, 'Where is the artifact you showed Roger Valente?'

'In the pocket of my jacket.' He touched the article, making sure it was safe. 'I thought you said that enemy of yours wouldn't try again.'

'Obviously, my assumptions were very wrong indeed.' Luca sighed. 'This new assault by the Peerless leaves me baffled.'

'Peerless,' Jackson repeated. 'Brussels isn't certain they actually exist.'

'The Peerless are very real indeed. But this clandestine band of Renegade Talents has survived so long by remaining invisible.'

'Something has definitely changed.'

'Indeed. But what? I have been their enemy for years.'

Jackson thought he could probably help with answers, but not yet. He knew without question that his internal barriers were gone. Just the same, he wanted to be seated in the same room, able to study the blind man as he related the full story. And see how Luca reacted.

Luca mused, 'The Peerless must have tracked my wards on the car. And attacked it, thinking I was still inside.' Luca was silent for a time, then asked, 'You are certain the car cannot bring you back?'

'Luca, the Bentley is now six inches high. Speaking of which, what happened to your shield?'

'Wards,' Krys corrected.

'Whatever,' Jackson said.

'The only reason the car exists at all is because of those wards,' Luca replied.

'So what now?'

'Stay on the line. I need to make another call.'

While he waited, Jackson related what Luca had said. When he was done, Krys frowned at the car and said, 'If we accept that Luca is telling us the truth . . .'

Jackson was very glad to have this in the open. He considered it vital for her to come up with the only way forward, as far as Jackson could see. When she remained silent, he pressed, 'It's time we accept him as an ally.'

'I know. I *know*!' Krys glared at him. 'But he's still got a lot of answering to do!'

'No argument there.' Jackson watched Krys stomp out into the field, muttering and waving her arms at the night. Which explained why Jackson was laughing softly when Luca came back on and announced, 'A helicopter is inbound and should be with you in fifty minutes. Keep your phone on; they are now linked to your GPS.'

Jackson and Krys spent the time scouting for possible attackers and drawing out their new implements, watching them gleam, studying the sense of connection, then releasing hold and letting them fade.

As they repeated the process, subtle elements gradually crystallized. These were no longer *things*. They were not *external*. With each emergence, the bonds grew stronger. Jackson felt as though he was studying how to use a new limb.

They talked about it at first, mostly exclamations over the sheer exhilaration that surged every time the powers were revealed. But gradually they went silent. The experiences drained them. When the chopper finally landed, Jackson felt scarcely able to cross the field and climb through the open door.

A limousine met them at Geneva airport. As they pulled up in front of Krys's building, she spoke for the first time since boarding the chopper. 'When are you going to tell Luca about, you know, the things?'

'I like that,' Jackson said. 'Not if. Not whether we should. I like that a lot.'

She offered a weary smile. 'When?'

'Tomorrow. First thing. Like you said, we need answers.'

'I want to be there.'

'Good. I'll phone you as soon as I'm up and moving.'

'Right.' She started to rise, then turned back from where the driver stood holding her door. Her eyes were as luminous as his hidden wand. 'I am so glad you brought me in on this.'

Jackson carried a warm glow all the way back to Rue Gambord. By the time he climbed the stairs around that massive central pillar, he felt as if his exhaustion was an anchor he had to haul up behind him. He groaned through the ordeal of undressing and showering, then collapsed on the bed and was gone.

Jackson woke sometime before dawn, utterly famished. He padded downstairs and made himself a sandwich from what he found in the fridge – butter and Dijon mustard and celery and pickles and four kinds of cheese. He drank a liter of water, then went back upstairs. He stood by the glass wall and stared out over the lake and the moonlit peaks beyond. All the windows were bordered by steel shutters. He had seen the bank of controls in the front foyer and duplicate set in the bedroom. The glass was several inches thick and probably bulletproof. Luca had no doubt put shields or wards or whatever they were around the place. He felt safe enough. He was fascinated by the view and had no interest in blocking it out.

Jackson had never cared much about money, saving it or spending it or being defined by it. He had been that way pretty much all his life. His father had been a gold-shield detective in Denver, shot while stopping a robbery and reduced to a desk job he hated. His mother had been a legal secretary. Money had always been tight when Jackson was growing up, something that had bothered his mother a lot more than his dad. Both were gone now, and sometimes Jackson felt as though his lack of interest in finances was a subtle means of honoring their memory.

Jackson's late wife, on the other hand, had found a unique pleasure in spending money. Sylvie had been very good at her herbal magic and loved being paid well. She reveled in shopping with a Frenchwoman's unbridled embrace of all pleasures. She adored the latest fashion, the ultra-chic destinations, the finest restaurants and clubs. She had a unique ability to treat the spending of her money as a personal achievement. Sylvie had found Jackson's lack of interest in the whole circle of earning and spending to be utterly baffling. She had loved him for finding pleasure in the joy it had brought her.

Now Jackson stood with his bare feet nestled in a plush carpet, staring at a million-dollar view, and willed the wand to emerge. He lifted his hand and studied the soft silver-violet glow, the tendrils that wove around its length, as though the implement fed off the starlight. He said softly, 'Will you just look at me now.'

THIRTY-SEVEN

Jackson's coffee maker formed an oddly comforting hint of normalcy as he prepared his breakfast. He called Luca and found the man as blandly alert as ever. He resisted a sudden urge to ask if Luca ever slept and merely said he and Krys were coming over.

He then called Krys and asked, 'How did you sleep?'

'Like a stone, except for the three times I woke up and made the ring reappear. How about you?'

'Good, and I made do with only once. I'm coming by to pick you up.'

'Give me fifteen minutes, I just got in from a run.'

Jackson showered and found a vague satisfaction in resuming his normal outfit of jeans and polo shirt. But when he entered the garage, the Jeep was gone. In its place, he found another new Bentley, this one pale blue with pearl hide stitched in a diamond pattern. The keys and papers were there on the passenger seat.

Simeon phoned as he pulled up in front of Krys's apartment house. 'I have the preliminary report on Bernard Bouchon, chapter two.'

Jackson cut the motor. 'Go ahead.'

'Bouchon indeed became an Acolyte with the Sardinian Institute. He died aged sixteen in what officially has been listed as a training accident. His records have been obtained in an indirect manner, as you requested. He was classed as a Warrior and received the highest possible marks. He was expected to rise to the level of Adept. Then he perished.'

'Your source is sure he's dead?'

'Sources, plural. Same intel received from the tax authorities and my friend in Rome.' Simeon paused. 'You were searching for something?'

'No, it's just . . .'

'Tell me.'

But he was too experienced an agent to deal in suppositions. 'What about the records on my house?'

'The answer, my friend, is another mystery.' There was the sound of papers being shifted. 'There was never anything on this property before. Not even a cow barn. The adjacent land held a farm. Your property was a pasture. Back in the sixties, the farmland was divided up. Gradually, the surrounding plots were sold off to the great and the not-so-good. Villas rose all around.'

Jackson spotted Krys emerging from her front door and waved her over. 'Why not here?'

'This particular plot changed hands eleven times. Once or twice, I could call it an investment. But eleven! Without someone building a house? On a rise with a view of the lake and the Alps? I talked to the builder, who claimed an architect gave him the design and the land. So I next spoke with the architect himself, who is one of our most famous planners of expensive homes. He was very vague, this man.'

Jackson waved as Krys settled into the passenger seat, motioning for her to remain quiet. 'Vague, as in cagey?'

'Perhaps, but I think . . .'

'Tell me.'

'*Mon ami*, we are returning to what I cannot openly discuss here in police headquarters. You understand?'

'All too well.'

'He had initially thought he might live there himself but, for reasons he could not explain, decided to remain in his current home. This architect seemed relieved that Luca had bought it from him. But I had the impression he was not clear on much of anything.'

'Thanks for this, Simeon.' He started the car.

'Where are you headed?'

Jackson pulled into traffic. 'Looking for answers.'

'That word has such a lovely sound. Answers. If you find some, share them with me, will you? I will sleep better tonight.'

Jackson drove to the lakefront in silence. He found a parking spot on the street a hundred meters from the Julius Brothers Bank. Only when they were approaching the building did Krys speak for the first time. 'Will you tell me what that was all about?'

'From now on, I intend to tell you everything.' He pointed to the building. 'But I'd rather wait and go through this with Luca as well.'

'Do you feel any resistance when you think about telling him?'

'Not since I called him last night.' Jackson scouted the perimeter, searching for Riyanna. The street and plaza were almost empty. When the hidden door clicked open, Jackson added, 'Even if the obstruction reappears, Luca has to know.'

Krys nodded, and he was grateful for her lack of objection. She asked, 'What if it breaks something, going against the barrier?'

Jackson had been wondering the same thing. 'Only one of us has to take that risk. You don't need to say anything.'

'Listen to us, discussing things we can't even name.'

When the second door slid open, Jackson said, 'Speaking of which, you were right.'

'About what?'

'Treasures,' he replied. 'There's no name that fits better.'

THIRTY-EIGHT

This time, Jackson felt no resistance whatsoever.

He laid it out carefully, taking his time, giving it to Luca in chronological order. He halted after describing the silhouetted figures within the deep cave. But Luca remained silent, immobile. So Jackson launched into the sighting of Riyanna outside Luca's apartment entryway. The nightmare. The sense of Riyanna's spells pressing him to commit murder, and the artifact's role as shield. Which led to their discovery of the artifact's true potential that previous evening. And the attack that followed.

He finished with a recounting of Simeon's report. When he was done, Luca sat and stared blindly straight ahead for a time. Then, 'They are certain Bouchon is dead?'

'Two independent sources came up with the same information.' When Luca remained silent, Jackson nodded to Krys. *Your turn.*

Krys followed his lead, describing her side of things in careful stages, beginning with the cavern elevator. The two of them sat opposite one another in a pair of white high-backed dining chairs, with Luca in the white leather settee between them. Krys's gaze held steady on Jackson as she gave her own version of a field agent reporting the impossible.

When she finished, and Luca did not speak, Krys asked Jackson, 'You didn't feel any barrier now?'

'Almost the opposite,' Jackson replied. 'Like it was time to bring him in. You?'

She nodded. 'Exactly the same.'

Jackson spoke slowly, testing the words as they emerged. 'Maybe we first needed to, you know, bond.'

Luca lifted his head and breathed deeply. Again. 'I detect no magical force whatsoever emanating from you or your artifacts.'

Krys demanded, 'Does what happened out there in the field mean Jackson is an Adept?'

'Allow me first to ask—'

'No, Luca. I'm sorry, but no. We've done a good job of filling you in. No holds barred. Now it's your turn. Is. Jackson. A. Senior. Talent?'

If Luca noticed the confrontational tone, he gave no sign. 'There are a few accounts of Talents coming into their abilities this late in life. I assume Bernard Bouchon was one. Most accounts I have read suggest that when it happens, the Talent's abilities remain stunted in their development. They find it almost impossible to break the bonds of logic and grow into their full potential.'

'That absolutely does not fit with what I witnessed last night,' Krys said.

'There is one other possibility,' Luca said. 'Where there is a deep love between an Adept and an ungifted, when the Adept dies, they may pass on a portion of their power. It is rare, but it happens.'

Jackson replied, 'Sylvie was not classed as an Adept.'

'Your late wife also married an Interpol agent. The Institute's examiners would have seen this as a punishable act. They might have quashed both her potential and her chances at further development.' Luca shook his head. 'The Institutes have much to answer for.'

Jackson was flooded by the old bitter fury. Sylvie's rejected application for senior training had come just a few months before her death. All the old unanswered questions about her passing resurfaced. Sparked with rage for all they might have known together, had she lived.

Krys asked, 'You OK there, partner?'

He did his best to shove it all aside. And nodded.

Luca asked, 'Will you both please show me?'

Again, Jackson tested the air and found no hint of resistance. 'I'll go first.'

He extended his arm in the gunslinger's motion, finding it easier to exert his will with that physical act.

Luca gasped aloud and jerked back in his seat. The shock was evident.

Jackson asked, 'You OK?'

'Yes. I . . . This is astounding.'

Jackson made the wand vanish. He said to Krys, 'Your turn.'

Luca was more prepared this time, but they could both see he was rocked when Krys made the ring appear. 'Remarkable. Before, I detected nothing. Now . . .'

Jackson said, 'What is it?'

'There is a certain flavor when I am in the presence of a senior Talent who is using his or her abilities. A unique signature. You both show this the *instant* your implements are revealed.'

'So . . .' Krys hesitated, then went on, 'You haven't heard of something like this before?'

'Never.' He asked them to reveal the implements together. He breathed several times, great shuddering breaths. 'You complement one another. Together, the presence of arcane forces is far stronger.'

Jackson stowed his wand away. Krys did the same. Luca breathed in, out, tasting the air. Then, 'One thing you should know about your acquisitions. Everything I've studied regarding the Ancients refers to how such magical implements and scrolls have what is called a "rightful position". Once they are used, once the spellwork is done, they return to these assigned stations.'

Krys looked at Jackson, who said, 'You've lost us.'

'Their *rightful position*,' Luca repeated. 'It appears that the scrolls and artifacts become anchored to a particular spot. They are brought forth, they are used, and they return. No mention was ever made, in any record, of them actually being *carried* back.'

'Hang on a second,' Krys demanded. 'Those artifacts just *went away*?'

'That is how it appears to me,' Luca replied.

'You mean, of their own volition?' A very real pain creased her features. 'So what happens to my ring when we finish this investigation? You're saying it might just *go back*? I can't keep it?'

'I have no idea,' Luca replied. He lifted his cane. 'I have had the use of this artifact for almost fourteen years. Through a countless series of quests.'

Krys subsided. 'That helps. Not a lot. But some.'

When Jackson was certain that topic was closed, at least for the moment, he spoke the name. 'Riyanna.'

Luca jerked a single nod. Or perhaps he just shuddered.

'You said we were safe from another attack.'

'And I was wrong.'

Krys asked, 'Was she the gargoyle I demolished last night?'

In response, Luca rose to his feet. 'Would you bring me my staff?'

Krys stood and walked to where it leaned against the wall by the stairs. When she handed it over, Luca touched the tip to his forehead, then ran it along the inside of Jackson's arm. He released

Jackson and made a slow circle around him, speaking in that slow deep monotone Jackson had last heard before Luca had read the vanished scrolls. The script along the staff's length glowed and swam.

Luca leaned back, set the staff on the floor by his chair, and said, 'Regrettably, Riyanna remains among the living. If she had been killed, the flavor of this spell would be different. I must apologize, Jackson. Profusely.'

'It's OK.'

'It is anything but. The spells of every senior mage carry a particular signature. I should have sensed her work.'

Krys asked, 'Why didn't you?'

Luca slowly shook his head. 'Riyanna. That woman has plagued me for years. But never did I think the Peerless would risk multiple assaults in a week. They have always valued secrecy above all else.'

Krys asked, 'So what has changed?'

'That is precisely the question I wish to ask. Could you both leave, please? I must cast the runes.' But as Jackson started to rise, Luca halted them with, 'Jackson, allow me to arrange a meal at your new home. Shall we meet there, say, in two hours?'

'Make it three,' Jackson said. 'First, we need to report in.'

THIRTY-NINE

They drove to Krys's home. Her apartment was small, which was hardly a surprise given the city's high rents. On a square-foot basis, a nice rental inside Geneva's old city cost as much as Manhattan's upper east side. Krys had a living-dining area, a separate kitchen, and a bedroom that Jackson did not ask to see. It was high-ceilinged and freshly decorated and impossibly neat. French doors opened on to a narrow balcony whose wrought-iron railing overlooked a park. Children's laughter drifted up from below as she positioned her laptop on the dining table. Jackson watched her code in for a secure and scrambled connection, then hesitate, her fingers poised over the keyboard. She asked, 'Jackson, what do we say? I mean, how much are we going to tell them?'

'Eventually, we give them the whole deal.' Jackson drew a chair over beside hers and seated himself. 'Right now, we're making an after-incident report. Hold to just the essential elements.'

The computer gave the soft chime of connecting, then Chief Meyer's face appeared. Her first words were, 'Is this secure?'

'And scrambled,' Jackson replied. 'We've had an incident.'

'Let me see if Barker is available. Hold one.' The screen went blank.

Jackson offered, 'Why don't you let me handle this first verbal report. You can observe how it's done, be ready for the next time.'

'Sounds good.'

When the screen lit up again, it was split so as to include Commandant Barker as well. Jackson launched straight in, keeping strictly to their meeting with Roger Valente and the attack in the countryside. He made no mention of anything related to their implements. Nor did he detail Riyanna's attempt to use him as a weapon against Luca. Both would have to wait. Jackson knew from experience that whenever new and unexpected magic appeared in an investigation, Brussels grew nervous. Their knee-jerk reaction was to pull the agents out of the field. Jackson did not want that to happen. Now was not the time to start talking about the treasures they secreted from a Swiss vault, or how those items had bonded with them both.

His report required six minutes and forty-one seconds. When he was done, Barker said, 'Do I need to inform you that this conversation and everything related to the case remain strictly confidential?'

Jackson knew Barker intended the query mostly for Krys. He answered for them both, 'No, ma'am, you do not.'

'This case will carry a long half-life. Which means it must remain in-house. Eyes only. Permanently.'

Krys replied, 'Understood, Commandant.'

'All right. First, the attack you experienced during your return journey. For several years we have received unconfirmed reports of a group of Renegade Talents.'

Meyer added, 'This goes far beyond individual Renegades studying the dark arts. This group is said to be organized and highly dangerous.'

'Luca called them the Peerless,' Jackson said. 'He claims they are his sworn enemy.'

'That is more than he has told any of us,' Barker said. 'Have him call me immediately.'

Meyer said, 'Perhaps you should allow Jackson to handle this for the time being.'

Barker did not like it. But in the end, she said, 'Luca Tami needs to understand how vital it is for us to receive a full report. This is the first direct evidence we have that the Peerless exist.'

'That and the hospital attack,' Krys added.

Barker shot her a measuring look, then demanded, 'Luca Tami thinks the Peerless were behind that assault as well?'

'He says there's no question,' Jackson replied.

'It is absolutely crucial for Tami to report on what he knows about this group.'

'Understood.'

Barker nodded once, twice, then said, 'Moving on. For the past six months, our informers have reported a heightened state of turbulence inside the Institutes.'

Jackson had always assumed Interpol maintained clandestine sources inside the halls of magical power. But this was the first confirmation. 'Which Institute?'

'All seven,' Bev Barker replied. 'Whatever this is, it is global.'

'You think this foment is tied to the Bouchon incident?'

'Quite possibly. Luca Tami's alert certainly suggests it. Which reminds me. It's time to speak with his superiors and see if they have any new intel.' She made a note on the pad, then asked, 'Where was I?'

'Global disturbances inside the Institutes.'

'Remember what I said in our last conversation. From its very inception, Interpol has been assigned a confidential remit.'

'Global checks and balances,' Jackson said.

'The world's governments rely on our assistance to maintain the status quo,' Barker went on. 'Globally, there are at present some two hundred and seventeen thousand registered Talents. They represent a sizable force, but because they are spread more or less equally, they do not pose a significant threat to any specific nation or regime. Their role in times of conflict is limited by the same sort of treaties as apply to the nuclear deterrent, with one notable exception.'

'Every country has access to magic,' Jackson supplied.

'We must maintain this balance of power,' Chief Meyer said. 'It all comes down to that.'

'Very recently, we have managed to confirm what Interpol has long suspected,' Barker continued. 'Some Institute Directors feel Talents have been docile and obliging for too long.'

Jackson said, '"Docile" and "obliging" are not words I would use to describe Talents.'

Zoe Meyer said, 'Some Institute Directors and their allies among the Adepts want to demand a leadership role in governments. *All* governments.'

Barker said, 'You can see the havoc these scrolls represent.'

'The power to go back and alter one element of our past, eradicate some opponent to stop them becoming a leading force in that nation's affairs,' Meyer said. 'The results would be catastrophic.'

Barker said, 'Our allies within national intelligence agencies have effectively been forced to share their intel because of the havoc these scrolls might cause.'

Jackson leaned back, recalling his first report, the lack of surprise shown by either woman, the way they had rushed to cut off the discussion. 'Why are you telling us this now?'

'You know the answer to that,' Barker replied.

Krys was the one who replied, 'You had to receive permission.'

'Which was granted very reluctantly. But your Bouchon incident has confirmed their worst fears.'

His chief added, 'Especially now that the original events have vanished from memory.'

'That brought the nightmare legends from our distant past directly into the here and now,' Barker agreed. 'Your initial report would most likely have been filed and forgotten, except for the timing of these incidents.'

'The details were too exact,' Meyer said. 'And you are too good an agent to have developed such an outlandish scheme.'

'Again, I am grateful for your confidence,' Jackson said.

Barker's features might as well have been carved from Alpine granite. 'You know what I am about to say, don't you?'

Jackson nodded. 'There are some governments who want to obtain the scrolls for themselves.'

'Which can't be allowed to happen,' Barker said.

'Roger that.'

Krys asked, 'Are these governments responsible for the deaths of field agents?'

'A question I only allow myself to ask in the dead of night,' Barker replied. 'And the answer is yes, quite possibly.'

Meyer said, 'If any of this ever got out, the radical anti-magic parties could well be swept to power with a landslide mandate to bomb the Institutes and imprison all Talents who survive.'

'Find the scrolls,' Barker commanded. 'By whatever means necessary. Destroy them. Those are your orders.'

FORTY

When the screen went blank, Jackson and Krys spent a few minutes standing on her balcony. It was just broad enough for two folding chairs and a small table. She had decorated the rim with flower boxes. It suggested a softer side that she kept well hidden around the job. Krys then excused herself, saying she wanted to dress up for the meal. When he asked why, she smiled and said that she thought gaining a power-ring was worth a little celebration.

Jackson took that as a clear alert that he needed to re-arm in the style department. He drove from her place to the men's store and picked up the two outfits he had left for tailoring. While there, he reluctantly decided to purchase duplicates of what had been destroyed in the field.

When he arrived back at Rue Gambord, he went upstairs and showered and dressed, then walked outside and inspected the house. The entire front yard was fenced in a head-high steel-and-glass wall, whose upper edge was honed to a razor edge. He spotted motion sensors embedded in the grass. The rear yard was only about forty feet wide and ended at a sheer rock face rising to a high ridgeline. Jackson knew attackers could easily rappel down. The flat roof would make an effective point from which to launch an assault. Not to mention what a pair of compression grenades could do with all that bulletproof glass.

Krys arrived wearing a midnight-blue pantsuit of what she said was Shantung silk. Her tensile curves turned the modest outfit into a frame for her allure. Jackson patted himself on the back for not relying on his standard evening wardrobe of khakis and an unironed shirt. 'You look great.'

'It's overkill, I know.'

'No, no, you're right. We need to mark the occasion.' He led her into the kitchen and confessed, 'I hope Luca tells the deli to pack some drinks in with the meal. All I've got is water and milk and coffee.'

'Coffee would be great.' She watched him prep the old apparatus and set it on the stove. 'I haven't seen one of those since I was a kid.'

'It can't be called an antique because it's too ugly to have any value,' Jackson said. 'How do you take espresso?'

'Same as the regular. Touch of milk.'

'Coming up.'

She leaned against the counter. 'Luca called me.'

That was enough to turn him around. 'Really?'

'I know. A first. He asked me how I'd feel about moving in here. With you.'

His movements slowed further. 'Luca Tami. Called you. And said . . .'

'He can't set wards around my apartment. A couple of retired Talents live two floors below. He said they'd be bound to notice. And he repeated what he said earlier about our new powers being stronger when taken together.'

Jackson nodded. 'That all makes sense.'

'I asked him to let me speak with you about it.' She crossed her arms. 'What do you think?'

He thought there were a hundred different reasons why her moving in could be a bad idea. But all he said was, 'Luca is right. We have to maintain a level of safety as we move forward.'

She studied his face, as though able to see all the emotions and reservations that boiled below the surface. 'You sure?'

'There are three empty rooms upstairs. Choose one for your bedroom and another for your office. We'll go by and pick up your things after we eat.'

She looked a little sheepish. 'I figured you'd say that, so I brought what I need with me.'

He tried for casual. 'Why don't you take some time now and settle in?'

Krys was still upstairs when two vans bearing the logo of Geneva's most famous restaurant pulled through the open gates. A chef and three assistants unloaded tray after tray of delicacies. They refused his offer to help, so he refilled his coffee cup and watched as they set bottles of white Burgundy and vintage champagne in his fridge and then decanted two bottles of Saint Emilion Premier Grand Cru Classe.

When Luca's limo pulled up twenty minutes later, Jackson's dining room had been transformed with starched linen tablecloths and six candelabra and sterling silver cutlery and bone china and crystal goblets. The chef was clearly accustomed to Luca's habits, for he did not offer to serve. Instead, he pointed out the various courses to Jackson and a wide-eyed Krys, all simmering in their silver-plated basting trays, and departed.

For starters, they dined on paper-thin slices of air-dried beef, a Swiss delicacy, and a mélange of lightly pickled vegetables. This was followed by filet mignon with the spring's first truffles, whipped garlic potatoes, and grilled chard. Chocolate torte for dessert. Cheeseboard.

Midway through the cheese course, Jackson was struck by a thought that left him hiding his smile in his glass. But Krys was too sharp for him. 'What is it?'

There was no way he was ever going to tell her what he'd just thought of, which was that his late wife would have keeled over at the sight of him. Here. Dressed like this. Playing host at this candlelit table. In this house. With his second Bentley of the week in his garage. Not to mention the wand now hidden up his sleeve.

When she saw he was not going to reply, Krys turned to Luca. 'Can I ask you something extremely personal?'

'You may ask whatever you want.' Luca had eaten little and drunk less. A taste of each dish and a sip from each glass. Nothing more. His cheese plate contained one cracker, a sliver of aged cheddar, a single stalk of celery, and three grapes.

'How much did you pay for this place?'

Luca said, 'Fourteen million euros.'

The idea of somebody paying sixteen million dollars for a house and then giving it away, even temporarily, silenced Krys. She drained her red wine, set the goblet down carefully, and stared into the candlelight.

Luca read the silence correctly, for he said, 'I will tell you whatever you wish to know.'

'Let's start with three things,' Krys said. 'How did you get your money? Why doesn't your wealth matter to you? And are you an Adept?'

He broke off a fragment of cracker, ate it with one more grape. 'The answers, as it happens, are interconnected.'

'So let's hear it.' The wine had softened her tone but raised her volume. She did not inquire. She thrust ahead.

'I was born the second son of one of Switzerland's most powerful banking families. Several of my ancestors were accomplished Talents; one even rose to a leadership position in the Singapore Institute. So they were hardly surprised when I began showing magical abilities.'

Jackson asked, 'How old were you?'

'Seven. For the next three years I was secretly tutored by Talents they smuggled in and out of Zurich. Then I was sent to Campione, where the European Institute runs an academy for the especially gifted or the very rich.'

Luca sipped from his glass. The level of wine did not appear to go down. 'My brother died when I was nineteen. By then I was already in Sardinia, completing my training as an Acolyte at the Institute. My mother perished in the same traffic accident that claimed my brother. My father retreated from his business and his world, then died of an overdose nine months later. The entire Tami fortune was left to me. I keep a distance from all business affairs. It suits the company's directors as much as it does me.'

Krys exclaimed, 'But why don't you *care*?'

'Two reasons. First, because when I was young, money was simply what paid for my imprisonment. You ask if I am an Adept. When I was nine, my tutors decided I had the potential, which was ten years earlier than this declaration is normally made. With my family's accord, these tutors caged me in terribly constricting rules and a discipline that I hated from the very first day.' He took another sip of his wine. 'You have no idea, you cannot imagine, what it was like. For ten excruciating years, I was tutored by men and women who hated me because I was already a more powerful Talent than they could ever hope to become. They created a military-style discipline and did so with my family's money and the Institute's blessing. Relocating to the Institute when I turned sixteen only made things worse. By my nine-teenth birthday, I despised them with a burning fury.

'The Institute wanted to be certain that any Talent with my sort of abilities was truly one of them. After I became an Acolyte at the Sardinian Institute, senior examiners regularly forced me to undergo excruciating assessments. The other students had no idea what this cost me. All they saw was that I was being granted special treatment. They hated me, and they made my life even more miserable than it already was.'

Krys murmured, 'Terrible.'

'Terrible indeed,' Luca agreed.

'What happened?'

Luca held up one finger. 'Before I answer that, I said there were two reasons why I did not care about the expenditures. You have both now experienced what many hear of but few ever realize: the bond between a gifted Talent and an artifact that carries some element of the Ancients' power. How did that feel?'

'You know how,' Jackson replied. 'It was amazing.'

'Exquisite,' Krys added. 'Explosive.'

'Beyond words,' Jackson added.

'I have known hundreds of such experiences. More. How do you think that might impact the way I feel towards the more mundane pleasures?'

Krys's response was to lift her empty wine glass without taking her gaze off Luca. She said, 'Barkeep.'

Instead of reaching across the table, Jackson rose from his seat and carried the bottle around. He recalled an older friend on the force once telling him to observe carefully how a woman handled her first tipple in his company, for it often revealed hidden elements in her nature. As he poured Krys another glass of the red, Jackson decided he liked this woman's inner nature just fine.

Krys asked, 'What happened to you, Luca?'

This time, Luca drained his glass. 'I fell in love.'

Jackson walked over and refilled Luca's glass. Perhaps it was the wine and the meal resting comfortably in his middle. But Jackson thought more was at work than a fine meal and a pleasant interlude. Jackson sensed a bond growing between the three of them, a link he had not known in years. The sort of connection that could make all the difference when things got hot. Surviving tight situations often relied upon trusting others to do the right thing at the right moment.

And something more was at work: a subtle energy that he had not recognized until that very moment. The more he bonded with his artifact, the stronger grew his shields. Jackson stood there at Luca's end of the table, straining to feel any hint of their adversary's spellcasting. It was there, he knew, but faint as a nightmare's final traces.

Luca said, 'Her name, as you know, was Riyanna. And she first came to me in a dream.'

Krys said, 'That sounds like the start of an epic poem.'

'A tragic one,' Luca said. 'By the age of nineteen, I was a rebel looking for the chance to destroy as much of the Institute as I could. Whether or not I survived mattered little to me at that point. I saw myself as a human bomb, just waiting for the right moment to ignite. Then, one night, Riyanna appeared and asked if I was ready to run free. Even before she spoke, I was lost. I begged her to take me with her, not because of the freedom she offered, but because already I could not see a life without her. What surprised her and all the Peerless was that Riyanna came to love me as well. But for Riyanna, love was a passing weakness. For me, it was everything. She cared far more for her growing powers of ensnarement than she ever could for any one man.'

Jackson walked around the table and resumed his seat. 'When she trapped me in that dream, I thought I was lost as well.'

'You were fortunate to escape,' Luca said. 'Riyanna has become their most powerful recruiter of men.'

Jackson said, 'Commandant Barker needs your report on the Peerless.'

'And she shall have it. It is a duty I have put off far too long.' Luca rose stiffly to his feet. He left his staff leaning against the table beside his place. He lifted his arms and began taking small steps around the space between the dining area and the living room. He touched each item he came into contact with, his fingers constantly shifting. Jackson had the impression he was marking his territory. 'Where was I?'

Krys replied, 'Loving Riyanna.'

'Initially, I was just another of many frustrated young Talents the Peerless brought in on a trial basis. Any Talent who is judged unworthy to join their ranks is erased.' Luca dropped his arms and began pacing, his actions precise now, his territory clearly defined. 'The first Peerless were all women. Men who join their ranks are required to make a sacrifice to show their loyalty. I have heard that this has nowadays become almost symbolic. Males give up contact with loved ones, they surrender a valued artifact, whatever. When I joined, the demand was draconian. At the time, most incoming males surrendered their manhood. But given the fact that love had brought me into their ranks, that was impossible.'

Krys whispered, 'Your eyes.'

'Just so.' Luca came within inches of the candles burning on the sideboard and wheeled about. 'The Peerless are bound together by three secret powers, a trio of spells that they claim date back to the Ancients. These spells, according to the Peerless leaders, were originally intended to be used by women. One of these is their masking spell; another is their wards. What makes these unique is that the more Talents who join together in creating the spells, the more powerful the cloaking and the shields become. And the third – well, you have already witnessed this.'

'The electric gargoyles,' Jackson said.

'Interesting. I have never thought of them as electric. But that fits well enough, I suppose.' Luca paused by the table and fumbled for his glass. He drank, then continued, 'Releasing the inner beast in that manner turns every Peerless into a Warrior. The spell magnifies their own life force with a power that some say creates a link to the people that are no more.'

Jackson asked, 'What about Riyanna?'

The pacing accelerated with his speech. 'The power of her allure continues to grow. She has the singular ability to fashion herself into an enticement few can resist. A few years after I arrived, Riyanna's infidelity had grown to include every male she brought in. By that point, Riyanna's power was so great that the incoming male Talents were no longer volunteers. They were her slaves.'

Krys said, 'It's amazing you escaped.'

'I was thinking the exact same about Jackson.'

Jackson said, 'It only happened because Riyanna started arguing with that guy.'

'The *guy*.' Luca's voice lowered to a soft murmur. 'Of course. The *guy*.'

'Tell us why that's important,' Krys said.

'Because when I was among them, the leaders were all women. No male was permitted to rise above their lowly status. Among the Peerless leaders, men were there to serve.'

Krys asked, 'Which is why you left?'

'Partly, yes. But if Riyanna had returned my love, I would gladly have remained their serf for all my days.' Luca stopped and turned towards the table. In the candlelight, the empty sockets appeared bottomless caverns. 'But she could not have cared less about my feelings or desire for a true relationship. So I left. And they have been hunting me ever since.'

FORTY-ONE

Luca phoned while Jackson was making coffee the next morning. 'The runes failed me. Occasionally, I need to repeat the process and cast them a second time. Not often, but it happens. Sometimes the first answer is incomplete. But always before I have known a sense of bonding.'

Jackson took his coffee over to the rear window. The rain was falling now as a heavy mist. The rock face beyond his back garden glistened. 'And now?'

'Yesterday afternoon and again this morning, the stones remained cold.'

Jackson thought he could see where this was headed. He asked, 'These stones of yours are from the Ancients?'

Luca said, 'An interesting question.'

'I'm asking because I was wondering if maybe it was something more than just cold rocks.'

Luca did not respond.

Jackson asked, 'Did you hit the wall as we described?'

'Until this happened, I was uncertain what precisely you meant by the barrier.' Luca sighed. 'I dislike this intensely.'

'Get in line.' Jackson heard footsteps on the stairs and pulled another cup and saucer from the cabinet. When Krys entered the kitchen, he lifted the pot in greeting. She nodded, so he poured her the second cup. He handed it over, then motioned to the milk he'd left on the cabinet. He cradled the phone with his shoulder and began preparing another pot. He said to the phone, 'So what happens now?'

'I have been thinking about how Krys described your connection to the artifact.'

'My wand.'

'She said you were granted a sense of higher awareness.'

'I don't know if that's a proper way to describe what happened.'

Krys mouthed the single word, *What?*

Jackson lowered the phone. 'Luca didn't get anything from the runes. He's wondering if maybe me and the wand, I don't know . . .'

Krys leaned forward and raised her voice. 'It's a good idea, Luca. Jackson needs to see how far he can take this.'

Jackson lifted the phone. 'You heard the lady.'

'Do nothing until I arrive,' Luca warned. 'This is very different from seeking a hidden element that is close at hand. I am preparing my initial report for Brussels. I must also report to my own superiors. This will delay my arrival at least an hour. Probably more like two.'

'We'll see you when you get here.' Jackson cut the connection, set the new pot on the stove, and leaned against the counter, his back to the window. He pointed to the envelope on the table. 'Those are for you. Cash and keys for house and car both.'

She set down her cup and opened the envelope. She flicked the bills with one fingernail. 'How much is in there?'

'Fifty thousand. Half of what Luca brought last night. I didn't notice it until this morning. He must have set it down on his way out.'

'Would it do any good to protest?'

'None whatsoever,' Jackson replied. 'Another coffee?'

'OK.'

He poured her cup, then his own. He seated himself across from her and filled her in on his conversation with Luca. 'We need to file a written report.'

'I volunteer. It will help me clear my head.'

'Keep it brief. One copy, every page marked "eyes only". Include mention of my contact with Riyanna.'

'What about, you know . . .'

'The treasures. Right. Hold that back for the end-of-action report.' He gave her a chance to object, then continued, 'Be sure to include Luca's assessment of the Peerless. Luca's preparing his own report this morning, but I want them to hear about the Peerless from us as well.'

'What are you going to do?'

He finished his cup and set it in the sink. 'I've always loved to run in the rain.'

'Wait for me, OK? I need to get the ya-yas out. Desperately.'

He had to smile. 'Give the lady keys to a Bentley and fifty thousand in cash, no reaction. Offer her a chance to go out and get cold and wet, she's all over it.'

'In a heartbeat.' She was already up and moving. 'I type super-fast. Fifteen minutes. Twenty tops.'

*   *   *

Jackson suggested they use the chief's home as their destination
and drop off Krys's report. He slipped the document into a zippered
waterproof folder, then they ran the six and a half miles there and
back.

Jackson's high school had been one of the few in Denver that
had offered boxing as a sport. The school had bordered one of the
rough downtown sections, and the principal had wisely considered
the ring an outlet for the rage-filled youths who filled her halls.
His coach had boxed for the Army, twice making it to the Golden
Gloves quarterfinals. He considered running in stormy conditions
an ideal way of testing his young recruits. Jackson had boxed
through college and the police academy. He was brash and
outspoken and liked to wade into trouble. Fights were inevitable.
Boxing gave him an edge.

When they returned to the house on Rue Gambord, Jackson
opened both garage bay doors. They stretched in the empty space
beside the Bentley. Beyond the open portals, the rain fell in an
almost continuous sheet.

Simeon called just as Jackson emerged from the shower. The
Swiss detective spoke with the mock resignation of an extremely
married man. 'I am instructed to invite you and Ms Duprey to
dinner.'

'I'll need to check with Krys. But that sounds great to me.'

'Apparently, Noemi feels it necessary to inspect your new partner
for herself.'

Jackson had been to their home several times and knew Simeon's
wife to be an exceptional cook. 'Long as I get to enjoy another of
her meals, Noemi can inspect all she likes.'

When they met up downstairs and Jackson told her about the
invitation, Krys offered one of her rare smiles and replied, 'Two
banquets in the same week. A girl could grow fat around you.'

They were enjoying another coffee when Luca's limo pulled
through the front gates. He refused Jackson's offer of coffee and
said, 'We need to gather in the safe. That is where the strongest
wards are located.'

Jackson and Krys carried chairs down from the dining room.
Jackson didn't like the idea of sitting where the three bodies had
been imprinted, even if they never actually existed. So he placed
the chairs at the rear of the safe, next to the painted concrete wall.
The remaining artifacts were gathered on two shelves to Jackson's

left. The golden saucer and all the other artifacts in which Luca had sensed a magical presence rested beside the objects with no hint of potency. Yet.

When they were seated, Luca told Krys, 'Engage your ring.' When she had done so, he went on, 'Your task is to hold Jackson firmly in place. His physical body must remain securely anchored. Now close your eyes. How do you see yourself?'

'A stone,' Krys replied. 'Big as the house. Bigger.'

'Good, very good,' Luca said. 'Grip his hand. See yourself connected by a chain that links him firmly to you and to this place. And to this life.'

Jackson felt the strength in her two-handed grip, the warmth. He asked Luca, 'What will you be doing?'

'Three things. First and foremost, I will serve as your shield while you hunt for answers. Second, I will observe. Third, I will instruct. Those are the three key duties of every senior Talent. To protect, direct, and ensure the forces being manipulated remain . . .'

Krys offered, 'Pure?'

'I was going to say "in correct alignment". But purity will do.' He continued to Jackson. 'I will ask questions and you will respond.'

'Got it.'

'It is vital that you *answer* me. Speaking aloud may prove very difficult, especially at first. But it forms a vital component of your link. You *must speak.*'

'Roger that.'

'One final warning. Do not under any circumstances search for answers about the Ancients. If anyone poses such a question while you are hunting, you must assume that they are your enemy. They seek to destroy you while you are at your most vulnerable. No Adept who sought answers to the Ancients' mysteries has ever survived. Their bodies, yes. But their minds . . .'

What resonated most intently was Luca's use of the word, Adept. But all he said was, 'I read you loud and clear.'

'Very well.' Luca planted the cane in the carpet between his feet. He touched the tip to his forehead. The entire staff shone with a golden-blue light, the pale wash of dawn on a clear sky. 'Let us begin.'

FORTY-TWO

Luca said, 'Touch your wand to your forehead. As you do so, mentally declare your intention to seek answers to the questions I will pose.'

Jackson deliberately slowed his motions to quarter-speed. But not from fear. He did not feel much of anything except a powerful sense of anticipation. He simply wanted to get everything exactly right. What was more, he wanted to *remember*.

The instant his wand's tip made contact with his forehead, Jackson felt his senses and his awareness break free.

The rush of awareness extended in whichever direction Jackson focused. As if in response, he heard Luca say, 'Here is your question, your task. Determine where the threat behind the attack on you and Krys originated.'

When Jackson started away, he sensed a lure to hunt for *other* answers. Ones to the mystery he had not been ordered to seek out. It would have been such a smooth and easy departure. The temptation was very potent. Awareness of the danger did not erase the lure. Jackson felt a softly burning hunger to forget all the mess of life, and ask the wrong question, and fly up, up . . .

Luca repeated, 'Determine the origins of this threat. Be precise about its physical location and the people involved.'

As soon as Jackson turned away from the forbidden lure, he saw the tracks laid out before him. They ran as straight and true as steel rails. Jackson played the high-speed locomotive and expressed himself away.

Luca said, 'You are commanded to *speak*.'

'There are two threats,' Jackson replied. He scarcely recognized his own voice. 'The Sardinian Institute is hunting you.'

'That is to be expected. And the other?'

'The Peerless—'

'*Do not approach them.*'

Jackson did not speak because Luca had not asked a question. He drifted over empty blue waters. Content.

'Approach the Institute. Remain undetected. Only go as close as you can while staying hidden. Under no circumstances are you to open yourself to danger.'

'The dangers are at the same place.'

'What?' The news rocked Luca. 'Peerless are on *Sardinia*?'

'Not far from the Institute.'

'Do not approach the Peerless!' Luca's breath sawed in his throat. 'What can you safely discover about the Institute's threat to us?'

The answer was to move forward. But when Jackson did so, 'There are wards blocking my way.'

Luca touched the base of Jackson's neck, spoke a word, then said, 'Proceed.'

Jackson passed through the invisible barriers as he would the surface of a clear pond.

A cell in the Institute's hospital wing formed a soft landing zone for Jackson's mental journey.

Jackson faced an elderly man lying in a narrow bed. In the instant of his arrival, Jackson knew the man's name was Clarence, and he had served as Luca's favorite tutor. Jackson also knew the old man was dying. This bare whitewashed cell in the Institute's medical clinic formed the last dwelling Clarence would ever know.

Even so, the elder's awareness was not trapped or dimmed by his failing body. Clarence lifted his head from his pallet and whispered, 'Who is there?'

A thousand kilometers away, Luca commanded, 'Speak!'

'I am with Clarence.'

'He is alive?'

'Barely,' Jackson replied. 'He has noticed me. He asks who I am.'

'So he was indeed an Adept. I always suspected it.' Luca sighed. 'They never let him train, of course. Still, this is a hint of good news in a day of grim tidings.'

Jackson asked, 'What should I say?'

'Tell him you are my friend.'

When Jackson did so, the old man moved his chin up and down, as if he was munching on air. He stayed like that so long that Jackson wondered if he had heard. Then Clarence whispered, 'You can hear me?'

'Loud and clear.'

Clarence's voice drifted down another notch. 'Luca, he is well?'

'Blind. But well.'

'He gave up his eyes to the Peerless?'

'For a woman,' Jackson corrected. 'But she was Peerless, so I suppose the answer is yes. He did.'

Luca said, 'Speak.'

Jackson did so while watching Clarence's own eyes leak tears. Clarence asked, 'He is with them still?'

Jackson passed on the question. Luca replied, 'Not for almost a decade.'

Clarence asked, 'How long was he with them?'

'Four and a half years,' Luca replied. 'Too long.'

'And the woman? What of her?'

Luca sighed. 'Tell him . . . Riyanna is addicted to the pleasure of enslaving men. Many, many men.'

'It happens,' Clarence replied. 'But how has Luca survived this long? Surely the Peerless hunt him.'

'I joined the CIA,' Luca replied. 'I am careful. I live within the ward-spells I learned from the Peerless. I am always armed. They deem me too expensive a target. Or, rather, they did. But something has changed. They have come after me three times in the past few days.'

'It is no longer just the Peerless who threaten him,' Clarence said. 'The Institute has named Luca a primary objective. They want him alive. He must not be captured. Tell him that. The dungeons here are very deep.'

'It was inevitable,' Luca said. 'They were bound to hear of my search. It threatens their aims. They can no longer pretend I died trying to escape.'

When Jackson repeated that for Clarence, the old man replied, 'You do realize the Institute use that same excuse when others vanish.'

'I suspected as much.'

'These days they lose too many Acolytes to class them as training accidents. But in your time, only a few managed to escape their clutches. Often these are the most gifted.'

'What are you saying?'

'Dark rumors, powerful enough to reach even me.' Clarence swallowed hard. 'They speak of a Warrior mage who escaped the year before you arrived in Sardinia. He approached the Peerless, only to reject their demand of sacrifice. Instead, he became a Renegade, moving from place to place, hunting the dark arts.'

Jackson could not be certain if he actually spoke the name aloud. But it felt as though he shouted it with all his might. Then Luca said it for him. 'Bernard Bouchon.'

'That is the name I heard. You knew him?'

'Not then. But our search includes him now. If he is alive.'

'Alive and dangerous, if the rumors are true. Actually, more than rumors. Several of my former students have now joined forces with the Peerless. Against my wishes, despite my desperate pleas. Their hatred of the Institutes knows no bounds.'

Luca softly pressed, 'Bouchon?'

'Recently, this dark mage approached the Peerless. Revealed his powers. Demanded a position of leadership. They agreed.'

'Bouchon,' Luca repeated. 'The reason for their attacks has become clear. And my new enemy has a name.'

Jackson saw no need to pass that on. Then Clarence asked, 'Has Luca found peace?'

When Jackson passed on the query, Luca swallowed hard, then asked a question of his own, 'You have allies you can trust with our lives?'

He watched the old man's chin wag up and down once more. 'Whoever would have thought such a question would be asked between Talents of the same Institute.'

'Between Adepts,' Luca corrected.

'Truly, you have joined their ranks?'

'In all but name,' Luca replied.

'I was right all along.' The seamed cheeks were streaked by new tears. 'And you were right to flee this horrid place.'

'I begged you to come with me,' Luca said.

'Who would have cared for the other wounded and vulnerable souls, the questing spirits, the fresh-faced Acolytes whose heart-fires were not yet quenched?' The words were ragged breaths now. 'Still, many were the nights I wished I had done so.'

Luca's breath was hot and tattered on Jackson's cheek. Krys kept a two-fisted grip on his hand and arm. A stone anchor.

Friends.

Luca said, 'Ask him if the Directors are aware of Peerless on Sardinia.'

'There have been rumors. Truly, one has infiltrated the island?'

'More than one,' Jackson replied.

'Tell Luca he must take care. You come to Sardinia?'

Jackson spoke the warning and question both. Luca demanded, 'Jackson, do you see the way ahead?'

Their next step was dramatically clear. Jackson replied to both

Luca and the old man, 'We must travel to Sardinia tomorrow afternoon.'

'Take the utmost caution,' Clarence repeated. 'The danger here, the intrigue. I am forced to keep wards on my chamber. Me, at death's door, inside the Institute's own clinic!'

While Jackson was repeating this, Clarence went on, 'I have someone who may be able to help. Her name is Asila.'

Luca asked, 'She is an Acolyte?'

'Only because the Directors doubt her loyalty.' The whispers dripped with old rage. 'Asila is the second finest Talent I have ever trained.'

Luca warned, 'Tell Clarence not to mention your abilities. To anyone.'

When Jackson passed on the message, Clarence asked, 'You are not an Adept?'

Jackson replied, 'I am not even an Acolyte. I'm an Interpol agent.'

Clarence laughed. 'The factor of surprise will certainly be in your favor. Ask my dear friend if he remembers the House of Mirrors.'

Luca replied, 'All too well.'

The old man offered a trembling smile. 'It deals in fake artifacts. But secretly it serves as a conduit for black-market items. For a time, the scamp you accompany was their finest thief.'

'Allegedly,' Luca corrected.

'Luca has always been a scoundrel,' Clarence said. 'Go there the day after tomorrow. Five o'clock in the afternoon. Asila will decide whether to trust you. I cannot make this decision, you understand? I can only ask. It is for Asila to decide. It is her life that she will be placing in your hands. And tell Luca not to try to see me. It is too dangerous. Tell him this is the last request I will ever make of the one who should now be leading this wretched place.'

FORTY-THREE

The limousine picked them up at eight thirty the next morning. Jackson carried a leather valise with a change of clothes and the saucer he had taken to Strasbourg. The final impression from his bodiless sojourn had been the need to carry this artifact with them.

Jackson disliked traveling without a gun, but since he no longer carried Interpol credentials, he could not risk a customs check. The odd little plate brought him a vague sense of assurance. But he doubted seriously it would help in a firefight.

The limo deposited them at Geneva's private-jet terminal. The Gulfstream's engines were revving before they passed through the customs gate and crossed the tarmac. The jet was pretty much what Jackson had come to expect from Luca. The seats were ivory doeskin and the tables burl. The co-pilot pointed out the galley with the chilled vintage champagne, the thinly sliced sirloin, the bread baking in the miniature oven.

After take-off, Krys studied a guidebook while Luca sat across from her, wrapped in his customary silence. Jackson made coffee and brought them mugs, then resumed his seat in the rear booth and reflected. He liked the way they were forming a team. There had been no live fire yet, but their methods reminded him of the battle-hardened squads of his past. Most agents Jackson knew tended to prepare by going inside. Making a thorough review of elements under their control. Taking time for a final gut check. Coming face to face with the very real prospect that some of their team might not be going home.

An hour into the flight, Krys closed her guidebook, walked back, and asked Jackson, 'Mind some company?'

'Not at all.'

She slipped into the seat opposite his and asked, 'Have you been to Sardinia before?'

'Once. I was ordered to give testimony before the Institute's so-called judiciary. Have you heard of them?'

'I know the seven Institutes want responsibility for self-policing,' she replied.

'They don't assign Talents to enforce any policy except the Institute's,' Jackson said. 'National laws regarding magic are basically ignored.'

'What was it like? Inside the Institute, I mean.'

'I have no idea. They insisted on meeting at my hotel. When I arrived back at the airport the next morning, a customs officer told me the Institute had phoned to say they needed more input. I was taken to a holding cell and left there for almost two hours.' He could still smell the dank, windowless chamber, scarred by the criminals and magic freaks detained there in the past. He went on,

'The three Talents treated me like I deserved to be chained to the central table.'

'That corresponds to what I've heard from other agents,' Krys said.

Jackson decided it was time to ask a few questions of his own. 'Your file leaves out more than it includes about your background. Where are you actually from?'

Krys nodded as if approving of his question. Jackson wondered if this was why she had come back to join him. 'I was born in Addis Ababa. My mother was from Cairo. My father was Canadian, but he never much cared for his homeland. I only met his parents once. They did not get along. My father trained as an anesthesiologist. But by the time I came along, he was mostly an administrator. He ran Médicins Sans Frontières in Ethiopia.'

Jackson nodded slowly. That news formed a piece of the puzzle her file did not supply.

Krys noticed his reaction and asked, 'You know what that means?'

'Doctors Without Borders are notorious for their hatred of magic,' he replied, using the English version of the name. MSF had been founded by a group of French doctors seeking medical volunteers to serve on a semi-permanent basis in some of the world's most difficult and dangerous regions.

'And for good reason,' Krys said. 'Magic can't directly heal human bodies.'

'Unless the ailment is caused by magic in the first place,' Jackson added. 'Otherwise, it does not counteract the process of disease or aging. But magic can and does instill greater power in herbs. Doctors who dislike natural remedies tend to point out that magic has little or no impact on manufactured pharmaceuticals.'

'You know this how?'

'My late wife.' He waved that aside. 'Another time, OK? Tell your story.'

'MSF positively loathe practitioners of magic. So much of their work takes place in regions where shamans still dominate the culture. MSF consider them killers armed with superstitions, who feast on fear and the purses of those too weak or ignorant to know better.'

Jackson asked, 'How did your father react when he learned of your abilities?'

'I never told him. Thankfully, my talent did not emerge until I was fourteen, old enough to know I had to stay quiet. We had moved to Canada when my mother's health started failing. She died the day before my fifteenth birthday. A few days after her funeral, my father put in for reassignment back to Africa. I knew I couldn't stay with him. Sooner or later, he'd discover my secret. I can't even imagine how he would have reacted. He agreed to let me stay on at boarding school. He died just before I graduated from university and applied to Interpol. Those next two years were the finest of my entire life. I was tutored by some of Interpol's best trainers, but only after they were sworn to secrecy.'

'And here you are,' Jackson said.

'Here I am.' For a moment her gaze healed, growing deep enough for him to dive into. 'Thanks to you.'

Two and a half hours later, they landed in Sardinia. A uniformed chauffeur transferred their luggage to a Lancia limo while their passports were given a perfunctory inspection.

The closer they came to Sardinia's capital city, Cagliari, the more bizarre grew the crowds. The main highway was lined by the curious, the yearning, the desperate. As the limo slipped on to the road fronting the harbor, they passed a group of *albinettes*, the name used for followers of an outcast Talent. The man had reaped millions by claiming to have discovered a means by which anyone could gain magical abilities. These would-be Acolytes dressed in one-piece white leotards, head to foot, and painted their faces the color of old bones. Their suits were adorned with magical signs and fragments of supposedly Ancient script. They writhed, they danced, they shrieked, and they beckoned toward the uncaring castle upon the peak. Jackson thought they looked both pitiful and resigned. As though they already knew their cause was hopeless.

The Institute was a gleaming white edifice that sprawled in careless abandon across a nearby ridge. Jackson thought it resembled a magical denture, placed there so it could gnaw a hole in the world.

Krys asked, 'Why are the Institutes all situated on islands?'

'Water reflects magic,' Luca replied. 'Enemies cannot hide.'

'We did,' Krys replied.

Luca's fingers illuminated the cane's hidden script. 'Are we enemies?'

Jackson stared up at the bone-white structure on the hillside and did not respond. But what he thought was, *Absolutely*. Gaining a magical ability of his own had changed nothing. The forces clustered up there were his foes, and they always would be.

'The Peerless hid their arrival as well,' Krys reminded Luca.

'The Peerless, the Peerless.' Luca stared blindly out of the side window. 'What I would give to know their intentions.'

Sardinia was the second-largest island in the Mediterranean, larger even than Cyprus. Only Sicily was bigger. It lay equidistant between Italy, the French Riviera, and Tunisia. It was also one of Europe's oldest landmasses. Sardinia's central mountains dated back to the early Paleozoic Era, over half a billion years. Geologists suspected the island had actually not been originally part of Europe at all but rather formed the last remaining fragment of a lost continent.

Most of the island's resorts were situated on white-sand beaches dotting the eastern coast. The capital city's only luxury hotel occupied a headland between the main harbor area and a newer stretch of seafront apartment buildings. As the limo pulled into the hotel's forecourt, they were greeted by a bizarre assortment of partygoers. Krys said, 'I've seen a program about this. Magical weddings are the latest high-society craze.'

Jackson offered to check them in and left Krys and Luca by the limo. He fended his way around a bizarre bridal party whose dresses turned translucent and shifted shape, revealing brief glimpses of stockings and undergarments that flickered messages before vanishing. The bride herself wore a blond wig that grew multiple snakes which hissed at Jackson as he passed.

When he returned to where Luca stood with Krys, he said, 'Call me old-fashioned, but I'd just as soon not be bitten by my wife's hair.'

'This hotel is drenched in magic,' Luca said, his words almost lost to the chaotic din that filled the vast lobby area. 'Our rooms were booked by a London travel agent I have used for years. Very discreet. Our actions and our presence will be lost in the chaos.'

Their suite occupied the top floor of the hotel's central section. Two modern wings jutted out to either side, filling every available inch of the rocky headland. Their parlor hearkened back to a different era, with a high-domed ceiling and parquet floors and double French doors opening to the sea breeze. They looked east over the Tyrrhenian Sea, which separated Sardinia from Italy's mainland. Beyond the pools and the sculpted gardens, sailboats and pleasure craft spun white froth from the jeweled waters.

Jackson called down for room service. They dined on *spezzatino di vitello con piselli* and *pecorino sardo*, two island specialties. After Jackson rang for coffee, Luca said, 'There is something I should mention. In his earlier version, Bernard Bouchon visited Sardinia. Once. For just four days.'

Krys demanded, 'Why are we only hearing about this now?'

'Until Jackson informed us of the need to travel here, I discounted its importance. Bernard came as part of a package tour. Very exclusive, quite expensive. The group stayed in this very hotel. They spent a full day inside the Institute, then toured the island by bus.'

'Institutes allow tourists entry?'

'Once a year, perhaps twice. Tightly restricted, the guests carefully vetted. It grants the Institutes a means to counter accusations their world is too shadowed in secrecy.'

Jackson watched a gull sail past their balcony. 'He was taking aim.'

'That is my judgment as well. As soon as Bernard returned to Switzerland, he began scouring the black market,' Luca went on. 'This was when his activities came to my attention. I worked backwards and learned of his trip to Sardinia.'

'So Bernard started hunting the scrolls, accessed the Island of Time, and rewound his life,' Jackson said. 'He gave up his current life and started over. Which leads him to the issue of where he landed for round two.'

Luca nodded. 'I would guess Bernard timed his return to the year his abilities began to emerge. And something more – an element that only makes sense now. Bernard's black-market acquisitions were not restricted to items required for his traveling through time.'

Jackson breathed, 'Battle magic.'

'Just so. While he searched for access to the Island of Time, Bernard Bouchon prepared himself. His aim was to become a Warrior, the highest and most exclusive caste of Talent.'

Krys said, 'So if Bernard's death is a lie, if he's alive and joined the Peerless . . .'

'Take great care in your meeting today,' Luca warned. 'Despite Clarence's assurances, I am very concerned for your safety.'

FORTY-FOUR

An hour later, Jackson and Krys left the hotel. Jackson suggested they walk. He liked being able to stretch his legs and have a look at the city. Some of the main avenues had been broadened to mock-Roman standards by Mussolini's egotistical demands. But the side streets held to the narrow winding pattern of bygone epochs, with cobblestones still split by shallow grooves meant for wagon wheels. Many of the buildings had been refurbished. They shone in the harsh afternoon light, a rainbow of pastels and ornate carvings and clay-tile roofs and wrought-iron balconies. A few still sported the shuttered verandas dating back to when Barbary pirates imprisoned their harems within brightly painted cages.

Jackson had spent his boyhood reading every available account of the Barbary pirates. Their mages could call up tempests that blew from all four corners of the compass or bring forth sea monsters large enough to swallow wooden vessels whole. For centuries, traders in the Mediterranean paid the pirates a tribute and added the cost to their bottom line. As a youth, Jackson had yearned to join those brave seamen who had finally vanquished the buccaneers. It was one of the reasons he had leaped at the chance to shift from being a Denver cop to a global Interpol agent. So he could hunt the world's dark corners for wielders of magical havoc.

At street level, the old city was one vast market for magic. Some of it was even real. Very little was legal. But Jackson knew the local cops were only too happy to turn a blind eye. As long as the stall-holders broke no local laws and paid their taxes, the Sardinian merchants were welcome to hawk whatever nonsense they wished.

Beyond the stone seawall, the bay sparkled and beckoned. The breeze was spiced with diesel and seaweed and fresh fish and wild sorrel and the yellow blossoms that lined the distant slopes. It made for a heady mix, so potent Jackson momentarily lost sight of approaching danger.

Which made Krys's watchful gaze more important than ever. 'We're being observed.'

The day snapped back into focus. 'Where?'

'Behind us. Five and seven o'clock. Two guys in their twenties.'

Jackson pretended to inspect a crudely painted hexagon whose center contained a mirror. 'Big guy and a skinny dude with glasses?'

'That's them.' Krys let a string of fake coral beads slide through her fingers. 'And maybe a third watcher. A young woman across the street at two o'clock pretending not to notice us. Red T-shirt.'

'I see her.'

'Heads up. Here they come.'

Jackson thought the pair looked like typical student geeks. One was rail-thin and wore thick black-frame glasses. The other was massive, taller than Jackson and carrying fifty more pounds, some of which might have been muscle. Both wore T-shirts from some online game and hiking sandals over socks. Both had bad haircuts. The thin one made a big deal of talking loudly enough to be heard by the crowd. 'Sir, you and the lady, you are the ones looking for tutors? You want to take the Institute's entrance exams, yes? You contacted the right website, I assure you.'

'We're the best,' the big guy said, scanning the crowd.

'The Institute has no age limit for new entries – that's what you have heard, yes? Newcomers are always welcome. And we can make it happen!' The thin guy rubbed forefinger and thumb together. 'As long as you can afford us!'

'We don't come cheap,' the big guy said, still scouting.

Jackson had to hand it to the pair. All the attention initially cast their way was gone now. This sort of offer must happen all the time. He asked, 'Which one of you is Asila?'

'Asila is a female-type Talent,' the big guy replied.

'Asila comes when she is ready,' the thin one said. 'Or not.'

Krys said, 'She wouldn't be the dark-haired lady across the street? The one in the T-shirt advertising my favorite ice cream?'

That surprised them both. The thin guy said, 'Our teacher didn't say anything about a second visitor.'

'Now you're talking about Clarence, right?' Jackson liked keeping the geeks off balance. 'Our conversation was cut short. I never got around to mentioning my partner.'

The big guy demanded, 'How did you contact our tutor?'

Jackson just waited.

The thin guy started to say something angry, but Krys cut him off with, 'I feel eyes.'

'This conversation is five seconds from over,' Jackson said. 'Either make it happen or go back to Clarence and explain to him how you missed your chance.'

The big guy cast one look across the street, then said, 'Café Rosa, on the harbor. Nine o'clock.'

When Clarence's contacts had departed, Jackson phoned Luca with an update. Luca thanked him for the intel but showed no interest in joining them. Jackson thought he sounded more distant than usual. But gauging Luca's mood was like trying to test the thickness of ice from a mile away. He went back to Krys and said merely, 'Apparently, our guy needs some time on his own.'

They dined at a waterfront restaurant on local oysters and sea bass brought in an hour earlier, or so the waiter claimed. The waiter also said his uncle ran a fishing boat, could sing the catch into his net, and invited Krys to come and see. Krys called him charming. Jackson wondered how many other women had heard his pitch that week.

After dinner they walked slowly along the waterfront, enjoying the night and waiting for the hour to arrive. When it was time, Jackson asked directions and was pointed north, away from the glittering lights and the high-end restaurants and the moored yachts. They passed a stone jetty that marked the older seawall, and beyond this floated the island's main fishing fleet. The waterfront was lined with drying nets and the pungent odors of men working the sea. The restaurants here were frequented by locals.

The Café Rosa was a students' dive, densely crowded and noisy. Jackson spotted the big guy because he stood head and shoulders over the mob. He watched Jackson's approach with hard, cautious eyes. 'Were you followed?'

'No,' Krys shouted. 'Why are we here?'

He gestured towards the rear. 'Go to the toilets. One at a time. There is a door leading to the alley. We'll come for you when it's safe.'

The guy moved gracefully for someone with his size and bulk. A shift, a smile to someone who shouted at him, and he was gone.

Five minutes later, Jackson met Krys out back. The odors were rank, but at least he could hear himself think. 'Anything?'

'All quiet.'

He merged into the shadows across the lane from where she stood. 'We'll give it another ten minutes.'

They needed only three.

An island van pulled up, blocking the alley's entry. In the street-lights, Jackson thought it probably had once been beige, but now it was mostly rust. The side door squeaked open and the young woman who had remained across the busy avenue that afternoon demanded, 'What are you waiting for, an engraved invitation from the Institute?'

FORTY-FIVE

Asila had agreed to make this journey because Clarence had urged her to trust them. And Clarence was the only outsider she had ever trusted in her entire life. Those were the first words she uttered after directing Krys and Jackson to join her in back. The van was driven by an older man she introduced as Carule, with the big guy in the passenger seat.

Jackson asked, 'You are from Sardinia?'

'For many generations.' She leaned forward and set her hand upon the driver's shoulder. 'Carule as well.'

The driver asked, 'You know Sardinia?'

'Not at all.'

'Then why have you come?'

'More importantly,' Asile added, 'why have you come *now*?'

'You are entering a dangerous place in perilous times,' Carule agreed.

Jackson searched for a decent reply and could only come up with, 'Because of Clarence.'

That silenced them for several miles as they charged up a winding mountain road. Finally, Carule said, 'Sardinia has not one popula-tion, but five. The tourists are one culture. The Institute is another. There are so many supplicants seeking entry that they make up a community all their own. And then there are two sets of locals. The city dwellers are parasites who would sell anything for a price and then steal it back. The other locals are a world apart.'

The big man spoke for the first time since their journey had begun. 'Our world.'

Asila took up the lesson. 'You know how many times the island has been conquered? No? Eleven! The town where we go, Arborea, is named after the *Giudicato*. Understand that and you begin to understand my people. Around the year 800, the Barbary pirates took over Sardinia's main ports. The Byzantine Empire was busy with other wars, so they ceded power to the *giudicati*, the hereditary judges. Most were corrupt leaders who oppressed our people. But one clan united the island for the first time in history. Our region was the poorest, a fishing district on the western coast between Logudoro and Cagliari. But in 1368, a judge named Eleanora conquered all but the two Barbary ports and united the island.'

'Arborea,' Carule repeated. 'It has been our battle cry ever since.'

Krys asked, 'Are you expecting a battle tonight?'

'We survive by being prepared.' Asila slipped a wicked blade from beneath her sweatshirt. 'This is the *resolza*, the Sardinian weapon.'

'The outsiders destroy, we rebuild,' Carule said.

Asila made the knife disappear. 'Conquered, yes. Destroyed, yes. Defeated, never.'

Jackson found himself liking her, the stubborn spirit that not even the Institute could tame. He thrilled at the hard, dark fire that burned in her voice and gaze. He liked how the others offered her the respect of silence and obedience. He replied, 'Thank you for trusting us this far.'

Their destination was a nondescript town hemmed in by tight cliffs. A pair of stone arms extended to form a natural harbor. The van halted by a waterfront plaza, where a group of old men played a late-night game of *boule*. Streetlights turned the surrounding trees into golden sentinels. The men's talk and laughter were as soft as the clicking balls.

One man broke away from the onlookers and hobbled over on bowed legs. Carule shook his hand, then Asila rose on tiptoes to kiss his grizzled cheeks. Jackson heard them speak the island patois. At Asila's signal, they alighted and followed her toward the seawall. They were joined by another dozen or so young people who drifted out of the surrounding shadows. No one spoke as they slipped into a wooden fishing vessel. The old man and Carule entered the cockpit, and the engine coughed to life. Asila untied the lines, tossed them over, and leaped lightly on board.

The night sea was oily calm. They chugged beneath the moon, away from land. An hour later, their destination came into view: an uninhabited island that rose from the still sea. The hump of rock was so encrusted with guano that it shone in the moonlight. Jackson could see no place for them to alight or for the boat to dock. But this must have been a regular run, for the old man sidled up to what looked like just another sea cliff, and Asila leaped ashore. She balanced on a ledge Jackson had not noticed until then. She held the lines while everyone else clambered out. She pointed to stairs that now scaled the cliff. 'Up there. Hurry.'

Carule led the way, the steps glowing softly as they climbed. Jackson saw Asila toss the ropes back and the boat pull away from the rocks. The cockpit illuminated briefly as the old man lit a pipe. When Asila looked up and hissed, Jackson kept moving.

A hundred meters or so above the waterline, a cave opened. As Krys stepped inside, she murmured to Jackson, 'The steps weren't there before we showed up. Or the landing.'

He nodded agreement. 'I wonder how long they've been using this as a gathering place.'

'For a thousand years,' Asila replied, coming up behind them. 'Longer.'

The cave's interior was alive with a soft and welcoming light. The sandy floor shone like golden ash; the walls were ivory, as were the ledges where the gathering perched. Asila glanced at a man standing by the entrance, who said, 'The wards are set.'

She faced Jackson and declared, 'You must tell us why we should trust you. Clarence has only brought you this far. We need more. We need to decide your fate for ourselves.'

Jackson suspected she spoke to assure the others. He had no trouble with her demand. 'My partner's only abilities are battle magic.'

Asila's dark gaze held Krys. 'You are a Talent? Trained at which Institute?'

'We have our secrets as well,' Jackson interrupted. 'She will reveal her weapons if you insist. Nothing about her past. But I have to warn you: with her, it's all or nothing.'

A faint rustle shifted the room. But Asila held to her silence. Finally, Jackson said, 'I'll answer for both of us.'

'If you can,' Asila replied.

FORTY-SIX

'Jackson . . .' Krys started to protest, then went quiet.

He understood her concern and shared it. There was no way he was going to reveal the wand. But during the boat ride over moonlit waters, he had received another distinct impression, that he might be able to draw forth some of the power – not much, but a little – without actually bringing out the wand. He hoped it would be enough.

He shut his eyes and concentrated on his empty right hand. Tighter and tighter, as intense as taking aim at a live target. When there was nothing else, no room for any other thought, he lifted the hand and touched his forehead.

The entire cave shared a gasp.

Jackson opened his eyes and scanned the gathering, or most of them. His awareness did not reach the furthest shadows. He also resisted a sudden urge to turn and inspect Krys. He would not do that unless she asked. And maybe not even then.

'One person must volunteer,' Jackson said. 'I will tell you about him or her until they say I should stop.'

Asila muttered, 'You will *tell* us.'

'They must volunteer,' Jackson repeated.

The big guy stepped forward. 'Do me.'

'Your name is Saunders.' Jackson spoke without hesitation. 'But your friends here at the Institute know you as Pepino, the famous Italian cartoon mouse. You were born in Edinburgh. Your family moved to London when you were nine, the year after you started showing magical abilities. You were trained there by—'

'Something personal,' Asila snapped. 'Something no police file will contain.'

Jackson was ready for that as well. 'You used to play the piano. Your first tutor in London made you stop. Her name was Agatha. You hated her for it, but you now understand the need to have made the choice. When you are very happy, you dream about piano music. But that doesn't happen often anymore. Only three times since you began your studies here—'

'Enough.' The big guy spoke to no one in particular. 'He's for real.'

Jackson had started to retreat. Then his waning attention alerted on a guy to his left.

To alert was a term from military canine training. It signified the moment when the animal sensed the target – bombs, drugs, assailant, whatever. Jackson's senses were *instantly* captured by that same awareness.

'I want to do one more,' he said.

'No need,' Asila replied. 'We accept—'

'I need to do this. For your sakes.' Jackson pointed to a young man hiding in the cave's recesses. 'The people here know you as Rupert. But your real name is Serge. You claim to be of English heritage but you were born in Austria. You are actually Serbian.'

'Lies!' He was a big guy pretending to be small. The roar pushed everyone away, exposing him.

Jackson went on, 'You are training to work as a craftsman, shaping weapons and wands and implements used by other Talents. But you really wanted to become a Warrior. The problem is—'

'You will stop this *now*!'

'You are double-gifted. And your ability as a Warrior is far weaker.'

Serge started for the opening. 'I don't have to listen to this!'

But Asila and Saunders and several others blocked his path. Asila said, 'Actually, you do.'

'He is a *liar*!'

Jackson went on, 'You hate your tutors for forcing you into a role you despise. This much you have shared with your mates. What you have kept carefully hidden is how last year you were recruited by a Peerless scout.'

Asila gasped, 'You're a *spy*?'

'He is more than that.' Jackson shouted to be heard over the man's curses. 'The Peerless are looking for a way through the Institute's defenses. They see Serge as the vanguard for an invasion. They have trained him, and now they have sent him here to see which of you would join their ranks. In return, the Peerless required as his ritual sacrifice that Serge give up his abilities with metal, which he despised anyway—'

The roar changed with the man. It started as a bellow so coarse it butchered the spell he uttered. The noise became an electric rush, like the crackle before a lightning stroke.

The gargoyle filled the cave with the stench of electric discharge. There was a solid consistency to the beast, though it was utterly without physical form. Jackson was close enough to see through the swirling reddish mist that formed its being. The creature reached one elongated claw for Asila, who stood frozen.

Krys shoved the young woman aside, screamed her war cry, and blasted Serge where he crouched.

The gargoyle evaporated, leaving behind an acrid stench and a pile of wilting red ash.

Jackson doubted very much that anyone else had noticed the ring come and go. Their attention had been on the beast, then Krys's assault had seared their eyeballs. He said quietly, 'Good work, partner.'

The cave came slowly back to life. A leather wineskin was passed from hand to hand. Jackson found a rich pleasure in the rough red swill. Asila accepted the skin from him, drank, passed it to Krys, and said, 'Tell us what you need.'

FORTY-SEVEN

It was after two in the morning when Jackson and Krys finally made it back to the hotel. Their entry went unnoticed, for the three ballrooms all rocked with wedding parties. The magic on display filled the lobby with a cacophony of sights and sounds. Jackson ignored it. Krys was so tired he doubted she even noticed.

Jackson arose before eight and ordered breakfast for everyone. He met the bellhop in the hallway and made a thorough inspection of each item. He signed the bill, then waited until the hall was empty before using the key and letting himself back into the room.

He made himself a cup of coffee and took it out on the balcony. He liked having this time alone. He needed to sit there in the sunlight, sip his coffee, watch the boats glide across the crystal waters, and take careful stock. Because something was definitely not right.

He had woken up with a sense of brooding anxiety, and the longer he sat there, the stronger it became. He was on his second cup when Krys joined him. She offered a soft greeting, made herself a coffee, then sat in the chair opposite and drew her legs up like a child might. She cradled the cup on her knees, lifting it to sip. When she reached over and set it on the table, Jackson asked, 'More?'

'I'll get it.'

'Stay where you are.'

He took both cups back inside and discovered Luca standing by the side wall. For the first time since that night at the obelisk, Luca Tami could not make it on his own. The cane in his left hand was just that: a white stick. The fingers of his right hand searched the air. Jackson walked over and gripped the weaving hand. 'We're out on the balcony. That sound good to you?'

'Are we exposed?'

'We're on the ninth floor with the Mediterranean straight ahead. A sniper on a passing boat could possibly make a hit. Or a very aggressive gull.' All the while, Jackson walked Luca out, matching his uneven steps. He settled Luca into a third chair, then asked, 'Coffee?'

'Is there tea?'

'Coming right up.' He went back inside, refilled Krys's cup, and poured a tea for Luca. He carried them out and said, 'There's a full breakfast spread. Waffles, eggs poached and scrambled, fruit, croissants.'

'Perhaps later,' Luca said.

'I'm not very hungry,' Krys replied.

Jackson went back inside, refilled his own cup, picked up a croissant, then put it down. His stomach rebelled against the very idea of food.

As he related the evening's events to Luca, Krys was staring worriedly at what appeared to be just another perfect day on the Med. When he went silent, Krys asked, 'Is there a storm coming?'

'A big one,' Luca said. He drew a long breath through his nostrils. 'Very soon.'

Krys said, 'We're not talking about a weather-type storm, are we?'

'No.' Luca felt his bare wrist. 'What time is it?'

'Quarter past ten,' Jackson answered.

Luca said, 'Call downstairs and ask when the first wedding begins.'

'Eleven,' Krys replied. 'I heard them talking while Jackson checked us in.'

'We need to use their ceremony to mask magic of our own.' Luca rose unsteadily to his feet. 'Let us move inside.'

Luca insisted they all eat something, explaining that the food would help anchor them during whatever came next. Jackson struggled through two awful eggs and a banana that might as well have been plastic. Krys fought her way through a portion of yogurt and blackberries, spooning it with the grim determination of a ditch digger. Luca polished off a minuscule bowl of granola, minus the milk.

Finally, Krys set her saucer on the sideboard and said, 'Yuck.'

Jackson said, 'Listen to the wedding.'

The sounds through the open balcony doors were discordant in the extreme. The band doing a sound check could not find the tempo. Then the cymbals fell over. A woman screeched in full-throated rage.

'Like a zoo at feeding time,' Krys said. 'That poor bride.'

Luca asked them to gather on the central carpet, then waited while Krys and Jackson moved the coffee table. Jackson helped Luca settle, then they sat cross-legged facing each other. Luca began, 'I have never heard of this being done. Not in modern times, at least. But I woke up to an image from my childhood, a painting from the early medieval era. Three sorcerers were seated at a table. Eyes closed. Casting their runes. As one.'

Krys protested, 'But runes are used by an individual. That's what concentrates the power. Even I know that much.'

'Indeed. And yet I sense we have perhaps forged ourselves into a single unit.' Luca drew the silk purse from his pocket and sat cradling it in his lap. 'These have saved my life on many occasions. When Clarence was taken from me and that loathsome tutor took his place, I planned to commit suicide. The runes showed me a better time ahead and a *purpose*. Now . . .'

The noise from below grew louder, more strident. It carried the tense alarm of coming battle. Jackson asked, 'How do you want to handle this?'

'Bring out your implements,' Luca replied.

When they had done so, Jackson said, 'Ready.'

'When I say, we will all touch the stones together. Then I will cast my runes.' Luca untied the clasp and let the stones gather in his hand. He cupped his palms together, then lifted them toward his forehead.

Then Jackson said, 'Wait!'

Luca lowered his hands. 'What is it?'

Jackson rose to his feet and said, 'I just thought of something.'

Jackson entered his bedroom and opened the satchel. His old-fashioned valise had been a gift from Sylvie, marking the last birthday he had celebrated with his late wife. The leather case had a metal band that ran along the top, sealing an accordion mouth. The valise was one of the nicest things Jackson owned and held a lot of very fond memories. He reached inside and pulled out the golden saucer.

He brought the artifact back into the parlor, seated himself on the carpet, and explained to Luca, 'As I was getting ready to leave the house, I had the strong impression we were going to need this. I felt the exact same thing when you started to cast your runes.'

Luca did not object. 'What do we do?'

It seemed to Jackson that the answer simply *arrived*. 'Choose a rune. Touch your forehead.'

'You are saying that I should connect with just one stone,' Luca said.

'Right. Then you reach out and touch it to the saucer. We do the same. Krys and her ring, me and the wand.'

'The pupil teaches the master.' The noise from below reached a terrible pitch as Luca selected one stone, spilled the rest back into the purse, then retied the catch-string. He touched it to his forehead, then held it out. 'Ready.'

'On three,' Jackson said. 'One, two . . .'

The saucer became a portal rimmed by fire.

Together they dove in.

And flew.

FORTY-EIGHT

Jackson was aware of Krys and Luca traveling with him. Their presence offered a strong sense of mortal comfort. As in, only because they had forged this bond was there a chance they all might survive.

Their objective was a ridge running between the Institute and the island's main mountain range. They halted in mid-air, perhaps a kilometer away and several hundred meters above the magic fortress, so that they looked down upon the peaked roofs and the towering pinnacles and the ant-sized wizards populating the interior courtyards. As they hovered, a dark miasmic cloud crawled up the ridge, carrying with it the molten stench of destruction. Jackson was filled with a malevolent sense of foreboding, of danger wrapping itself around the world.

At a silent indication from Luca, they traveled back together. Krys slipped through the portal formed by the golden saucer, then Jackson heard an old man's voice calling out to them. He had the sense that Clarence had been signaling for some time, and that Luca heard it as well. He and Luca departed once more.

The failing tutor struggled feebly to rise from his pallet. Jackson saw both Asila and Carule there in the room with him. Clarence cried aloud, 'Do my senses deceive me, or is the enemy truly coming?'

'No, old friend,' Luca replied. 'The enemy is already here.'

Jackson heard Luca and Clarence make plans regarding the tutor's young allies. But their discussion seemed fragmented, as though Jackson's ability to hear was shredded by some outside force. Luca finally noticed and demanded, 'What's the matter?'

But Jackson was already plucked away.

He was drawn against his will, out of the Institute and along the outer perimeter. Jackson passed Warrior Talents on patrol around the boundary wall. He saw how they surveyed the city below with the same bored contempt a child might show a colony of ants.

Jackson dropped over the ledge and slipped down to where a cave's mouth came into view.

Instantly, Jackson was filled with the flash of *knowing.*

He *knew* that Bernard had learned while still an Acolyte of this secret entrance. The cave led into the Institute by way of ancient tunnels. For a time, it had been used by rebellious students to escape their school's suffocating oppression.

Now the Peerless were hiding here. Gathering strength. Preparing for battle.

He sensed the presence inside and fought more fiercely. But there was no way of escape, no power strong enough to free him from the sucking maw.

Riyanna sat alone in a circle she had drawn in the sand. The runes were cast before her. Jackson could see shadow figures around the

cave walls. He knew these were other Peerless who waited for
Riyanna's report. Jackson was also aware that Riyanna was the one
casting runes because the Peerless spies inside the Institute were males
she had enslaved. Jackson realized he had become trapped by the
terrible confluence of his being extended beyond physical boundaries
at the very same moment she asked her question. He knew . . .

He knew he was lost.

Riyanna gasped at his arrival. '*You!*'

Jackson felt contained within the same force that had gripped
him the first time they had met. He willed the wand into his hand.
But there was no hand. Nor wand.

One of the shadow figures spoke. He could not hear or see
anything beyond Riyanna's rune circle. Riyanna was not especially
beautiful in her human form. But her magnetic potency was immense.
Jackson faced a woman who had distilled her essence to the one
trait that defined her existence: the captivating sexual allure that
made men her slaves.

Riyanna snapped at the ones beyond Jackson's field of vision, 'I
asked to have revealed any possible threats to our plans, and *this
one* appeared.'

He could not speak. The body he no longer possessed felt
incapable of drawing breath.

'You, an Interpol agent! You have neither training nor connection
to the Institute!' Her gaze held the intensity of a probing blade.
'You failed to do my bidding before, and yet you are the one drawn
by my spell!'

Riyanna slapped the stone floor. Jackson felt his entire being
vibrate from the power of that blow. 'I *demand* to know. Why are
you here? Why are you here *now*?'

He felt words rise with the gorge. Ready to be plucked from him.
Jackson was gripped by forces he could not overcome, until . . .

A ferocious wind blasted through the cave-mouth.

Even Riyanna was caught unawares by its force. The storm
hammered the rocks until they hummed like tuning forks, louder
and louder . . .

A small fragment of Riyanna's rune circle was erased.

Instantly, the cave came into sharp focus.

The mass of Peerless surrounding her circle shielded their eyes
from the blast. And at their center stood Bernard Bouchon.

Even now he was not fully in human form. He stood a full head taller than the other Peerless, his features stretched and elongated into a predator's mask. And there on the left side of his face, his neck, down to where the collar of his robe hid the rest of the damage, were scars resulting from Krys's attack in the field. Jackson did not *think* this. He *knew.* Just as he was certain Bernard had been transformed through his study of dark arts, into something *other.*

And now Bernard was here. Intent upon leading the Peerless into battle. Waiting for Riyanna to give them the final word.

Only now Riyanna's features rippled from the shrieking wind ramming its way into her circle.

Her eyes widened with alarm, and she shrilled louder than the wind, '*It is Luca!*'

The wind became a fist that gripped Jackson more tightly than Riyanna, pulling him from the cave, across the arid plains, through the city, into the hotel, up through the saucer . . .

The impact of his return was so strong that Jackson was flung across the parlor.

He tumbled to the carpet and lay there gasping. When he finally focused on the scene, Luca was already up and moving. Jackson managed, 'Thank you.'

Krys cried, 'What just happened?'

'No time.' Luca moved as though fighting against unseen currents. 'We flee, or we die.'

FORTY-NINE

Jackson was still recovering as they stepped through the hotel entrance and found the convoy organized by Clarence and Luca parked along the street's opposite side. Jackson counted eight vehicles in all, plus about a dozen mopeds. Luca, Krys, and Jackson piled into the first van. Asila was seated in the front passenger seat while Carule drove. Jackson sat behind the driver, Krys by the right window, with Luca seated between them. The van's rear hold was crammed with everyone's luggage. Whatever happened, they were not returning to the Institute or the hotel.

Once they were underway, Asila said, 'My great-grandmother told me stories when I was a child. Of the shadows that crept across our island when Mussolini's troops landed. She had heard of such forces from her own grandmother. And on back through time. The storm that could not be seen.'

'Asila was the one who first sensed the danger,' Carule pointed out. 'She dragged me into Clarence's room just in time for us to witness him make plans with a Renegade Talent who was not actually there.'

Jackson said, 'Clarence told us you were the most gifted Acolyte he had ever known, after Luca.'

She waved that aside. 'Luca, why did you flee the Institute?'

'They took Clarence from me. I endured seven more years and three more tutors. But the day Clarence left, I knew someday I would escape.'

'I too would run,' Asila agreed. 'If Clarence was not there. If I did not have Carule. If there were not other Acolytes to help. If we had not hoped we would one day fight them from within.'

'You were the one who hoped for such a time,' Carule said. 'For myself, I have yearned for nothing more than a life beyond the Institute's walls.'

'And yet you stayed,' Asila said.

He showed her dark eyes. 'Your love made even that dread place bearable.'

As the road climbed steeply up the island's central massif, Asila described the moments after Luca had spoken with their tutor. The old man had ordered Asila and Carule to depart and take every possible Acolyte and Talent with them. All they could trust, and any they hoped to bring to their side. Meet Luca and the others at their hotel. And do whatever Luca said. Asila had tried to question him, but Clarence had simply replied: do this for him, or die.

Luca asked, 'And our teacher?'

'He refused to even discuss it,' Carule said. 'I begged. He pretended not to hear me.'

'Clarence is without pain only because of spells that are replenished each hour. He ordered us to fly for him.' Asila wiped her face. 'He said to tell you that he would rest peacefully, knowing you have grown into your own.'

Carule slowed. 'We have trouble.'

The highway leading inland from the island capital passed a set of monolithic gates, the only break in the Institute's vast outer wall.

The steel gates were open now, revealing a bevy of dark-robed Warrior wizards with a woman at their head. Her steel-gray hair was cropped short, her jaw square, her gaze as hard as her cry. Through the van's open window, Jackson heard her screech, 'Halt or be fired upon!'

Luca said, 'I know that voice.'

Carule's voice shook slightly. 'It's the Director Agatha.'

'They made that woman a Director?' Luca snorted. 'This confirms every bad sentiment I have harbored about the place.'

Asila asked, 'You know her?'

'All too well,' Luca replied. 'She was my tutor. And my nemesis.'

'I see you there, Carule!' Agatha's every word rose and fell like fractured glass. 'How dare you consort with those outlaws. You and Asila are under arrest! Warriors, seize them!'

'Carule, Asila, stay where you are.' Luca shifted over. 'Let me out.'

The instant Jackson pulled open the van door, Krys crowded her way past Jackson, following Luca from the van.

At Luca's appearance, the Director crowed, 'When the Monitors told me you had been sighted, I thought to myself, not even you would be that monumentally stupid. And yet here you are!'

Luca waved the hand not holding his staff. 'Get out of our way, Agatha. We don't have time for your nonsense.'

'It's *Director* Agatha to you, Renegade!' Her rage billowed with her robes. 'I'll see you in chains where you belong!'

For an instant, Jackson thought Luca had collapsed. He did not lower himself so much as fall to his knees. The movement halted the rushing Acolytes, who clearly were uncertain how to handle a blind man who could not remain upright.

Their hesitation was enough for him to intone the one deep, low word and slam his staff into the ground.

A cone of dust and heat *surged* outwards, a triangular force that *blasted* the Institute's wizards off their feet.

All but Agatha. Her wards shimmered from the impact but remained intact. 'Try your mischief with me, will you!' She shoved her sleeves back from wrists bound in copper and ink. 'I told them arresting you was a waste of time! Now accept the fate you should have received years . . .'

The sight of Krys flaming into warrior vixen mode and screaming her war cry froze the Director. Her eyes went round as Krys fashioned a giant's fist of fire and fury and *hammered* down.

Agatha squealed and crouched, though her wards held. But there was little comfort in this, as Krys continued to pound the Director as she would a shimmering nail.

Jackson remained where he was in the van, which bounced slightly with each fiery impact. He could not help but grin. His partner's latest trick made for great entertainment.

When the Director was mashed down to where she was at eye level with the pavement, Krys noticed the Warriors preparing to retaliate. '*Stay down or die!*'

All movement froze. Even Agatha stopped trying to clamber from her hole in the cracked asphalt.

Luca called, 'Hear me, all of you! The Institute is soon to be under attack!'

Agatha's protest was somewhat muffled by her lowered stance. 'Don't listen to that Renegade! He—'

'Krys, if she speaks again, obliterate her.' Luca called to the gaping Warriors, 'Heed my words. I did not destroy you as I could only because the Institute needs you. The Peerless are coming!'

As though in declaration to Luca's words, a shuddering roar struck them through their feet and chests and ears. Instantly, a new claxon sounded, a metallic warning that repeated the same word over and over. *Breach. Breach. Breach.*

Luca shouted, 'They are here! See to the Institute's defenses while you still have time!'

All but Agatha scampered back through the Institute's open gates.

Jackson helped Luca back into the van, but Krys remained standing by the open door as Carule started forward. She walked alongside the van as they passed the Director.

Agatha remained as she was, buried chin deep, until the convoy rounded a corner and drove out of sight.

When they crested the first rise, a thunderous rumbling echoed from all the surrounding cliffs. Luca said, 'Can you see the Institute?'

'Not yet,' Carule said. 'But there is an overview about four kilometers ahead.'

'That's our destination,' Jackson said. 'When we reach it, pull over.'

Asila complained, 'We have rushed and fought and defied the Institute, and now we stop?'

'So you can observe and learn and remember,' Luca replied. 'If we survive.'

The road climbed through a pair of steep-sided canyons. Then the walls to their right opened up, revealing the dramatic vista Jackson had last seen in his bodiless state. The lay-by was marked with a *Scenic View* sign in four languages. Their train of vehicles turned into the parking area, and the people staggered out, stunned to unsteadiness by what they witnessed.

A massive battle raged all around the gleaming white structure. Jackson watched as several dozen of the electrified gargoyles scaled the hillside. Directly above the Institute swirled a putrid green tempest, similar to the one that had attacked them in the French countryside.

The dark-green clouds shot out a continuous stream of dragon-headed vortexes. None, however, managed to break through the Institute's wards. The buildings' shields sparked and crackled. Even where Jackson stood, he could smell the electric stench of magic against magic.

Warrior Talents and Acolytes stood atop the Institute's main battlements, while more clustered by the stone boundary wall. They fired lightning blasts at the invaders, whose own wards deflected the assault in all directions. The surrounding hills were scarred with red-hot wounds. Rocks flowed like lava.

Jackson described for Luca what they were witnessing. Luca asked, 'What is your assessment?'

Krys said, 'The Peerless are outgunned and outmanned and going up against a fortified stronghold.'

Jackson guessed, 'They probably gathered on Sardinia hoping Serge and Riyanna's other spies would find them a way in.'

'Which failed, thanks to you,' Carule said.

'I was the one who recruited Serge to our cause.' Asila shook her head. 'I was so certain about him.'

'Then I showed up in Riyanna's rune circle, and Luca broke me out,' Jackson continued. 'The Peerless were left with two choices: either they snuck away or they tried a suicide run.'

Luca said, 'I would not give up on the Peerless just yet.'

As he spoke, the ground beneath their feet began to rumble.

A gout of flame and smoke blasted from a point below the Institute's central section.

The ridgeline holding the Institute heaved upwards, then a massive slab broke off and crashed into the gorge below. About a fifth of the whole structure. Swallowed by the fire and the dust billowing up from below. Jackson saw bodies go pinwheeling down and heard distant screams.

A far larger group of gargoyles appeared from the cave midway up the ridge. They swarmed in electric fury, while above them crimson lightning blasted the defenders.

Luca gripped Jackson's arm and said, 'We must go.'

Asila spoke to the others, then called more loudly. Reluctantly, they all headed back toward their vehicles. Luca asked Carule, 'Do you have a place where the others can go and be safe?'

'My village,' Carule said without hesitation. 'My brother and uncle will see they are sheltered.'

Asila needed a moment to shape the words. 'And for you?'

'We have to leave now. The airport will be under siege. Can you get us a boat that will take us to the mainland?'

Carule was already on the move. He called to the others, urging them to greater speed. Only when he was certain they were galvanized into action did he say, 'Get in.'

FIFTY

Carule and Asila spent the entire journey working their phones. Three times Luca broke in, saying he would finance whatever they required.

An hour later, they entered a seaside village dominated by seafront hotels. The harbor was full of ultra-expensive yachts and colorful tourist boats. Carule halted at the quayside where a massive power-boat idled. He cut the engine and warned, 'My friend will carry you to Civitavecchia in record time. But he is expensive.'

'And I am telling you that cost is not the issue,' Luca replied. 'Your safety is the critical factor. Readying yourselves for what comes next.'

'And what is that?' Asila swiveled in her seat. 'Can you read the future?'

'Given what I know of the Institutes, I can make a solid

prediction.' Luca's fingers ran up and down the length of his staff, causing the hidden script to flame and dance. 'They will make every effort to create an illusion. The attack by Peerless never happened. Today's casualties were all victims of a sudden illness. They will do their utmost to hide this as they have masked so much else, and resume life as they want it.'

Carule asked, 'And what of us?'

Luca nodded. 'You have a choice. You can go back now. All of you. Pretend you were there, you managed to survive, and resume your lives.'

'No,' Asila held her lover's gaze. 'No.'

'Then you need to gather and prepare.'

'For what?'

'I have no idea.' Luca's fingers moved faster still. 'As soon as I see the way forward, I will be in touch. Until then, find a place where you can remain hidden and safely build your magical abilities. A villa on Corsica, perhaps. Someplace where you have allies, and where outsiders will be noticed. Remember, cost is no longer an issue. Let me know what you need, and I will send the money.'

They climbed out and gathered on the stone quayside, their movements slow and measured. Asila told them, 'We are your allies in whatever comes. I hope you know that.'

'And wherever we land, you have a refuge,' Carule said. 'Whenever you need one.'

'A new era begins,' Asila said. 'There will be the redefining of many things. I pledge my life to this.'

'This is what I have spent my life yearning for,' Luca replied. 'Friends and allies in whom I can trust.'

Asila slipped the sheathed knife from her belt and handed it to Jackson. 'This resolza has been carried by my family for generations beyond number. It is yours now.'

Jackson had no idea what to say. He took the knife and accepted embraces first from Asila, then Carule. He watched them return to the van, open the doors, and then just stand there. Unable or unwilling to end the event. Jackson lifted his hand in farewell and again gave the Sardinian cry, but softly.

Arborea.

The seas were calm, the day windless. They arrived in Civitavecchia at sunset and were swept by limousine straight to Rome airport. After they passed through Italian customs, Jackson placed a call to Simeon. When the detective answered, Jackson asked, 'Can you talk?'

'I am seated in the stands, watching my son's team lose a football match. My son is not even playing. I would pay good money for a diversion,' Simeon replied. 'Where are you?'

'Rome.' Jackson gave a swift recap of the events. His recount was punctuated by the faint sound of cheers.

Simeon said, 'There has been no report of an attack on the Sardinian Institute.'

'Luca said they'd erase any hint of threat,' Jackson said.

'How could they possibly succeed? The first direct assault on an Institute since the world wars? It will make headlines around the world.'

'You don't know the Institutes,' Jackson replied. 'Luca does. If he says they're going to hide this assault, we need to believe him.'

'You are certain you saw Bernard Bouchon among these Peerless?'

'He led them. His study of the dark arts has twisted and warped him into something *other*. But it was him.'

Luca remained locked in some internal struggle for the entire flight. Twice Jackson asked what the matter was. Both times Luca gave no sign he had even heard.

When they landed in Geneva, another limo was waiting to take them into the city. Jackson's companions looked as exhausted as he felt. When the limo pulled up in front of the bank's side entrance, Jackson took Luca's satchel from the trunk. He followed Luca down the narrow passage and up the stairs and into the white apartment. He asked a third time, 'Will you tell me what is going on?'

'I am missing something,' Luca replied. 'A vital component.'

'You want to do the runes? I could call Krys—'

'It is not the runes I require.' Luca fumbled his way to the white settee. 'I need time alone.'

When he returned to the limo, Krys asked, 'Is everything OK with him?'

Jackson stared out of the side window at the featureless slate-gray structure. 'Hard to say.'

They arrived back at Rue Gambord well after midnight. Jackson checked several of the news feeds, but no mention was made of an attack on the European Institute. After ten minutes of watching Jackson's futile search, Krys said, 'Tomorrow.'

*   *   *

The next morning, Jackson woke feeling on target.

Every successful case reached such a definable juncture. At this point, things started coalescing. Events and evidence and even the actions of his opponents, everything began focusing upon the end goal.

Jackson usually sensed this long before he could actually frame it in a logical sequence. But he knew it was there. Just out of sight. He had picked up the first faint whiff of his quarry. He was on the hunt.

He phoned Luca while making his first cup of coffee. The blind wizard tried to beg off, but Jackson ignored the man's morose tone and insisted he come over that morning.

It was crucial for them to do another search together, the three of them seated around the Ancients' saucer or whatever it was. And Luca himself had said the safe was the location with the strongest wards. The clock was ticking, Jackson said repeatedly. Finally, Luca relented and agreed to meet them in an hour.

Jackson went upstairs, knocked on Krys's door, then returned to the kitchen and prepared a breakfast of fruit and cheese and nearly-stale bread. He opened his laptop and started work on the eyes-only report.

Sequencing was crucial to such statements. Jackson used the painstaking step-by-step procedure as a means of sifting through all the events. He sought to clarify the various elements from the perspective of their target. Both the Peerless and some faction of the Institute hunted scrolls with the power to change reality by shifting past events. They had to assume these two enemies were also now hunting them.

As he was finishing, Krys entered the kitchen. She saw what he was doing and said, 'I thought you were leaving the reports to me.'

'This is a rough draft of our end-of-watch account. I'm looking for something. This helps me think. When I'm done, I need you to write your own account. Then read them both through. Compare the two versions. See if you can find it.'

'Find what?'

He shook his head. 'It's better if I don't say.'

She seated herself across from him. 'That almost makes sense.'

'You decide what stands out.' Jackson rose from the narrow breakfast table. He moved to the stove and put a fresh pot on to brew. 'We need to adjust our thinking. There are multiple issues to resolve here. It often happens with investigations involving magic.'

'Scrolls with the power to go back and change the past, and through the past change the future.' Krys slid the laptop around to face her. 'Where are they, and how do we get our hands on them? Did Bernard Bouchon survive the battle on Sardinia? Is he planning another attack on Luca?'

'All good questions,' Jackson agreed. He watched the coffee percolate. 'At this point, it all comes down to asking the right ones.'

'Here's another. Going back to our first meeting in Luca's home: He insisted the Peerless have managed to survive by staying below the radar. Why did they make such a major assault now? Was it because we showed up?'

'I've been wondering about that as well.' Jackson pulled down a fresh cup from the shelf and poured a coffee for Krys. He refilled his own and then pulled his chair away from the table. Making room between them for all the questions. 'For the Peerless to make that full-on attack, they had to be preparing long before we even knew we were going.'

'So we're assuming the attack had nothing to do with us?'

'That doesn't work either. It's too coincidental. Field officers hate coincidences. It implies motives and actions we're not taking into consideration.'

She frowned as she typed. 'Like what?'

'I have no idea. But we need to keep an open mind. We can't become so focused on one construct that we lose sight of other possibilities. For example, Luca assumes Riyanna is behind it all. What if he's wrong? What if Bernard is the real enemy?'

Krys pondered that a long moment, then resumed typing. Jackson checked the clock and decided, 'I'm going for a quick shower.'

As he was finishing, she called from the bottom of the stairs, 'You need to hear this.'

Jackson slipped on jeans and a sweatshirt, and went barefoot back downstairs. As he entered the kitchen, Krys said, 'I decided to check with our Sardinian friends before signing off on the report. Asila wasn't available. Carule's on the line.' She lifted the phone and said, 'Jackson's here now. I'm putting you on speaker.'

Carule asked, 'Is this phone secure?'

'Luca set up wards,' Krys replied.

'What do you hear about the attack on the Institute?'

Krys looked a question at him. Jackson pointed at her. Telling her to handle this. Krys replied, 'The news is quiet. I've just checked online. There are some unconfirmed reports. A couple of websites said they had videos of an attack, but I couldn't download them.'

'They are being magically erased,' Carule said. 'We have heard the same from allies around the globe. The Institute has been completely repaired. It looks as though nothing ever happened. The police have been ordered not to pursue inquiries. We lost twenty-nine Acolytes, eleven Talents, four Adepts, and three Directors. They have officially been declared victims of a terrible disease.'

Krys asked, 'Are you safe?'

'For the moment. Our opponents are so busy building this elaborate lie they have no time to bother about us. Asile thinks they have counted us among the dead. I hope she's right.' Carule paused, then added, 'We will soon need money.'

Jackson said, 'You heard Luca. Whatever you need. Can I tell him what it's for?'

'The Sardinian Institute is a boiling hive of discontent. More disaffected students are leaving every day. A few senior Talents as well. We need a safe haven large enough to take them all. We've located a farmhouse in the Corsican highlands, much land, good water. Asila has gone to check it out.'

Ten minutes later, Krys was still typing. She felt his gaze and said, 'Almost done.'

'Luca's late. That's never happened. The man has an inherent Swiss respect for time.'

'So call.'

'I have. Twice. He doesn't answer.' Jackson felt a faint crawling sensation of unease. 'Another first.'

Jackson walked through the front rooms, checking the windows. The forecourt was empty. The day was beautiful, the sunlit waters sparkled, the mountains rose in silent majesty. The thick glass reduced the highway traffic to a gentle hum.

He decided to give Luca another five minutes, then head over and make sure everything was OK. No matter how morose the guy might have been, Jackson could not imagine he would renege on an appointment. He re-entered the kitchen and said, 'Luca might have given us a crucial piece of the puzzle. The resting place for the Ancients' scrolls and artifacts.'

'I've been thinking about that.' Krys revealed the ability to type and talk, something that Jackson had never managed. 'Like the caverns where we found our treasures.'

Jackson started to remind them both that the treasures were not theirs, legally or otherwise. But he merely said, 'Maybe Bernard Bouchon discovered the location of the scrolls' resting place.'

Krys stopped typing and looked at him. 'Something you said that first day, when you walked me into the downstairs office. You said Luca read from scrolls that weren't there.'

'He just read the one scroll on top. The other two were underneath.'

'Right. Three scrolls that had already gone back to their resting place. He was reading just the residue.' She shook her head. 'I wish I could have seen that.'

Jackson started to say this was behind them and they needed to focus on the scrolls' location *now*. Then the idea hit him, strong as a slap to his face. *Bam.*

Jackson hurried from the kitchen and was midway across the front foyer when Krys called, '*Wait!*'

He stood there, poised like a hunting cat ready to pounce. Knowing the whole case was about to blow wide open. He was not halted by Krys's request, but rather the fact that he was still missing that one element to bring it all together. He needed, he needed . . .

Krys rushed up and said, 'I'm your partner. Tell me what you're thinking.'

Jackson forced his mind to slow down enough to frame the words. 'The obelisk.'

'Right. So?'

'Bernard Bouchon did not erect the obelisk. We know this how? Because if he had—'

'Of course,' she said.

'It would have vanished with everything else of his.'

She opened the front door. 'It was there all the time.'

Jackson said, 'And something more.'

'What?'

'It remains as a conduit for magic.' Jackson recalled climbing up there for the stroke of midnight and watching a new reality unfurl, one only visible while he gripped the black stone. 'Luca said an obelisk like that is mentioned in all the accounts he's read of the island's appearance. But no one knows for certain why.'

She gave him a minute, then pleaded, 'Talk it out, let me help.'

'The same is true for the desk. Luca said it was probably carved from rock the house stands on. I'm thinking for the safe as well.' Jackson described observing the ring of fire rimming the safe while Luca had read the scrolls. 'Luca ordered me to ignore it. As far as he was concerned, nothing mattered but the scrolls.'

'You think he was wrong.'

'What I think . . .' A growing unease tightened his gut. Jackson did not mind the pressure. It amplified the sense that the case was reaching the juncture when the swirling events coalesced into a logical pattern. He reached for his phone.

Krys asked, 'Who are you calling?'

'Luca. If he doesn't answer, I'm heading over there.'

'Right.' She opened the front door and stepped outside. 'I want to take another look at the fountain.'

Jackson hit the connection and was put straight through to voicemail. Luca's message was one word long, 'Speak.'

He started to say he was driving over. Then a shadow crossed the front windows. Swift as a bird, but large enough to blot out the sun from an entire room.

Then Krys screamed.

FIFTY-ONE

The instant Jackson bulleted out of the front door, Krys shredded the blue-sky day with her second scream.

'That's right, my lovely.' The woman's voice was slightly distorted, as if it was being played through a faulty loudspeaker system. 'Tell Luca it's time to come out and play.'

Jackson made it to the first step before a second attacker swatted him to the gravel. The force was strong enough to rattle his brain. The massive weight landed on his chest and pinned him to the rocks.

The gargoyle with Riyanna's voice snarled, 'Where is Luca?'

Jackson was having difficulty getting air into his lungs. The weight shifted slightly, and he heard the gravel rustle, as though a heavy load was being maneuvered. He was clenched in what felt like a fist of branding irons. He could feel his clothes smolder as he was hefted aloft. He gasped, 'Not here.'

Riyanna held Krys pinned with one set of talons as she lifted her head and howled. Jackson felt the visceral screech in his bones.

He willed his wand to appear. Nothing happened. His struggles only caused the gargoyle holding him to tighten its grip. Jackson watched Krys struggle and fail to light her ring. 'Let her go!'

There was no real body to the gargoyle, not in the sense of blood and flesh. Jackson faced an image forged from pure energetic potency. He smelled his skin begin to blister. He had never felt so helpless.

Riyanna's shape showed hard human traces embedded into perilous fury. She remained poised like a bird of prey over Krys. Riyanna looked from Jackson to her captive and back again, savoring their vulnerability. Then said, 'I want you to deliver a message to Luca.'

Jackson watched as one of her talons grew into a curved red blade as long as his arm. He realized what she intended and did his best to shout, '*No!*'

'Tell Luca this is the fate that awaits—'

A third gargoyle leaped through the front gates and swiped Riyanna with enough force to send her tumbling. 'Tell him yourself.'

FIFTY-TWO

Everything about Luca was an astonishment.

The gargoyle holding Jackson flung him aside, a casual gesture that sent him flying across the forecourt. Jackson hit and rolled and came up in one continuous motion, not wanting to take his eyes off the unfolding events.

This newly arrived gargoyle was definitely Luca. And yet the man had *changed*. The difference went far beyond how he wore an electric skin and a monster's form.

Luca's gargoyle had eyes.

Gone was the reticent blind man best suited for the back row.

In his place stood a beast with yellow lightning strips over his back and shoulders. Luca leaped at the gargoyle that had pinned Jackson and smashed him back through the house's front portal. The creature took out the door, the frame, and the two side windows.

Luca's head reappeared in the demolished entryway. He said, 'Run.'

Riyanna shrieked her war cry, gathered her limbs beneath her, and pounced. Luca caught her, flipped her high overhead, and then he roared.

Luca's cry carried a blast of force that blew Riyanna higher still. She crashed into the wall bordering the property and took out a fifteen-foot segment. Luca tracked her with a snarling leap of his own. The gargoyle who had gripped Jackson emerged from the house and raced after them.

Krys clutched her chest with one hand and fumbled for a grip on the gravel with the other. Jackson lifted her and scrambled for the house. As he passed through the mawing gap where his front door had stood, he heard Riyanna shriek, '*Sisters! To me!*'

But there was no safety inside the sunlit house. The foyer was filled with rubble from the creatures' impact. They picked their way carefully towards the stairs. Jackson could hear Krys grunt softly from the pain of breathing and assumed she had several cracked ribs.

'Cellar,' he said.

There was an almighty *crump* from overhead, strong enough to cause the home's steel-and-concrete foundations to shake. Then a second blow struck the roof. Actually, Jackson decided, it was four together, but so close they felt and sounded like a single elongated blast. Ba-ba-ba-*BAM*.

All the glass walls on the main floor shattered.

The impact sent Jackson tumbling. Krys managed to stay partly upright by gripping the stair railing, though the motion caused her to gasp with pain.

Jackson regained his feet, looped Krys's free arm around his shoulders, and together they stumbled down the steps. More blasts struck the roof, the garage, and then directly in front of the house. The last sight Jackson had of the main floor before rounding the corner was of two gargoyles slamming into what was left of his front portico, tearing away the entire wall. Overhead, they could hear the upstairs exploding. A cloud of dust powered down the steps after them.

They were coughing and limping as they struggled across the downstairs landing, through the office, and into the vault. Jackson eased Krys to the carpeted floor, coughed against the dust, and asked, 'Can you try your ring?'

She remained crouched on her knees, coughing feebly and then gasping against the pain, her right arm wrapped around her chest. Streaks of burn marks creased her from neck to waist.

Jackson heard a series of shrieks from out front and knew Luca faced an entire army of gargoyles. Jackson's gun and Taser were both upstairs. If there was any upstairs left. The vault was filled with dust and the rending screech of his house being torn apart.

Then Jackson spotted the blade.

He had placed Asila's resolza on the top shelf across from the artifacts. He brought down the knife, pulled off the sheath.

He had to try.

Krys coughed, then managed, 'Jackson . . .'

Jackson drew out his wand. 'Luca needs me.'

He touched the wand to the blade.

FIFTY-THREE

Luca's wards worked well enough to keep the house's central pillar intact. The stairs were a jumble of concrete, knotted together by twisted steel and what was left of the carpet. Overhead, the house groaned in mortal agony as it kept taking direct hits. But Jackson couldn't worry about that now.

As he passed through the remnants of his front foyer, he caught sight of his reflection in what was left of a tall mirror. He glimpsed a warrior of old, dressed in gleaming silver armor. He held a long, curved sword of blue fire in a two-handed grip. His head was encased in a helmet encircled by what might have been a golden ringlet. Jackson's mind flashed back to his boyhood dream of fighting the Barbary pirates and their evil mages. Then he was out of the door and into the battle.

Luca was almost lost beneath a furious swarm of gargoyles. He and Jackson exchanged a single look, then Luca flashed yellow fire that seared through the two gargoyles crouching to the left of the demolished front stairs. The remaining foes gave a unified howl of anguish as the pair disintegrated into crimson dust.

Jackson launched himself into the fray. He knew he was yelling, but he could hear nothing so clearly as the blood singing through his veins. He sliced the sword at claws reaching toward him and took the limb off cleanly with one stroke. He swung the blade in wild arcs, taking another two creatures with the next blow, a third, a fourth. On and on he powered into the mob with Luca at its center.

Riyanna clawed her way to the top of the band fighting Luca. She shrieked at her enemy, and one talon grew to the length of a venom-laced spear. She shrilled again as she rammed the blade through Luca's hip.

Luca howled in pain, then swiped and took Riyanna's talon off a hand's breadth from her claw. But the spear remained embedded in his flesh.

Jackson used two of the gargoyles as a launching pad and leaped on to Riyanna's back. She was busy growing another talon, or else she would have eliminated Jackson in the instant he required to gain his balance. When she did turn to him, however, it was too late.

He yelled as he swept the blade in a vicious arc and took her head in one stroke.

Riyanna turned to crimson dust. Jackson tumbled and righted himself and took another gargoyle off at the knees.

But there were so many.

An electric red army howled from the roof of his demolished home. Each blow connected, and each wound carried the force to eradicate another beast. Yet there were more. Always more.

Jackson felt himself take a hit. A talon managed to pierce between the juncture where his neck met his shoulder. He chopped off the claw and drew the talon from his flesh. Jackson felt no pain. But he could feel his blood draining down warm and wet inside his armor.

The entire forecourt was ankle-deep in silt the color of drifting rust. And still they came. Jackson knew Luca fought bravely. Every flash of yellow fire took out more of the beasts. But the two of them could not vanquish an entire army.

Gradually, Jackson felt his strength begin to ebb with the blood that now dripped between the armor plates and stained the rust at his feet. Then he discovered he was on his knees.

How he had arrived there, he had no idea. Only that his sword had become impossibly heavy. It lay there in the dust before his face, and yet he could not grip the haft and raise it. Not even when a new gargoyle launched itself in for the kill.

Bernard Bouchon's gargoyle was a head taller than the others and held an electric parody of the man's original face. He lumbered across the forecourt, shoving aside the last remaining fiends. Aiming for Luca.

Jackson's friend and ally knelt in the dust, chest heaving, and watched helplessly as Bernard strode forward. 'We meet at last.'

Jackson willed himself to rise. Join battle with their nemesis. But his body refused to obey.

'This one is mine.' Bernard's elongated talons readied for the kill.

Then a new scream froze the entire battle. A sweet sound, despite its harsh note. Jackson managed to lift his head. Krys stood with her ring-hand stretched overhead while the other gripped her ribs. The light flowed from her ring and surrounded her entire being in a shimmering golden shield.

Krys did not try to aim her force. Instead, she stabbed the sky.

All around Jackson, the air caught fire.

That was how it seemed to him, as though the only safe havens were the tiny spot where he knelt and the one to his left where Luca sprawled. Everywhere else became encased in flames.

Shrieks and wails rose all around him, but Jackson remained untouched. The destruction carried a whirlwind force, a raging tumult that spun all about the three of them.

Then it was over.

When Krys released her flame, there was nothing left save drifting clouds of pale red ash.

Jackson felt his body grow so heavy that all he could do was accept the earth's embrace. His last images came together in a confused muddle – Luca slumped in human form just beyond the reach of his left hand, Krys stumbling towards Jackson and calling his name, and police sirens on swift approach.

The crimson silt made such a soft pillow for his head.

FIFTY-FOUR

Jackson came to momentarily when they loaded him on to the ambulance. He was drawn from the black depths by Krys, strident even when wounded. She insisted on being allowed to journey in his vehicle. Then the medic inserted a needle into Jackson's arm and flooded his system with an icy salve. As he drifted away that second time, Jackson realized he was in a lot of pain.

Awareness came and went in fleeting snatches. Jackson could not be certain he woke at all. Perhaps his dreams merely knitted together in some coherent fashion. Twice he thought he heard Krys and Simeon talking, and he wondered why Luca did not respond. The blind man's absence troubled him, though he could not piece together a reason.

He woke for certain when a bright light shone directly into his face and a coldly officious voice demanded in French, 'This one also has no papers?'

'Destroyed in the assault on his home,' he heard Simeon reply. 'A tragedy.'

'Tragic. Yes. Even more so if they bring their danger and destruction into France.'

'Which is why I accompany them,' Simeon replied. 'To assure you this is not the case.'

'Forgive me for questioning your judgment, Monsieur—'

'Detective.'

'But you are Swiss, and this is France, yes? And we have been alerted to the battle on the lake's southern rim. What is more, we *saw* it. Here. In Divonne. The attack lit up our sky.'

But Simeon kept his cool. 'The former despot of Benin resides two houses east of Monsieur Burnett's former residence. The citizens of Benin, as you are no doubt aware, were cruelly oppressed. The International Courts of Justice issued an arrest warrant for this former ruler, on the grounds that he used outlawed magic on his own populace.'

'And now he whiles away his days on the shores of Lake Geneva,' the customs officer sneered.

'Indeed so. Another tragedy. But we were speaking of these innocent victims. My country has no doctors who have specialized in the healing of magical wounds. The Divonne Clinic has a world-wide reputation—'

'Yes, yes, I am well aware of all this.'

'And the clinic has alerted you to our arrival, no? So if you will be so kind as to stamp my papers and lift your barrier, we will endeavor to save these lives while there is still time.'

*   *   *

When Jackson next awoke, he lay in a hospital bed. What he could see of the room showed expensive furnishings. A spray of orchids stood in a stylish vase on the table to his right. Simeon sat in a leather chair, reading from a file bearing the official Swiss seal. The drapes to his window were pulled open, revealing a darkened window. Jackson licked dry lips and asked, 'What time is it?'

'A quarter past nine.' Simeon held the cup while Jackson sucked on the straw, then set it down and said, 'Your partner's burns were treated and her ribs were taped. She was here until a moment ago. She claims you saved her life, by the way. How are you, my friend?'

'Sore.'

'Then you have come to the right place. I am assured by the doctors that their assorted pain remedies are unrivaled. Shall I call someone?'

'Later.'

'I have been told you will make a full recovery. But you lost a considerable amount of blood, so you will need to take it easy—'

'You might as well say it.' When Simeon did not reply, Jackson pressed, 'You're not sitting here just to make sure I get all the meds I want.'

Simeon made a process of closing the file. 'Luca is not expected to survive the night.'

The night and the setting and even his own pain crystallized in a flash of loss. 'There's no chance they're wrong?'

'He was poisoned. By what, the doctors have no idea.' Simeon shook his head. 'Krys has just walked down to check on him. I am to call her the instant you awake.'

'I want to go to him.'

'Of course you do. The doctor has insisted that he check you over first, however.' Simeon pressed the call button, then realized Jackson was pulling off the monitor cables and struggling to rise. 'What are you doing?'

Jackson said, 'Find me a wheelchair. And some clothes.'

'My friend, I just told you, we must wait—'

'There isn't time. We have got to move *now*.'

Simeon rose, started for the door, then turned back and said, 'At least tell me what it is that cannot wait for the dawn.'

Jackson tried to stand, but the world spun, and he was forced to sit back down. He hated the weakness. But he had to work around it. He had no choice. He asked, 'Tonight is the full moon, correct?'

Simeon gave him a hard look, then checked his phone. 'And if it is?'

'In that case,' Jackson replied, 'we are going to try to save Luca's life.'

FIFTY-FIVE

K rys arrived while Simeon was making arrangements. Jackson's first question was about Bernard. Dead, she replied with evident satisfaction. All of the remaining gargoyles were rendered into dust by her blast. How, she had no idea.

Twenty-seven minutes later, they left the clinic. Simeon drove the ambulance with Jackson strapped into the passenger seat. Krys was seated in the back, across from the mobile stretcher holding Luca. Jackson wore surgical blues and a pair of rope-soled sandals Simeon had stolen from the doctors' ready room. The sandals were half a size too small and pinched. Jackson merely added that discomfort to all the others. Climbing out of the wheelchair and into the ambulance had been a serious challenge. He had a plastic baggie holding a variety of pain meds in his pocket, but he had not yet taken anything. He needed to stay as sharp as possible for as long as he could.

Signing Luca out over the doctor's dire warnings took as much time as obtaining a driverless ambulance. When the doctor tried to override them, Simeon replied that if the doctor insisted on keeping Luca there and the patient died, he would personally ensure the doctor was brought up on a charge of willful manslaughter.

The border station proved no difficulty. The French were only too happy to see them leave, and the Swiss saluted Simeon's badge and waved them through. On the other side, Simeon said, 'We are going to your residence? Truly?'

'Fast as you can,' Jackson replied. Waking Luca had been a trial. But the blind man had fastened upon Jackson's words and used magic to recover, at least temporarily. Jackson asked, 'Is Luca awake?'

'I am,' came the weak reply.

'Hang in there.'

Simeon said, 'You are, of course, aware that your house is a complete and utter wreck. Not to mention a crime scene.'

'It doesn't matter. What time is it?'

'A quarter past ten,' Krys replied.

Simeon demanded, 'And just exactly why is the time so important?'

'The bridge can only be formed on the blue moon and the one that follows. Luca, isn't that what you said?'

'Correct.'

Simeon used the rearview mirror to examine each face in turn, 'Dare I ask what bridge you mean?'

'It's complicated,' Jackson replied and was rewarded by what might have been a laugh from Luca. Weak. But still.

Simeon went on, 'Just to be certain, you are drawing me further into a project that will undoubtedly require me to break even more laws of my country?'

'A whole mess of them,' Jackson replied.

'On that one word we most certainly agree,' Simeon said. 'This is indeed a mess. One of Alpine proportions.'

The ambulance was top-heavy and swung harshly around corners. Jackson stifled a grunt as he was pressed against the door. 'Think of it this way,' Jackson said. 'If I'm right, in a couple of hours, none of this will ever have happened.'

'It will all just go away?'

'Poof. Gone. Not even a cloud of smoke,' Jackson replied.

'I have your word on this?'

From his position on the stretcher, Luca said weakly, 'And mine as well.' He murmured something more that was lost to the rumble of a passing truck.

Simeon demanded, 'What was that?'

Krys replied, 'He said, once again the pupil instructs the master.'

'Well, then' – Simeon ground the gears – 'I suppose that will have to do.'

FIFTY-SIX

As they turned on to the lakefront highway, Simeon said, 'Explain to me why we are headed back to the crime scene.'

'The obelisk,' Jackson replied. 'And the safe.' Jackson did

not mind tracking it through. Talking helped keep his discomfort at bay. 'They were components of Bernard Bouchon's earlier existence. Which means they should have disappeared with everything else.'

Simeon frowned at the night. 'And yet they are still there because . . .'

'The magic is stronger than time,' Luca murmured, his voice somewhat stronger now.

'So the obelisk and the cellar-safe, these are your objectives?'

'No,' Jackson replied. 'We also need the scrolls.'

'The ones Bouchon was after,' Simeon said. 'Which you do not have.'

'Right.'

Luca chuckled softly. 'Of course.'

Simeon glanced in the rearview mirror. 'Krys, are you laughing as well?'

'Not yet,' she replied. 'But I'm hoping.'

'Bouchon built the house there,' Jackson explained. 'He planted the obelisk there. Because this—'

'Of course!' Krys exclaimed.

'—Is the entrance to the Ancients' lair,' Jackson said. 'Down through the centuries, each time the scrolls were rediscovered and used, they went back to the place where they were anchored.'

Luca coughed and then might have muttered, 'Brilliant.'

Jackson went on, 'Bouchon did not construct a safe. He built a portal. And he hid it by constructing a house on top of it.'

Luca laughed again – a wet sound, but welcome nonetheless. Jackson went on, 'Luca told Commandant Barker that the spell scroll he read that night was for building the bridge to the island. He called it an Ancient's method of opening the unseen portal. We assumed it was part of the time spell. We were wrong.'

Krys murmured, 'Of course.'

'And you?' Simeon demanded. 'You have located a different way into this mysterious portal?'

'Let us hope so,' Luca replied.

'Obviously, my understanding anything is of little significance compared to this magnificent drama of yours.' Simeon opened his door, rose from the ambulance, and remarked, 'A fog is gathering over the lake.'

'It's not fog,' Jackson said. 'Hurry.'

FIFTY-SEVEN

The house was an utter ruin. The roof was smashed into giant cement flakes, all linked by a web of steel rods. No window remained intact. Thick shards of glass glittered in the ambulance's headlights. The top two floors were essentially compressed into one. The central column rose from the wreckage like a square fist.

Krys emerged from the rear and opened Jackson's door. Simeon came around and helped her ease Jackson from his seat. Between the loss of blood and the general battering he had received from the gargoyles, there was no way he could have made it on his own. His arms around their shoulders, he straightened slowly, testing each muscle and joint in turn. Simeon said, 'We could leave you here—'

'No,' Jackson said. 'I'm good. And I have to do this.'

From the rear of the ambulance, Luca murmured, 'The forces are gathering.'

As they climbed what was left of the front stairs, Krys said, 'One thing I don't get.'

'Just one?' Simeon said from Jackson's other side. 'In that case, I lag so far behind I can scarcely see your dust.'

Krys said, 'Neither the Peerless nor the Institute ever came after the scrolls. Why?'

Jackson timed his words to each tight exhale. 'Our first visit to his home, Luca told us a Talent can only reach the island once. Bouchon had no chance to reshape his world another time. There was nothing to be gained by revealing what he knew to others. My guess is that knowledge of the scrolls died with him.'

The ceiling was bowed down like a concrete and steel hammock, forcing them to walk at a crouch. Krys said, 'And the Peerless attacked him now because . . .'

'They tracked his magic. Multiple times.' Jackson let them guide him down the rubble-strewn steps. 'They attacked him in the hospital because they assumed he would be vulnerable. When that failed, they struck at the car because they knew only a former Peerless could set up their special wards. Then they discovered he was on

Sardinia at the same time as their failed attack on the Institute. And
they decided it was time to go on the offensive, regardless of the
cost.'

Thankfully, a segment of each stair remained intact. As they
threaded their way, Simeon said, 'I suppose now would be a good
time to hear why it is so important to come here at all.'

'This takes us back to our first visit.'

'The murders that never happened.'

'Right. After Luca ordered you and your men away, we came
down here. While Luca was reading the scroll's shadow, I saw
the vault become ringed by fire. Luca told me to forget the vault.
He said it wasn't important. He was wrong.'

'So the vault . . .'

'Is the portal,' Jackson replied. 'It's why the house was built here.
And my guess is that the obelisk forms part of the key to gain entry.'

The basement foyer was a rubble field. The office was missing
its ceiling. The carpeted rear wall was gone. From the doorway,
they looked straight into the vault. Which remained untouched.

Jackson took a step away from the others. He could not hold
himself straight, for to do so pinched the neck and shoulder muscles
that had been lacerated by the gargoyles. As he fashioned his wand,
Jackson tried to push aside his injuries and all the lingering doubts.
For Luca's sake, he had to succeed.

Simeon gasped, 'Is that a—'

Krys replied, 'Hush now.'

Jackson touched the wand to his forehead.

A few moments was all he required. He released his hold on the
wand and turned around. Stricken by far more than his physical
pain.

Krys saw the change. 'Jackson?'

His breath sounded ragged in his own ears. When he was ready,
he met his partner's gaze and said, 'I know what we have to do.'

What was more, he knew why.

FIFTY-EIGHT

Jackson limped into the vault and retrieved the little golden plate. When he stepped back out, he asked Simeon, 'Are you willing to play a role in this?'

Simeon's gaze swiveled back and forth between Jackson's face and the hand no longer holding the wand. 'What do you call everything I've done up to now?'

Krys said, 'He means, are you willing to take part in a magical event?'

Simeon wrestled momentarily, then decided, 'I have walked to the cliff's edge; I might as well jump.'

Jackson handed Simeon the plate and said, 'Hold this steady.' When Simeon took a firm grip, Jackson said, 'Krys?'

The light from her ring filled the ruined chamber. 'Ready.'

Jackson held out his wand. 'On my count. One, two . . .'

The fire began to encircle the vault's portal the instant they touched the plate.

The little golden plate now gleamed like a beacon, illuminating the stairs that flowed down into impenetrable shadows. Jackson hobbled over to where he could peer down and down and further still. There was no way he could make it down, much less climb back out.

Krys moved up beside him and asked, 'How far do they descend?'

Simeon responded from Jackson's other side, 'Deep as the caverns in our treasure rooms, I suspect.'

'I'll go,' Krys said.

Simeon scoffed, 'Don't be absurd. With your ribs, you would never climb back out.' He peered into the shadows. 'So this is what the other side of the cliff's edge looks like.'

But at that moment, Jackson realized the climb would not be necessary. 'Step back,' he said.

As they did so, the first figure entered the room.

*　　*　　*

The little being only stood a few inches taller than Jackson's knee. As before, the streaming lights silhouetted its small form. The figure bore itself with intense dignity. Of that, Jackson was certain.

Then a second figure appeared behind the first. And this one held three scrolls.

Jackson took the plate from Simeon's limp fingers and grunted with the effort required to bend down and set it on the rubble before the being.

The two figures stood there, observing him and making no move.

Jackson wished there was some note of triumph to this moment. Knowing that the time had come to relinquish his treasure and let it return to the holding place. But all he felt was a loss so deep it overwhelmed his body's multiple agonies.

He held up the wand. He stared at its gleaming silver length.

Krys moaned, 'Jackson. No.'

The treasures are not ours, he wanted to say, but just then he could not utter the words.

Bending down and handing the figure his wand was the hardest thing Jackson had ever done.

Behind him, Krys moaned.

He straightened slowly, utterly bereft. He feared he would go through the rest of his days feeling like a cripple.

The first figure made the wand disappear, then the two of them turned and looked at Krys.

Dripping tears, Krys stepped up and wrested the ring from her finger.

The second figure walked forward and set the scrolls at Jackson's feet.

FIFTY-NINE

Krys was still struggling for composure when they made it back to the forecourt. Jackson did not mind. In fact, he found a meager comfort in how at least one of them honored their loss in this fashion.

When Simeon opened the ambulance's rear doors, Luca neither moved nor gave any sign of life.

Krys exclaimed, 'Don't tell me he's dead.'

'Still here,' Luca murmured. 'Barely.'

'The scrolls,' Jackson said. 'I have them.'

There was a long pause, then Luca lifted his right hand and searched feebly about him.

'Allow me,' Simeon said. He entered the ambulance and handed Luca his cane.

Luca touched the tip to his forehead. It glowed feebly at first, then gradually strengthened until it was hard to look at directly. What was more, Jackson felt the glow enter his bruised and battered frame, soothing and energizing both.

Krys whispered, 'Do you think it might heal a broken heart?'

Jackson could think of nothing to offer, except to reach over and take her hand.

'Help me sit up,' Luca said.

Simeon cranked the lever on the side of the metal stretcher, raising the back section. When Luca reached out, Jackson leaned into the ambulance and handed him the scrolls.

Luca unfurled one and began tracing his fingers over the illuminated text. The words writhed and swam and revealed their secrets.

Luca unfurled the second scroll, then the third. His hand flew over the text, then he sighed and said, 'Someone needs to touch the obelisk and identify the bridge's location.'

The fog became so dense they could no longer see the house from the forecourt. As Luca droned the spell's first portion, Simeon helped Krys scale the fountain's outer wall. From his position by the ambulance's rear doors, Jackson watched her touch the obelisk. Despite the blanketing mist, she cried, 'I see it!'

Luca's voice remained weak but clear. 'Ask her where the bridge connects.'

She must have heard him, for she called back, 'Almost directly in front of your bank.'

'It is only fitting,' Luca said. 'Let's be off.'

SIXTY

They drove along deserted streets. Geneva appeared completely void of life. The fog parted reluctantly at the ambulance's approach, then sealed up firmly behind them. Simeon asked, 'Luca, are you doing this?'

'Of course.'

'I cannot see where we are,' Simeon said.

Luca replied, 'Someone let in the night air.'

Jackson rolled down his window. Other than the rumble of their engine and the hiss of tires on rain-slick streets, there was no sound whatsoever.

Lightning flickered almost constantly over the lake, flashing odd swirling shapes into murky existence. But there was no thunder. Now and then, Luca drew in a long slow breath. Finally . . .

'Stop here,' Luca said.

Simeon pulled to the curb and cut the engine. They could see nothing except the swirling gray mist. He and Krys rolled out the stretcher, then transferred Luca to Jackson's wheelchair. Luca murmured, 'Krys, make a light, please.'

Her voice fractured. 'I can't.'

Luca turned sightless eyes to her, his face wracked by unaccustomed emotions. He fumbled for a moment, then extended the hand holding his staff. 'Here. Take this.'

'But . . .'

'Touch it to your forehead and call silently for light.' When she had done so, and the surrounding mist was turned golden, Luca added, 'May it serve you well, my friend.'

They started off together. Luca held the scrolls firmly in his lap. Simeon pushed the wheelchair. Krys supported Jackson with one arm and held the staff aloft with the other. The light continued to part the fog, revealing the bridge straight ahead.

When the chair touched the bridge's boundary, Luca asked, 'Jackson, are you able?'

'Yes,' he replied, hoping it was true.

Simeon stepped back, and Jackson took his place. The two of

them started forward. A few paces on, Jackson glanced back. Of the shore and his friends there was no sign except a faint golden glow, almost lost now.

Lightning flashes surrounded them, revealing a bridge made of what appeared to be unadorned black granite. Up ahead rose an obelisk identical to the one on Rue Gambord. It drew fire like a lightning rod, illuminating the island upon which it stood. As they approached their destination, Jackson found himself flooded with a healing energy. And apparently, so did Luca, for his voice solidified as he asked, 'You knew I was searching for this chance to begin anew?'

'From the very first day,' Jackson replied.

'And yet you helped me.'

Jackson nodded. 'We all have our hidden motives.'

When the chair touched the island, Luca said, 'I can manage from here.'

'What will you do with the scrolls?'

'They will be left on the island, and hopefully vanish when it does.' Luca turned sightless eyes his way. 'You gave up your wand? For me?'

'You said it yourself,' Jackson replied. 'It was only on loan.'

Luca reached out his hand. 'Farewell, my dearest friend.'

SIXTY-ONE

They stood there together, Jackson and Krys and Simeon, and watched. The lightning flashed almost continuously, illuminating the silhouetted figure who rose from the wheelchair and walked forward and touched the obelisk.

Instantly, the lightning stopped. The mist cleared. The night became just that, another night along the placid waters of Lake Geneva.

Of the island, there was no sign.

Together, they returned to the ambulance and joined the traffic streaming along the shorefront avenue.

SIXTY-TWO

At Jackson's insistence, they drove straight to police head-quarters. Simeon settled him and Krys into an interrogation room, then Simeon left to disable all recording equipment. They accepted the detective's offer of tea. Jackson took one of the pain pills and Krys another. Then they got to work.

Simeon proved an excellent typist, and personally wrote both of their testimonies. Two hours and thirty-one minutes after their arrival, Jackson signed the document, then Krys. He then took a second painkiller.

Jackson remained encased in a medicinal fog during the drive back to his studio apartment. Simeon and Krys helped him upstairs, where Krys bid him a sad goodnight.

At the door to the elevator, Simeon turned back and asked, 'Will I remember anything tomorrow?'

'I don't know if any of us will,' Jackson replied. The ache of loss burrowed through his internal mist.

Simeon tapped his wedding ring on the elevator's door. 'Then let me say now that I am indeed grateful for being included in this investigation.'

Jackson waited until the door sighed shut, then said softly, 'This quest.'

SIXTY-THREE

But the next day, they all remembered.

That night they gathered together in the forecourt of the ruined house. Simeon's wife Noemi was with them. Simeon had told her most of what happened, and she had asked to witness this for herself.

Even if the next day she forgot everything, Noemi told them, still she would forget with her husband.

Noemi was compact and dark and lovely. Being also extremely French, she had brought three bottles of vintage Margaux, along with a basket containing pate and fresh-baked loaves and grapes and a quarter-round of Gruyere cheese. They sat on the rubble and ate and drank and watched the fog roll in. When the time came, they helped one another clamber up the fountain's outer rim and across the hidden path.

They gathered by the obelisk and stared across the lake, as an island appeared and became silhouetted once more by the silent lightning. They watched a man push another man in a wheelchair. They saw the two shake hands. Then the one crossed back over the bridge to where he touched land and was gone.

The other man rose from the wheelchair, deposited scrolls on the ground, reached forward, and touched the obelisk. It all faded then: the island and the man who was no more, lost to myth and fable and time.

Afterwards, they embraced one another with the fierce abandon of friends who had known both triumph and hardship, and now faced the very real prospect of never seeing one another again. Because even when they did meet, the events and the emotions and all the shared endeavors . . .

Gone.

SIXTY-FOUR

B ut to Jackson's utter astonishment, he was again proven wrong.

Instead, he awoke the next morning with his memories intact.

He and Krys returned to Rue Gambord together. The house was restored, pristine. What was more, their bodies carried no bruises, nor aches, not even a scratch. Her ribs were healed, his wounds gone, their strength restored.

And yet they remembered. They both remembered *everything*.

As they stood by the open front gates, Krys asked, 'Why haven't we forgotten?'

Jackson shook his head.

'The ones who stole our treasures,' she decided. 'It has to be. Nothing else makes sense.'

'They didn't steal anything,' Jackson replied. 'Do you want to go in?'

'No. Definitely not. You?'

He thought of the wand he had laid upon the rubble and said, 'I'm good.'

They drove to Interpol's Geneva office, where yet another astonishment awaited. For Commandant Barker and Chief Meyer both remembered as well. They even recalled the eyes-only file regarding Bernard Bouchon, sealed in Barker's magic-protected safe. The safe containing all the cases that had never existed.

Krys was offered a full reinstatement, commendations, and an invitation to return to Brussels. Jackson urged her to take hold of the offer with both hands. Krys thanked them one and all, and replied that she needed time to reflect.

Jackson, on the other hand, was asked to go rogue.

They did not put it like that, of course. They said simply that black-market activity was going through the roof, and Jackson had proven adept at handling the most sensitive of cases. They offered him a deep-cover assignment, full backing, direct connections to the CIA and Sûreté, the works. They *begged*.

Jackson responded the same as Krys. He needed time to reflect.

Krys went back to pulling regular shifts. But at Chief Meyer's urgings, Jackson remained on voluntary lock-out. He wrote a longer report that was passed on to other intelligence agencies. He attended several briefings and began making contacts within the global clandestine arena. Many of the officials with whom he met were already working on the assumption that Jackson had accepted the appointment. He decided to remain silent and wait until he had a clear indication before declaring one way or the other.

He spoke with Krys a couple of times each day. She said the Geneva office remained the quiet backwater it had always been, but claimed she did not mind, and Jackson believed her. They went to a concert. They enjoyed their belated dinner with Simeon's family. Simeon and Noemi both retained their memories, which spiced the shared hours with an almost palpable flavor.

On the twenty-fourth night, just before midnight, Krys called and said, 'I think I'm going to take the Brussels posting.'

'Good,' Jackson said and meant it. Now that it was out in the open, he sensed this was what he had been waiting for at some deep level. 'This is definitely the right move.'

'What about you?'

The musings that had carried him through the days and nights finally solidified into a definite, 'I'm staying undercover.'

'For real?'

'Yes. I've just decided.' He breathed freely now. 'I've been wanting to return to fieldwork. But at the same time, I don't want to go back to another regular posting. I want something different.'

'A new beginning,' she said.

'Exactly.'

'I'm glad for you,' she said. 'It's something you can do better than anyone else.'

'Maybe,' he agreed.

'No, Jackson. I *know*.'

They said goodnight, and Jackson sat where he was, reflecting on how right this all felt. How *fine*.

Then the sensation returned, strong as the first time down in Switzerland's secret treasure rooms. And before Jackson lifted his hand and willed it back into existence, he knew . . .

There in his hand was the wand.

He was still sitting there, staring dumbly at the shimmering silver staff, when his phone rang.

When he answered, Krys sobbed so hard she could hardly draw breath, much less share the news.

'I know,' Jackson said. 'Me, too.'

SIXTY-FIVE

Three days later, Jackson emerged from his studio. He had agreed to help Krys pack up her belongings and prepare for the next day's return to Brussels. But when he exited the building, he found a Bentley Flying Spur pulled up in front of his door. This one was a silver-tan. The rear door opened and a woman in her forties stepped out. She was dressed in a Chanel outfit of knitted silk and looked as polished as a jewel on display. 'Mr Burnett?'

'Can I help you?'

'Actually, sir, it's the other way around.' She gestured toward the car's rear door. 'Would you be so kind as to join me?'

When he entered the car, Jackson discovered there was no driver behind the wheel. 'What's going on?'

'Sir, I am here in an official capacity. You may refer to me as Sandrine. You have recently been asked to go undercover and tackle the rising flood of black-market magic. I am here to urge you to take that position.'

Jackson demanded, 'How did you hear about that?'

'Sir, I represent a collective of concerned citizens. Many of whom are very highly connected. Because Switzerland has outlawed magic, their identities must remain strictly confidential. You may refer to them as the Forest Council. In 1291, leaders of the three Forest Cantons, Uri, Schwyz, and Unterwalden, gathered in a highland meadow. They formed a defensive alliance to combat anyone plotting against the greater good. Sir, members of this new Forest Council are convinced this is happening again today. The new enemies are within the seven global Institutes of Magic. They also include the Peerless and several other groups.'

Sandrine opened a briefcase and extracted a series of documents. 'The Council wishes to offer you their unqualified support. To demonstrate what this signifies, they have acquired a house on Rue Gambord and named you as owner. These documents assign you title to both the home and this car. And these papers represent a series of accounts that have been opened in your name, with holdings amounting to . . .'

Jackson scanned the document with her. 'Eight million dollars.'

'Actually, sir, the holdings are in euros. They total approximately ten million US dollars.' She offered him a silver pen. 'Please sign the highlighted spaces.'

'But I haven't officially agreed to anything.'

'Nonetheless, the Council wishes to offer this as a goodwill gesture. You may, of course, return the holdings to them in the unfortunate event that you decline the position. I should also mention that the Commandant of Interpol has been informed of this move and has given her approval.'

When he was done signing, Sandrine tapped the papers back into alignment and shut them in her briefcase. 'Do you know the Banque Genevoise?'

'Of course.' It was the biggest private bank in Geneva and the third-largest in Switzerland.

'Go to the main entrance. Give the guard your name. Your liaison within the Council would like to meet you.'

'Now, or after I decide?'

'This very instant if you would be so kind.' Sandrine handed him a card. It contained merely her first name, a phone number, and an email address. 'We urge you to accept the position without delay, Mr Burnett. You may contact me day or night. You should assume no request you might care to make is beyond the Council's abilities to fulfill.'

Jackson was still working on his response when she opened the other door and rose from the car. 'Good luck, Mr Burnett. And good hunting.'

Jackson left the car parked in front of his apartment building and strolled down the quayside, taking his time, trying to work out exactly what had just happened. He stopped for a coffee, pondered whether he should call someone – Krys, Simeon, the chief, anyone. But in the end, the phone remained in his pocket. He paid for his coffee and continued walking.

The Banque Genevoise occupied its own island in the middle of the Rhone River. It was a classical structure fashioned from blocks of Alpine granite. Jackson entered by the main doors, gave his name to the guard, and was instantly passed to a hovering young man. The aide released a velvet rope and ushered Jackson into the director's elevator. He was whisked to the penthouse level, where an elegant silver-haired woman escorted him straight through the reception area and into an empty office that could only be described as palatial. She told him, 'The Chairman said to be alerted the instant you arrived.'

'No rush,' Jackson assured her.

'Thank you, sir. The Chairman won't keep you a moment. Would you care for a coffee?'

But Jackson was unable to respond. For he had caught sight of the man in all the photographs lining the credenza behind the desk.

The man stood arm in arm with a smiling wife. With three children. With friends. With world leaders.

Jackson was astonished to discover that Luca had gray eyes.

The door opened behind him, and an even tread crossed the room.

Jackson turned and faced a man his own age but cloaked in wealth and worldly power.

'My name is Luca Tami,' he said, offering Jackson his hand. 'By any chance, do you remember me?'